Slow Burn Summer

Slow Burn Summer

a novel

JOSIE SILVER

DELL
NEW YORK

This book is a love letter to the mighty
romance reading community. You're the best readers
ever and I'm forever grateful for your support.

Slow
Burn
Summer

1

"SORRY ABOUT THIS, CAN YOU JUST HOLD HIM FOR A SECOND WHILE I wipe this off me? It's like he has this wild sixth sense that I'm wearing clean clothes, must throw up all over him straightaway."

Kate glanced at the familiar green door behind the harassed young guy thrusting the baby out toward her, knowing the fastest way to get round him was to refuse, but old parenting instincts die hard. She recognized the exhausted look in the guy's eyes, and the I'm-holding-on-by-a-thread-here tone in his new-dad voice. Sighing inwardly, she held her hands out for the red-faced, squirming baby.

"I'd keep him at arm's length, he's just filled his nappy. He's like a grenade, goes off at either end without notice."

"Yeah, they do that," she said, trying to surreptitiously check her watch without tipping the baby to one side. "Hello, you," she whispered, thrown straight back to Alice's baby days by the unexpected weight of a baby in her arms. He was surprised enough to stop crying and stare up at her, silent when she stroked the pronounced curve of his cheek with the back of her finger.

"I think he likes you, you should keep him. I'll come back for him in about eighteen years," the guy said, finally finding a pack of baby wipes in the bottom of his overstuffed changing bag and scrubbing ineffectually at the baby sick down the front of his hoodie.

"Trust me, you'll look back when he's eighteen and wish he was this small again. He'll still be throwing up, just beer-induced rather than milk," Kate said.

"God, I'd kill for a beer right now," the guy sighed, giving up on his scrubbing and shoving the wipes back into the bag. Kate caught his eye and he shook his head and laughed. "I don't mean it."

"I know," she said. "It gets easier."

Lifting the baby onto her shoulder, she waited while he re-clipped his baby carrier in place and gave himself a shake.

"Thanks for being cool," he said, wrinkling his nose as he took his son back. "We better go and find somewhere to change you, hadn't we, bud?"

Kate glanced sideways as he moved away into the lunchtime crowds and found the shoulder of her black jacket covered in baby sick.

"Shit balls," she muttered, dragging it off to examine the damage. She'd spent the last two days deciding what to wear for the job interview, and none of her plans had involved baby sick.

Sighing, she did the only thing possible: shoved her jacket in the nearest litter bin, reassured herself she wasn't underdressed, then threw her shoulders back and turned toward the painted green door again. It was open, an older guy heading out just as she headed in. She stepped aside with a tight smile, giving him a wide berth.

"Don't worry, I won't vomit on you too," he said, having clearly witnessed the whole incident.

She shrugged lightly, an it-happens gesture designed to move things along.

"I think you have some in your hair," he said, peering at her.

Kate touched her curls and groaned when she found them damp. "Oh, for the love of God." She'd stashed a hair band in her pocket earlier and reached for it on autopilot, patting herself down and belatedly realizing she wasn't wearing her jacket anymore.

"In the bin," the guy said, rueful. He looked like someone never likely to find themselves in such a ridiculous situation, well put together from his suntan to his tweed jacket to his polished shoes.

"Well, that's that, then, isn't it? Message received," she said, glancing up at the skies in surrender. "I can't go into a job interview with no jacket and sick in my hair, can I?"

He looked at her for a moment, then silently unknotted his tie and handed it to her.

"For your hair," he said.

Kate looked at it, surprised, and then at him.

"You've come this far," he said, by way of explanation.

She swallowed hard and nodded. He was right. She could salvage this. Tying her hair back, she took a deep, grateful breath.

"Thanks," she said.

He nodded and held her gaze for a second, then stalked away into the London street scene.

UNAWARE OF THE DRAMA PLAYING itself out on the street below, Charlie Francisco sat at his late father's desk with Kate Elliott's letter smoothed flat in front of him. It was addressed to Jojo Francisco, as much of the mail still was, despite his father's untimely death a few months previously. Known around town as the "starmaker," Jojo had been a charismatic talent agent who'd operated solely on his famous gut instinct, his killer negotiating skills disguised by his lovable, eccentric demeanor. His sudden passing had come as a shock to everyone, clients, associates, and rivals alike, but most of all to Charlie, his only child and the slightly unwilling heir to his agenting throne.

Kate's handwritten letter had arrived the week previously, a thick white envelope addressed in black ink—fountain pen by the loops and slopes of the letters. He'd turned it over a couple of times before opening it, with a strange sixth sense that it wasn't going to be something run-of-the-mill. An echo of that gut instinct his father was so famous for, maybe.

Dear Jojo,

I'm one hundred percent certain you won't remember me, I was one of your clients twenty years ago. God, I feel old writing that, it's a lifetime, I know! A literal lifetime, actually— my daughter, Alice, has just turned nineteen and gone to university, not that that's the reason I'm writing to you (by hand, you'll note, because I remember how much you always hated technology. I draw the line at purple ink though!).

Or maybe Alice leaving sort of is the reason I'm writing to you, at least in part—she's left home for a new adventure, and I'm about to turn forty and recently left my husband, so there you go.

If you do remember me at all, it'll be for chucking my career in to get married and move abroad—"a monumental mistake" you called it, as I remember. I was offended at the time but it turns out you were right. He had that clichéd affair with his secretary— it's fine if you're rolling your eyes. It's taken twenty years, but I guess the joy of "I told you so" never gets old, right? Permission to revel in it granted.

I feel embarrassed to be writing to you after all this time. A bit of me hopes this letter is returned to sender because you're drinking rum punch on a beach in the Bahamas, but obviously more of me hopes you're still the best agent in town and willing to let me buy you lunch and apologize in person. We're talking a sandwich in the park rather than shepherd's pie in the Ivy, though, just to set your expectations at a realistic level! That's kind of the point, to be honest. I've left my husband and he's kept all the money— damn me and my lovestruck pre-nup! You did try to warn me, I wish I'd listened.

Is it unrealistic to hope there might still be a place for me in the acting world, Jojo? I know I'd have to start at the bottom again and most likely stay there, but I'm okay with that.

I've found myself living in a studio flat and for all I know I might not even remember how to act, so I'm sealing this now and shoving it in the post box before my nerve fails me. And yes— I'm trying to shamelessly curry favor by writing instead of emailing! If by any chance you've given up on purple ink and joined the digital revolution, you can find me at kateandclive@blinkmail.com.

Hope to be in touch soon,

Kate

(BTW, Clive is the tortoise my sister and I have co-owned for the last thirty-three years. I set the email up just after my breakup, and I admit there was wine involved. Clive appeared just as I was choosing an email address and it seemed funny at the time because he's the only guy who I've always been able to count on, but now I have to explain who Clive is all the time and it's not very funny at all really, is it? Will change it to something more professional, obvs.)

Whoever Kate Elliott was, she clearly hadn't heard about his father's demise. Her frank letter had been intriguing enough for him to ask his secretary to pull Kate's paperwork from Jojo's meticulously maintained archive. It landed on his desk within minutes, a slim manila file with a headshot clipped to the outside.

"Thanks, Felicity," he'd murmured to her retreating back. She'd worked for the agency for at least twenty-five years, her time split between Jojo on talent and Fiona Fox across the hall on literary. They'd been a formidable double act for decades, Felicity the human bridge between them, manning reception and running the ship.

A note had been pushed beneath the photo clipped to the file, his father's unmistakable purple handwriting.

Foolish child! All that talent down the drain, plug pulled just as she was getting started. Rising star, falling star. Crying waste of talent. And for what? Some misplaced notion of love being willing to give up your dreams for someone else's? She'll be back, no doubt.

Charlie sighed. His father had always been an astute judge of character, and nothing had upset him more than wasted talent.

Jojo's portrait had watched him from the wall opposite; Charlie had practically heard his father telling him to connect the dots. In one hand, a letter from an unknown actor. In the other, a job specifically requiring an unknown actor, someone to pose as a romance author for PR purposes. He studied Kate's headshot. Clear green eyes, auburn hair falling around her shoulders. It was twenty years out of date, but maybe, just maybe, she had the look of a romance writer. Her letter had pulled no punches—she was freshly divorced and desperate for work, and to be frank he'd have an uphill battle selling the job to anyone more established. Clicking into his email, he'd copied Kate's address with a resigned sigh. He might be Jojo Francisco's son, but he drew the line at purple ink.

Glancing at the clock now, he sighed and folded Kate's letter back into its envelope. It didn't matter whether she was right for the job or not. She hadn't even bothered turning up.

2

SAME "FRANCISCO & FOX" ETCHED ON THE HALF-GLASS DOOR AT THE TOP
of the narrow, winding wooden staircase, same sickly mix of fear and
excitement in the pit of her stomach when she was buzzed inside. Kate
could almost feel the echo of her younger self taking a seat on what was
quite possibly the same battered leather sofa in reception, and she was
pretty certain she'd been greeted by the same secretary as all those
years ago too. The time-capsule effect did little to settle her nerves.
Would Charlie Francisco be a carbon copy of his father, as familiar as
all of the other fixtures and fittings, likely to barrel out of his office and
bark her name even though she was barely five feet away?

She glanced up when the phone on the secretary's desk
buzzed, and a sharp female voice echoed around the room de-
manding coffee, stirring decades-old apprehension in Kate's gut.
Her eyes flickered to the closed door bearing Fiona Fox's name in
shouty capitals. Jojo's long-term business partner was still in situ
then, and by the sound of it, every bit as sharklike as she'd been
twenty years ago. Kate had been eighty percent terrified, twenty
percent in awe. Jojo and Fiona had been like the world's most
fear-inducing parents back when she was a teen, and whenever
she'd been faced with difficult occasions over the intervening
years, she'd asked herself what Fiona Fox would do. What she

really hoped Fiona Fox *wouldn't* do in that exact moment was step out into reception and spot her sitting there, because she was already hanging on to the last shreds of her dignity by her fingernails.

She was in luck. Charlie didn't keep her waiting, which she was grateful for. She'd googled him, of course, and seen his corporate headshot, but his complete dissimilarity to his father came as a jolt all the same. Jojo had been a terrier of a man, a huge personality packed into a compact package, although he'd strained his shirt buttons thanks to too many swanky lunches. Same office, same secretary, but this was a very different Francisco. Taller, certainly. No barreling, either. He strolled out and extended his hand, radiating a self-assured confidence that felt more California beach bar than London office.

"Kate?"

No barking either, then, and the only thing straining his close-fitting white shirt was his biceps. More wolf than terrier, throwing her off her stride even more than the sicky baby and the ruined jacket.

She shot out of her seat with her hand outstretched, wishing she'd wiped it on her trousers first in case it was clammy. If it was, his business-like half nod didn't show it. His inquisitive eyes swept over her mildly disheveled appearance and seemed to make a snap judgment on her non-suitability for whatever role he'd had her in mind for, the briefest flicker of disappointment, perhaps.

"Sorry I'm a few minutes late," she said. She resisted the urge to elaborate, because baby vomit was hardly the ideal conversational opener at a job interview, was it? Besides, his quickness to jump to the wrong conclusion had pulled on her already-frayed nerves.

"Come through," he said, ushering her into his office and closing the door.

Same green-leather-top desk, same captain's swivel chair behind it. A different smell, perhaps. Back in the day there had been a linger of cigar smoke and industrial end-of-the-day sweat, in contrast to Charlie's subtly expensive cologne and fresh coffee, as if he'd just wandered in from his post-run morning shower.

"Your father always said to trust him to steer the ship from that chair," she said, her mind rolodexing back through the decades at the sight of it.

"Did he also tell you he'd steer you clear of icebergs?" Charlie gestured for her to take the seat opposite.

She laid a hand over her throat for dramatic effect. "You mean I wasn't the only one he used that line on?"

Charlie patted the arm of the captain's chair as he sat down. "He commanded his entire fleet from this thing."

"Like Napoleon," Kate said.

He raised his eyes to his father's portrait. "I think he'd get a kick out of the comparison."

"Well, he was usually right," Kate said. "And in my case, he definitely was. As I said in my letter, I've managed to steer myself spectacularly onto the rocks."

Charlie's gaze didn't flinch. He didn't seem embarrassed by her candor or seek to make light of her situation.

"It sounds like you've had a tough year."

A small, wild laugh bubbled up her windpipe. "Just a bit." She swallowed and cleared her throat, remembering she wasn't there for a stroll down memory lane. "Your email mentioned a job I might be suitable for?"

It could have been a trick of the light, but something shifted momentarily through Charlie's dark, watchful eyes. Was he regretting inviting her in, deciding whether to even bother telling her about the job he'd called her there to discuss? He glanced down at his desk. Kate did the same, seeing her file, the twenty-years-out-of-date headshot, Jojo's flamboyant purple ink. Charlie quickly slid a thick, blank-covered, spiral-bound book over the top of it.

"This book is in need of an author," he said, splaying his hand flat on its plain front cover, summer bronze against snow white.

She frowned, unsure what he meant. "Doesn't it already have one?"

His expression said *yes*, but also *no*. "Not one prepared to have their name across the front of it."

"Is there something wrong with it?"

Charlie shook his head. "Quite the opposite. It's a love story for the ages."

Kate was trying, but the pieces weren't slotting into place. "I'm sorry, I'm not clear what you're saying," she said eventually, a tiny shrug to imply it wasn't her fault he was being vague.

He steepled his fingers over the book cover, a small sigh suggesting she should try harder. "It's the work of an extremely established author, but it doesn't fit their brand. It's a one-off diversion from their usual genre, and they're not willing to see it published under their own name."

"So why don't they just use a fake name, a pseudonym?"

He took a moment to consider his words. "It's a little more complicated than that. They don't want to be connected to this book in any way. They're not prepared to risk a pseudonym that might be linked back to them at some point in the future."

"So my name would be on the cover and my photo on the jacket?"

He nodded, watching her wrap her head around the concept.

"Do I have to actually do anything?" she said, trying to decide if it was something she could sign up to. "Besides get a new headshot?"

"Something less teenage might be a start," he said, just on the right side of sarcasm.

"I was nineteen, actually, and a fool," she said, prickled. "And now I'm thirty-nine, and still a fool, apparently."

Awareness flickered through his eyes; he opened his mouth to reply and then seemed to think better of it. He turned the manuscript over in his hands instead, dark lashes hiding his eyes, a reset back into professional mode before he spoke again.

"So it'll be classed as a debut novel, which in the usual run of things shouldn't mean face-to-face interviews, but your photo would be on social media pages, you could expect online interviews, podcasts, that kind of thing. Nothing too strenuous and the publisher will give you all the background info you need." He paused. "You'd need to be on time for things, obviously."

"Wow," she said. "If you must know, a baby was sick on me on the street right outside. I had to put my favorite jacket in the bin." He narrowed his eyes, almost as if he didn't believe her. Reaching a hand behind her head, she pulled the tie from her ponytail, closing her eyes for a second as a waft of baby sick hit her when she flapped her curls around her shoulders.

"Some guy gave me his tie to fasten my hair back, but here, let me share my sour, crispy curls with you as proof."

He sighed and passed her an elastic band from a pot on his desk.

Kate resisted the urge to flick it at him, feeling like a moody teenager as she fastened her hair back again to stop herself from gagging. If it wasn't for the fact she really needed the job, she'd have got up and walked out just for the satisfaction of the flounce. As it was, she put her shoulders back and acted like the grown-ass mature woman she was.

"Would I need to use my actual name?"

He paused and gave her question due consideration. "Would you prefer not to?"

She chewed the inside of her lip, thinking. "If I'm going to view it as playing a role, I think I'd find it easier if it's not my real name."

"I'd suggest you keep Kate so it feels natural when someone addresses you, but I can help you settle on a different surname, perhaps?"

The idea of reinventing herself as a completely new Kate wasn't entirely without appeal.

"Can I know who the actual author is?"

"No. And I think that's for the best, because then you wouldn't need to guard the secret."

She folded her arms and looked at him levelly across the desk. "Is it you?"

His eyes opened a little wider, startled. "Why do you ask that?"

She raised her eyebrows. "You look like a guy who wouldn't admit to writing love stories."

"I'd be proud as hell if I'd written this one," he said after a few silent seconds.

"But what if I have questions about the story? Surely I need to know it inside out so I can field anything that's thrown my way?"

He loosened the knot of his tie a fraction as he swallowed. "Perhaps a good first step would be for you to read the book?" He pushed the manuscript toward her. "Think of it as being sent a script to read, see if you connect with it, if it gives you the magic feeling."

"Now you *do* sound like your father," she said, because however different Charlie was from Jojo Francisco, "the magic feeling" was a phrase she'd heard in this office several times before.

"I learned from the best," he said. "I realize it's an unconventional role, not what you came here expecting. I'd make sure you're well remunerated for your time, if you decide to take it, naturally."

His words grounded her, a reminder that her pockets were light and her options were limited.

"Can I take a couple of days to read it before I decide?"

"Of course," he said, getting to his feet to see her out. "Take as long as you need."

Charlie Francisco wasn't at all like his father in appearance or demeanor. Jojo had been paternal but unpredictable; being around him had set her nerves on edge. Charlie was a different Francisco altogether. Definitely not paternal, and he set her nerves jangling in a whole other way.

SHE'D BEEN CONCERNED THAT SHE'D be one of several people up for whatever role Charlie Francisco had her in mind for, but as she headed toward the train station with the manuscript stashed safely in her bag, she had a sneaking realization that he didn't have anyone else anonymous enough for the job on his books. He was asking her to be a ghost author.

3

CHARLIE BARELY HAD TIME TO SIT DOWN AFTER SEEING KATE OUT BE-
fore Fiona Fox came striding through, no knock on his closed door.

"Well?"

"Come in, Fi," he said, with a resigned half smile.

"Did she say yes?"

He swallowed, watching Fiona pace. "She's going to think
about it."

"Think about it?" Fiona said. "The woman is on her knees
with a twenty-year gap on her CV, and she's going to *think* about
it?"

Sometimes it felt as if his father hadn't left the building at all.

"Let's just give her time to read the book," he said. "We need
her to genuinely love the story first, which I'm sure she will."

"She was dressed like a bloody waitress, that's going to need
work. Looks bohemian enough to carry it off at least," Fiona said,
gripping the back of the chair opposite his with her expensively
bejeweled fingers. "I mean, was that a man's necktie in her hair?
Did she roll in here late, fresh from a bunk-up? We need someone
we can rely on for this, Charlie. Is she that person? And as for all
that clanky jewelry . . ." There was an implied shudder to her
words, a distaste for anyone who didn't share her own taste for

power dressing and heavily lacquered hair. Fiona Fox had perfected her signature look in the nineties and never deviated from it for the sake of fashion. Kate Elliott hadn't struck Charlie as especially bohemian, but in truth he understood what Fi meant. She had an individuality about her that even her blank-slate white shirt couldn't disguise, from the hastily tied-back curls to her musical silver bangles when she shook his hand. He'd found her candid honesty refreshing; there was no air of desperation even though life had chucked her into the deep end of late.

"Do you think it's a fair thing to ask of her?" he said. "The element of subterfuge?"

"Is the woman an actor or not?" Fiona threw her hands up in the air. "Don't be gauche, Charlie, it's dull. Writers use pseudonyms all the time, you've been around this business long enough to understand it's just semantics."

"Not usually like this, though," he pressed. "If it ever came out, it could be a PR train wreck." He was trying to find an angle Fi would care about, because she definitely didn't give a hoot about Kate Elliott.

"Then make damn sure it never comes out," Fi said, steel-eyed. "It comes down to putting the right person on this job in the first place, Charlie, a safe pair of hands, because there's no room for second chances. Does she have the balls or not?"

He'd only met Kate Elliott once, but he found himself very much hoping that she did. She'd breezed through the office this morning like fresh mountain air, no side order of sarcasm or sense of game playing.

"Let's wait and see how she reacts to the manuscript first, one step at a time."

Fi shook her head. "Get her on the phone. We don't have time to work to her schedule, she works to ours."

"Fi, she only left the office ten minutes ago. She hasn't even had time to get to the train station, let alone read the manuscript."

"She doesn't need to read it. We need someone who thinks on their feet and makes decisions based on gut instinct. Is she going to be a rabbit in the headlights when she's put on the spot? Because she will be. She won't have a week to make her mind up what to do or say then, will she?" Fiona sat down opposite him. "Call her, Charlie. Let's see what she's made of."

Charlie found himself conflicted. Fiona had been in the backdrop of his life for as long as he could remember, his father's oldest friend and business partner. She was about as bendable as an iron rod and as warm as freshly churned gelato, but he happened to know she kept a dog-eared copy of *Chicken Soup for the Soul* in her desk drawer and gave monthly to a local cat sanctuary, both facts she'd deny. Fiona Fox was a stalwart in the publishing world, and in Charlie's world too, and right now she was using their complicated relationship to her advantage, as usual.

"Fine," he said, reaching for his mobile with a sigh. "But for the record, I think we risk losing her by pushing too hard."

"If she's going to jump, better now than when her name's on the front of that book."

Fiona took the seat opposite and watched him place the call, speakerphone on. He privately thought it would be better for all concerned if it went to voicemail. He imagined Kate standing on the train platform searching for her mobile in her oversized bag, bangles jangling against the plain white cover of the book.

"Charlie, so soon," she answered after a handful of rings, sounding bemused.

Fiona's eyebrows shot up, as if Kate should be more respectful.

"Thanks for coming in today, Kate, it was good to meet you."

She sighed. "Are you calling to say you've changed your mind because I arrived late, even though I explained why?"

"Well, that wasn't—"

"Or has Fiona Fox vetoed me because—"

Charlie closed his eyes, unwilling to look across the desk. "Fiona and I are here together just now, Kate," he cut across her so she wouldn't lose herself the job before she'd even accepted it. "We both think you're a great fit for the role, so shall we fix up a time for you to come back in and dot the i's and cross the t's?"

She fell silent for a few beats, the bustle of the train station evident through the phone speaker.

"I'd prefer to take some time to read the book first, as we agreed?"

Fiona rolled her eyes and tapped her blood-red nail against the face of her slim gold watch. "Give her twenty-four hours," she stage-whispered.

He shook his head. "What, to live?" he shot back, hopefully quiet enough for Kate not to hear.

"I'll call as soon as I've read it," she said, cool. "Monday, maybe?"

Fiona threw her hands in the air, even though it was already Friday.

"Monday it is," he said, wishing he'd refused to call her at all, because he'd ended up unnecessarily compromised in both women's eyes. He placed his mobile down and looked at Fiona. "There. We'll know she's the right person by Monday."

Fiona got to her feet. "Your father would have known she was the right person within thirty seconds of meeting her," she said, turning on her heel.

Fiona drew unfavorable comparisons between Charlie and

his father all the time; he was really hoping it'd ease off as she recovered from Jojo's loss and adjusted to Charlie's less shoot-from-the-hip agenting style. In truth, Charlie was still working out what his own agenting style was going to look like. Being his father's understudy had never been part of his life plan; if it hadn't been for his all-too-messy divorce, he'd still be in L.A. now, knee-deep in scripts and studio meetings. Being married to the daughter of one of Hollywood's sharpest agents had been great until it wasn't—L.A. was a big place, yet it turned out there wasn't room enough for the both of them. His father had been cock-a-hoop when he'd proposed to Tara, the only child of one of his oldest professional friends. The coming together of two legendary agenting dynasties, her father had said in his wedding speech, misty-eyed and champagne happy. And it'd felt that way to Charlie too, as if he'd found his place and his people and his purpose. Neither he nor Tara were interested in agenting, but they'd grown up around the acting industry, and they turned their own love story into a lucrative writing duo telling other people's love stories.

He'd hit the wall hard in the aftermath of their breakup, so much so that his father had finally pitched up on his L.A. doorstep and not left until he agreed to come home to London with him. *Home.* Therein lay the rub, really. Nowhere felt like home. Not his soulless L.A. beach house, too showy and void-like without Tara. And not his father's stuck-in-a-time-warp London townhouse either, decorated over thirty years ago by Charlie's late mother and untouched since. To give Jojo his dues, he'd done his best to take care of his son at a point when he really needed taking care of, even if Charlie didn't accept the help as graciously as he might have at the time. Talent agenting was never on his radar as a career option; he'd agreed to work alongside his father as a stop gap, going in to work at Francisco & Fox to avoid his father hiring a housekeeper to make sure he didn't have whiskey for breakfast. And then Jojo had gone and bloody died, keeled over in his beloved shepherd's pie at the Ivy, leaving Charlie alone in the captain's chair, whether he liked it or not. And whether Fiona liked it or not too, which on most days, she didn't.

4

"I've written a book," Kate said, flopping onto the other end of the sofa to her sister, careful not to lose any Pinot from her glass. She'd been back from London for a couple of hours, and all she'd done from the moment she'd sat on the train was read the mystery manuscript.

Liv looked at her sharply. "Have you? When? On the train home?"

Kate shrugged. She'd made the decision within the first few pages that she was going to say oh-my-God-this-is-heartachingly-beautiful yes, so technically, perhaps, she had become an author on the train. "Kind of."

"Is it a gory thriller about an adulterous twat called Richard who catches his tie in the shredder while doing his secretary and gets yanked face-first into the blades? Or maybe he gets dragged into a dark alley by his ex-wife's violent kick-ass sister? I'd pay good money to read that."

Liv had taken Richard's adultery almost as hard as Kate herself—she was the elder sister by two years, and she took her position seriously. They'd lost their mother as small children and been raised by the kind of father whose "eccentric scientist" approach bordered on unintentional neglect. He'd rarely remembered to turn up at parents' evenings when she'd been small, and he'd chosen to appear at an overseas convention rather than attend her wedding to Richard. It hadn't hurt her as much as people might have imagined; he'd never exceeded her expectations as a father.

It had been Liv's brain wave to move Kate into the flat above her fancy-dress shop in the aftermath of the separation, making decisions because her sister couldn't face it. It was a far cry from the five-bedroom detached Kate and Richard had shared—or rather she'd *thought* they'd shared it, until she'd walked in on him in bed with his secretary and realized he'd stitched her into a pre-nup so watertight that she'd been lucky to leave with her own clothes.

Damn those love goggles. She'd driven away from that house with a few cardboard boxes and a suitcase, her dignity in shreds as curtains around the gated community twitched with barely concealed excitement. She'd headed blindly to Liv and Nish's overcrowded three-story terrace, where the welcome was all-encompassing and she'd had to talk her mild-mannered brother-in-law out of paying Richard a visit to relieve him of his teeth. Turkish veneers, not that it was relevant.

"I've been working out," Nish had said gamely. "And I cycle to the office three times a week now, better for the planet."

Kate tucked her legs beneath her, already in pj's even though it was barely six o'clock.

"It's a love story," she said. "An incredibly beautiful one."

Liv put her head on one side, studying her sister. "You've lost me."

Kate reached behind the sofa cushion for the plain-covered book she'd stashed there when she'd answered the door to Liv ten minutes ago.

"This one," she said. "It's an orphan at the moment, and I've been asked to be its mother."

"You didn't actually write it, though?" Liv said, trying to understand. "You haven't blown the dust off those old romances you used to write and gotten secretly famous have you?"

Kate swirled the wine in her glass, watching the concentric circles. It had been a long time since she'd written anything, fragile dreams squashed by the reality of life as Richard's wife, life organizer, and hostess. She'd quietly channeled her soul-deep need for creative expression into writing rather than performing for a while, but even that had fallen by the wayside after Alice was born.

"God, I wish I'd written it because it's stunning, but no, these aren't my words."

Kate had already made two decisions about the book. One, she was going to take the job. She could have called Charlie to let him know, but he'd wound her up by badgering her for an answer before she'd even caught the train home. And two, her immediate family needed to be on board, because she wasn't prepared to lie to them. Liv refilled their glasses as she listened to the details of Charlie's unusual job offer, flicking through the pages of the manuscript balanced on her knees.

"So you basically moonlight as the author online and on the cover, kind of like the book's official representative?"

"That's about right," Kate said. "But we'd need to keep the fact I haven't actually written it between ourselves. Nish can know, obviously, but I was wondering about Stevie and Arun . . . would it be easier to just not tell them I haven't actually written it, so they don't need to keep any secrets?"

"My kids will have very limited interest in the whole thing anyway, unless you go viral on social media or something," Liv said. "If it doesn't happen on their phones, it doesn't happen."

"I'm not planning on becoming a meme any time soon," Kate said. "I better tell Alice, though, it feels too much to keep from her."

"She called me last night to see how you are," Liv said, finger-combing her blonde hair back into a knot at the base of her neck.

"I spoke to her myself," Kate said.

"Yeah, she told me. She was just double-checking you weren't faking it for her benefit."

Kate sighed. "I hate that she feels as if she needs to worry about me."

"She doesn't need to. She chooses to, because you're her mother and she adores you."

"Did she tell you she thinks I should go solo traveling in Thailand to find myself? She bombarded me with links this morning."

"Yes. Asked me to badger you into going."

Kate sighed. "Oh to be nineteen and think the answer to all life's problems can be found on a tropical beach."

"Can't they? I can think of worse places to look."

"I'm forty next birthday, bit late for my gap year," Kate said. "I don't want to run away, Liv, but Alice does have a point. I need to do something to spark my life up, and I think it might have just landed in my lap."

Liv topped up their wineglasses. "So what did you think of Charlie Francisco?"

Kate huffed. "Nothing like his father, that's for sure."

"He was a one-off, to be fair," Liv said.

Jojo had been in Kate's life for barely two years, but in that time he'd been a wise teacher, an unpredictably brilliant agent, and sometimes a fatherly shoulder. He'd certainly guided her well, straight into the casting department of one of the country's longest-running soaps. She remembered his joy in personally delivering the news that she'd landed the part she desperately wanted, his pride when she won Most Promising Newcomer at the Soap Awards the following year. He'd helped Liv out back then too, putting her in touch with TV and film costume departments she'd never have gotten a foot in the door with otherwise. He was that sort of man, expansive and generous with his knowledge and his little black book of contacts; he'd taken both sisters under his wing, and Kate's resignation like an arrow to the heart.

"Charlie's overconfident," Kate said. "Suntan. Bit flash."

Liv sniffed. "I did some digging. Word is he cheated on his wife, Tara, more than once."

Liv had a direct hotline to Hollywood gossip through her indiscreet circle of costume department friends; she'd known about several movie-star scandals before even the pushiest of journalists. Not that she ever told anyone but Kate, which didn't count as they were two sides of the same coin.

Kate sighed. "I'm not shocked. He didn't exactly remind me of Richard, but there's something about him I didn't one hundred percent trust."

"He's hot, though, right?"

"Oh God, yeah. Seriously hot."

"There's that," Liv said.

"I thought he was the secret author at first. It's no big leap from writing rom-com movies to novels, is it?"

"Who knows." Liv shrugged. "I bet Tara wrote the movies anyway and let him take the credit."

It was a disappointing but not altogether surprising idea. Richard's infidelity had layered cynicism into Kate's everyday thought patterns, her rose-tinted love goggles flung into the nearest dustbin.

"Watch yourself around him," Liv said. "All that"—she pointed toward her own face and made circles in the air—"can be distracting."

Kate knocked back the last of her wine. "He should watch

himself around me," she said, then laughed. "Don't worry, I've got his number. He might be wolfish, but I'm no Red Riding Hood."

Liv gathered her stuff together to head home. "You do look good in red, though," she said. "That dress I made for your engagement was killer."

Kate handed Liv her keys. "Shame it didn't actually kill Richard, it would have saved me a whole heap of trouble."

She didn't mean it. Not entirely. Without Richard there would be no Alice, and in truth the early years of their marriage hadn't been without their good times; but the shock of adultery and divorce had rattled every bone in her body.

Alone again, she flopped back on the sofa and picked up the plain white book, writing her name on the cover with her fingertip. There were few silver linings to her reduced circumstances, but at least there were no inquisitive neighbors or close friends to explain her sudden new author life to. As ghost authors go, Charlie Francisco couldn't have picked a better person for the job.

Hi Charlie,

Thanks for seeing me last week, and even more so for offering me such an incredible opportunity. I've read the book (twice—I couldn't sleep last night for thinking about Leanora's story, she's jumped off the page straight into my heart) and you were right, it's ... I don't even have the words for how much I'm in love with it.

It would be an absolute honor to be its official representative, if the offer is still open. Please let me know what I should do next.

All my best,

Kate

Hi Kate,

That's great news, I was very much hoping to hear from you today.

Give me a couple of days to discuss things in-house and I'll get back to you.

Let me know if any days and times are better at your end.

Best wishes,

Charlie

5

"ARE YOU SURE YOU DON'T WANT ME TO COME WITH YOU? I CAN CLOSE up here, it's deathly quiet." Liv looked up from her sewing machine when Kate appeared downstairs ready to head into London. "I can sit at a separate table and keep an eye, send you a discreet signal if you start the verbal diarrhea thing." She drew a finger across her throat to demonstrate.

"Don't even say it, you know I'll be worse if I worry about it."

"You can't help it, it's all part of your charm. Same as my barely concealed inner rage."

Kate breathed in slowly, counting, holding, releasing again as per the meditation app she'd been using to try to foster calmness. "Besides, it's not the kind of place you can just turn up and get a table." She'd checked the restaurant online and studied the menu so as not to be caught out; reviewers often gloated about finally getting a table after months of impatiently waiting. "What does this outfit say to you?"

Kate gestured down at her slim black cigarette pants and cornflower-blue silk blouse. She'd gone with a ruby red lip too, for confidence.

"Successful author type does lunch. Can you walk in those boots?" Liv said, eyeing Kate's black heels.

"Trainers ready, just giving you the full effect," she said. "Is this lipstick too much?"

She'd bought the too-expensive lipstick not long after she'd broken up with Richard. The assistant had informed her the shade name was Ruby Slippers, in case she ever needed a refill. She'd cried as she left the shop and caught the train in the opposite direction to her old house, "no place like home" ringing in her ears. Today was the first time she'd actually felt able to take the lipstick from its fancy box and use it.

Liv stood to shake out the peacock-feathered bodice she was working on, a costume commission for a sci-fi fantasy movie.

"Hang on," she said, taking the pins from her mouth. "Take this for luck."

She slid their mother's slim silver bangle from her wrist and added it to the similar one Kate always wore. They were their only keepsakes from their mum, one each, and over the years they'd fallen into the habit of doubling them up if either of them needed an extra shot of protection.

Kate touched it briefly, glad of the quiet, bell-like reassurance that had accompanied her through exams, her driving test, her wedding day. Job interviews too, if that was what today's lunch could be classed as.

"I think I'm going to suggest Dalloway for my new surname," she said, switching the boots for her trainers. "Kate Dalloway. What do you think?"

"Will you buy yourself flowers on the way home too?"

Kate shrugged into her coat. "I considered Havisham, but there's no way I'm risking getting caught in a wedding dress ever again."

"But you made such a beautiful bride," Liv said.

"Because you made my dress, and walked me down the aisle, and helped me plan it all," Kate said. "Everything about the day was perfect, except the groom."

"You can't write love off forever because of one bad apple," Liv said, plucking a loose thread from the shoulder seam of Kate's coat.

"Um, a twenty-year bad apple," Kate said. "That's a whole orchard of bad apples. It'll be on the *News at Ten* tonight—national apple shortage declared due to one massive manky apple called Richard bloody Elliott. There will be a cider shortage and the nation will go after him with pitchforks."

"I'll be the one at the front with the really rusty one," Liv said.

"I've never been big on apples anyway," Kate said.

"Me neither. Not even in that cheap cider we used to drink as teenagers."

"Especially not that cheap cider." Kate shuddered. "God, I can taste it now. Fizzy cat piss."

Liv opened the shop door. "Go, Mrs. Dalloway, take your leave."

"Miss Dalloway, in my case," Kate corrected, buttoning her coat to fend off the early April chill. "Wish me luck."

"You don't need it," Liv said, leaning on the doorframe. "Remember, they need you more than you need them—Charlie Francisco needs to show you the money."

Kate looked knowingly at her sister. "Been watching *Jerry Maguire* again?"

Liv laid her crossed hands over her heart. "If he says 'You complete me,' marry him."

"That's really terrible advice."

Kate shook her head, laughing as she set off toward the train station at a brisk pace, already wishing she'd remembered to bring a hair band. Would she ever feel like a fully-fledged grown-up? She could only hope that her high-heeled boots and Ruby Slippers lipstick would be enough to hide the fact that inside she was forever in her pj's with her hair scraped up, eating a family bag of Cheetos in front of the TV on her own.

6

KATE WALKED THROUGH THE POLISHED BLACK DOOR OF THE POSH MAY-
fair townhouse restaurant in a last-minute flap, because it had suddenly occurred to her that she'd offered to buy Jojo Francisco lunch
in her letter. Did Charlie plan on holding her to it on his father's behalf? It was the kind of place where someone in uniform opened the
door and quietly ushered you in; she was glad of her expensive boots
to make her look more well-heeled than she actually was. She'd be
washing up for at least ten years to clear a lunch debt in here, and
God, the shame of her card getting declined would be hard to come
back from. Should she ask him outright before they ordered? She
couldn't possibly. She could always slip back outside again unseen
and call him to cancel, say some unavoidable thing had suddenly
come up. Except that suggested flaky, and she was already on dodgy
ground after baby-sick-gate. A safe pair of hands was a basic necessity for the job she was hopefully about to be hired for.

"Kate." Charlie materialized beside her, taller by a head. No
slipping away unseen, then. "I spotted you coming in." He nodded *I've got this* to the approaching maître d', who smiled and
veered away to do something else.

"Just a heads-up." Charlie spoke quietly, close to her ear, as he
guided her through the shady, intimate dining room toward their

table. "Fiona is with us for drinks, then heading off to another meeting."

Kate nodded, appreciating the forewarning. Her recollections of Fiona Fox from twenty years ago were of a hard-boiled woman who seemed to be the only person in the world Jojo Francisco deferred to. Would time have mellowed her? Not that she'd ever been woundingly sharp with Kate, perhaps out of deference for Jojo's soft spot or some maternal protection for the motherless teenager she'd been back then. Maternal was possibly overstating it. More raptor-like, with Kate as one of her eggs.

"Two minutes late by my watch." Fiona removed the trio of tiny olives from her martini and laid the stick beside her glass, eyebrows arched, no handshake.

Not mellowed, then, Kate thought, knowing full well she was at least five minutes early, because she'd loitered outside for a while rather than come in and risk being here before Charlie. Fiona appeared to have defied the decades, looking exactly as she did the last time Kate had seen her. Hair straight out of the Bonnie Tyler playbook, and she was almost certainly wearing the exact same chunky diamond beetle on her lapel.

"I realize we might have met before but I haven't the faintest recollection of who you are," Fiona said, setting the tone early. Kate swallowed the implied forgettability, and didn't add that she remembered Fiona's ferocity and occasional bone of kindness. She looked around, wondering what to do with her coat. She didn't have to wonder for long: a member of the staff appeared and wordlessly whisked it away as Fiona batted her hand toward the seat opposite. "Sit, before someone asks you to fetch a bottle of Bordeaux."

The none-too subtle attempts to unsettle Kate landed as intended, but she just smiled tightly and took her seat beside Charlie.

"Drink?" Charlie said. "The martinis here are excellent."

Kate found herself conflicted. She loved a good martini, but feared the alcohol might loosen her tongue a little too much. She needed to stay sharp, to look cool on the outside even if she was a hot mess on the inside.

"Have one, he's paying," Fiona said, which—unbeknownst to the older woman—was a considerable weight off Kate's shoulders. Enough to make her nod in agreement, and within moments an ice-frosted martini glass appeared in front of her. Now. To olive or not to olive? She was a fan in general, but Fiona had laid her olive-laden cocktail stick down beside her glass. She reluctantly placed hers on the table too before sipping too much of her drink in one go and almost spluttering on the throat-stripping strength. Goodbye, nerves; hello, confidence.

"I hope you understand the gravitas of the role you've been offered," Fiona said, fixing her with a stare. "Frankly, I need to be convinced of your commitment."

Kate ran her tongue over her teeth to remove any stray ruby lipstick traces and tried to keep Liv's *Jerry Maguire* pep talk at the forefront of her mind—although asking Fiona Fox to show her the money might not be the best way to demonstrate commitment right now.

"Well, I love the book with my whole heart," she said, taking another good mouthful of martini before plowing on. "My own love story came to a sudden and unexpected end last year, so I can relate. I ugly cried my way through it, in a cathartic sort of way. Not that my husband died—I walked in on him having sex with his secretary, to be totally honest—but I've experienced some parallel emotions as a result. The shock, certainly, and the abrupt tear in the fabric of my life. It's the big things, of course, like living alone for the first time as an adult, but the million small things even more so. I didn't realize the exact moment of our final argument over what to watch on TV. Who knew that having the freedom to watch back-to-back episodes of *Married at First Sight* would be one of the upsides to divorce? That and not having to buy hummus anymore. Honestly, I'd rather eat grout. I'm still figuring out who I am without him, really. I'm nobody's wife, and I don't have to do much mothering now my daughter's away at uni. You could say it's just me, alone at sea, looking for a life raft to climb onto. I'm Kate Winslet clinging to that door. This book"—she picked up Charlie's copy of the manuscript and clutched it to her chest—"this book is my door, Fiona, and I won't let it sink, I promise you."

Kate laid the book slowly down on the table and knocked the rest of her drink back in one long gulp, wishing Liv had been at a nearby table giving her the cutthroat sign. Half a violently strong martini and she'd let the hot mess out.

Fiona stared at her, momentarily slack-jawed, and then delicately picked up her cocktail stick and dropped it in her empty glass. She glanced at Charlie with a sigh, then back at Kate.

"As soliloquies go, it was hardly Shakespeare, but we're tight on time so you'll have to do." She scraped her chair back and someone instantly appeared with her coat. "Media training, Charlie, and fast." Fiona stalked away between tables, leaving a trace of old-school Opium lingering over people's lunches.

"Well, that went well," Kate said, finally eating her olives as she sagged in her chair.

"Sorry not to have intervened," Charlie said. "It was kind of hard to get a word in."

Kate sighed. "I said too much, didn't I?"

"I mean, the *Titanic* reference was a little out there, but I admire that you committed," he said. "Hungry?"

Kate sat up straight and rolled her shoulders, relief and alcohol softening her bones. "Martini on an empty stomach was a really bad plan," she said. "I'm actually starving."

"Go crazy," he said. "Order a bunch of sides, the whole works. Business credit card."

"SO, IS GHOST AUTHORING SOMETHING that happens a lot behind the scenes?" Kate said, after they'd ordered far too much food for two.

Charlie filled their water glasses. "Not exactly," he said. "Pseudonyms are not unusual, of course, or ghostwriters, where someone writes the book on behalf of someone else. Autobiographies, for instance—people in the public eye often get help putting their memories into a cohesive narrative. It's become more commonplace in fiction too in recent years—the famous name on the front isn't necessarily the person who wrote the words inside. What we're planning to do with this book is an unconventional twist on that, I guess."

"Smoke and mirrors, you mean," she said, testy because he sounded like a politician trying to persuade her that his party's underhand dealings were par for the course.

"Publishing is no different from any other business in that sense," he said. "Fluid, always evolving. It needs to stay dynamic to survive. At the end of the day, people want to read brilliant books, so everyone wins."

"It'd certainly be a tragedy if no one else ever got to read this," she said, resting her fingers on the blank book cover. "Is there anything I need to know about the actual author? Anything they'd like me to include when I talk about the story?"

Charlie paused while their food was delivered to the table, making easy conversation with the waiter as the various dishes were served. Kate watched him closely, trying to discern if he'd deflected her question to give himself time to think of a convincing answer.

"The only thing you need to be sure of is that the author doesn't want to be involved at all," he said once they were alone again. "Not in the PR, not on the cover, not at all."

"Okay, I get it. Well, I don't, obviously," Kate said. "Because if I'd written this, I'd be shouting about it from the rooftops with a megaphone."

He looked at her levelly over the rim of his glass. "You did write it, remember?"

She picked up her cutlery. "I wish I had. I tried to write a novel before Alice was born, but life kind of got in the way, as it does."

"Or maybe it gets in the way for people who let it, who don't want it enough?" he said.

She put her knife and fork down again. "I'm not sure that's entirely fair," she said, feeling judged. "Or maybe it's fair for men, but not for women who're trying to juggle work and little kids and home life. Trust me, spare time is spent sleeping."

He let her words sit in the air between them as he loaded his plate.

She didn't retract or soften them; he wasn't a parent, but that didn't mean he couldn't understand how all-consuming it could be. She changed the subject instead, flipping the spotlight onto him.

"Was following in your father's footsteps always your long-term plan?"

"Not exactly. Not at all, in fact." He sighed, putting his water down in favor of his wineglass. "Life doesn't always go to plan, though, does it? My father was very much a roll-with-the-punches kind of guy. I'm trying his approach on for size."

The guarded expression on his face suggested there was a lot more to that conversation he didn't feel inclined to share.

"Right. And how's that going for you?"

"Up and down."

"It sounds as if we've both found ourselves traveling down unexpected tracks," she said, offering him an in if he wanted one. Finding out what made Charlie Francisco tick was high on her priority list, because earning her trust had gotten a whole lot harder since the Richard debacle.

He raised his glass and touched it to hers, awareness of her subtle attempts at digging reflected in his dark eyes.

"And now you're all alone at sea, clutching a metaphorical door and hoping for rescue," he said, seesawing the emphasis right back onto her.

"Fiona must think I'm a loose cannon," she said. "The connection between my brain and my mouth goes on the blink sometimes, words come out of their own accord." His fork stilled midway to his mouth and she jumped in before he could ask the obvious question hovering on his lips. "In unscripted situations, I mean. It never happened when I was acting, obviously. I'd like to plan for all possible Kate Dalloway conversations in advance, so I'm prepped and ready for anything."

"Dalloway?"

She'd said it so often in her own head as to not remember she hadn't floated it officially. "What do you think?" She helped herself to spring greens and creamy mash.

"Kate Dalloway . . ." he said. "Let me think on it? It needs to feel natural, almost invisible, given the circumstances."

Would it have killed him to just say yes?

"You really don't remind me of your father very much at all," she said, laying her cutlery down.

He narrowed his eyes a fraction. "Is that a good or a bad thing?"

Ideas and energy had crackled in the air around Jojo Francisco. He was a morning sunrise to his son's midnight sky. If there were stars in that sky, Charlie was doing a good job of obscuring them.

"Neither, it's just an observation."

"They're big shoes to fill," he conceded, then after a beat added, "or maybe you're remembering him through rose-colored glasses. Your opinion of him might have been different now you're . . . older."

Ouch. "Old enough to realize Kate was totally right to let Leo float away from that door, if that's what you mean," she said, snarkily.

The corner of his mouth twitched as he refilled their glasses. "Knowing when to let go is no bad thing."

"Sometimes you have no choice." Kate reached for her glass, because the conversation felt something like picking her way over an active minefield. "Do you have any siblings?" she asked, wading toward safer ground. She hoped he did for his sake, because she could imagine that being Jojo's child must have been quite an intense experience.

Charlie shook his head. "Just me."

Kate flinched; she didn't want to think of a life without Liv.

"I lean on my sister more than I should, probably," she said, touching the silver bangles around her wrist. "I honestly don't know how I'd have gotten through the breakup of my marriage without her."

Charlie sighed, his dark eyes melancholy. "Alcohol and bad decisions, if you're anything like me, which I'm sure you're not."

The starkness of his unexpected reply caught her off guard. "Experience in the divorce trenches?"

Charlie made a sound somewhere between a cynical laugh and a groan. "The trenches sounds about right. One too many skirmishes. No winners in that particular war."

Liv's gossip-hungry L.A. contacts had Charlie down as a

walking red flag, enough to keep her guard up around him. Not enough to make her walk away from the job opportunity, though—she was getting into business with him, not into bed.

"Except the lawyers," she said. Her credit card would probably never recover from the shock.

They fell silent, both aware they'd strayed from professional to personal.

"Anyway," Charlie said, clearing his throat and the heavy mood, "I have a draft offer for you to look over." He slid a slim document from the black leather folder on the table beside him. "We've been back and forth with the publisher a fair few times because of the slightly unusual arrangement. They suggested a flat fee given the unknowns involved, but we've pushed back for a signing fee plus traditional royalty percentage. Lower than the usual percentage, of course, as the author themself needs to get paid, but enough to give you some skin in the game if it sells well."

In truth, the details went over Kate's head, and she wasn't sure if she should read the offer right there at the table or wait until she was alone on the train home. Curiosity won out and she flipped the front sheet, skimming the numbers.

"The signing fee is relatively modest," Charlie said, watching her face. "But given the quality of the book and a decent marketing plan, I'm confident the percentage cut will work in your favor."

Kate nodded, running her fingertip over the paperwork. The signing fee wasn't especially modest given her current financially precarious position; it offered her a much-needed level of security to cover her bills and life expenses for the next six months or so, if she was cautious.

"Have you got a pen?" she said.

"You don't need to sign it right away," he said. "Take it home, look it over."

"Is there anything in there designed to catch me out?"

"Kate, it's my job to make sure no one tries to catch you out."

"Then I guess we need to trust each other," she said. "Pen?"

He passed his hand over his face, scrubbing his eyes. "Can I say something before you sign it?"

She took the pen he held out, then sat back a little in her chair, waiting.

"You already know that being a talent agent was never my life plan. Things had gone very badly for me over the last couple of years. Working with my father was the backup plan I didn't see coming. And then he died and, cards on the table, a lot of his clients either left the agency or were poached. My list is pretty small right now—a couple of big names who stayed out of loyalty because the work comes to them, and a handful of lesser-known faces. And now you, if you sign this contract. You're not signing up with Jojo Francisco, and all of the associated razzamatazz that went along with his name. You're signing with me, Charlie, the guy left holding the reins."

Kate nodded slowly. "Well, now I've heard your soliloquy too, so we're even." Clicking the pen, she flipped to the back page of the contract and signed it with a flourish. "There, all done," she said. "So what happens next?"

Charlie slid the contract back into his file. "Now the fun starts."

He held her gaze, then cleared his throat and signaled for the bill.

CHARLIE WATCHED HER PICK HER way through the tables, auburn curls bouncing, not noticing the heads turned in her direction or the second glances over shoulders.

We need to trust each other. She couldn't know how impactful her words had been.

Sighing, he pulled his phone from his jacket pocket. As expected, a flurry of voice messages from Fi, because why would she type when she could just shout into her mobile? An email from the author's editor, Prue, too, checking he'd tied things up with the actor and outlining a barrage of ideas the PR team were excited to discuss. He placed his phone face down and poured the last of the wine into his glass with a sense of unease. He wished he'd been blessed with his father's infamous gut instinct; he seemed to spend too much time questioning his own decisions these days.

He wasn't Jojo Francisco, yet here he was attempting to walk in his daily-polished brown-leather brogues, sitting at his worn-smooth-by-deals desk and living in his outdated house. Every decision he made was governed by the question of what would Jojo do, say, think. This was his father's furrow, his father's life. He finished the wine, unable to shake the thought that just as Kate was a ghost author, he was a ghost agent.

7

"YOU DIDN'T NEED TO DRESS LIKE AN ACTUAL BURGLAR," KATE SAID, EYE-ing Liv's head-to-toe black outfit as she parked the car a few doors down from her old house.

"You said inconspicuous," Liv said.

"I meant more double-glazing salesperson than black widow, but it's fine."

Liv shot Kate's outfit a scathing look. "Well, you nailed the brief. I'll have two bay windows and a replacement back door, please."

Kate couldn't relax enough to laugh; being back in her old neighborhood had her rattled. The cul-de-sac was deserted, as usual. It wasn't the type of place where kids kicked a ball or rode bikes. Even the cats were indoor pure breeds, gazing at the world from the safety of upstairs bedroom windows.

She was pretty certain the house would be empty. Alice was at university, and unless hell had frozen over, Richard, never one to knowingly miss an opportunity to schmooze and show off, would be at the Geneva trade fair.

"Right, let's be clinical, in and out as fast as possible," Kate said, sorting her key ready to insert into the front door. "I'll ring the bell to double-check, then once I've let myself in you get out and follow straight behind me."

It worked exactly as she'd said, and she breathed a sigh of relief when the old alarm code beeped its approval.

"Trust him not to change the locks," Liv said. "Underestimating you as usual."

"For once, I'm glad," Kate muttered, pausing in the hallway to recalibrate and notice unfamiliar scents, subtle differences layered across overwhelming sameness. The paint colors she'd picked out, the furniture she'd chosen, a watercolor she'd never seen before. There was a time when she'd loved this house, in the early days when Alice was still a child. Now it felt like someone else's home. Because that's what it was.

"Come on, let's get this over with," she said, one hand on the balustrade.

"Shall I leave my shoes by the door?" Liv said.

Kate shook her head. Richard was a shoes-off fanatic, and the small act of rebellion felt satisfying. Upstairs, she paused by the closed master bedroom door, then couldn't resist pushing it open.

"So clinically tidy," Liv whispered, standing beside her. "Didn't it drive you nuts?"

Kate shrugged. The twice-weekly cleaners Richard retained had seemed like a help at the time, but with the benefit of hindsight she could see they were paid to ensure he lived a clutter-free existence. He'd always been someone who liked things neat and well organized; his parents were exactly the same. The night she'd walked in on him with his secretary in that exact same room, one of the first things she'd noticed was Belinda's mismatched underwear. God knows how much it must have played havoc with his mood, he'd have been straight on to John Lewis to order her some expensive new matching sets. She'd no doubt have seen it as a gift of passion, his subtle message delivered in a froth of lace and satin.

Kate clicked the door quietly shut, glad not to be sleeping in there anymore.

"In here," she said, opening the guest bedroom door. Fitted cupboards lined the walls, and for a second she stood still and just stared at them. "Give me a minute," she said, scanning the room. "I'm sure they're in here somewhere."

She'd been thinking a lot lately about the manuscripts she'd started before Alice was born. Their mother had been creative, an artist and silversmith; the bangles she and Liv wore were her handiwork. Both of her daughters had inherited the creative gene. Liv expressed it through the clothes she designed and made, while Kate had always felt destined for the bright lights of the stage. When she abruptly turned her back on that world to follow Richard to Germany, she'd found herself compelled to write instead, scripts and manuscripts, crafting words for others to perform if she wasn't going to do it herself anymore. She hadn't looked at those manuscripts in over fifteen years, but something in her had made her hold on to them. Looking after her future self, maybe. It was a phrase she'd used often when Alice was younger: "Do your homework early rather than leaving it to the last minute, look after your future self"; "Eat some healthy stuff in among the crisps and chocolate, look after your future self." Maybe by keeping the manuscripts away from Richard's twice-yearly shredfests, she'd been subconsciously doing that for herself. If she could lay her hands on them, that is.

"What are we looking for, exactly?" Liv said, ready to get stuck in. "A box covered in hand-drawn love hearts and cherubs?"

"I don't want to go rooting through everything," Kate said. "I'd rather no one realize we've been here at all."

"We wouldn't need to break into your own house if your ex-husband would be more reasonable," Liv said. Kate had considered just asking for the manuscripts but knew he'd probably have made it as difficult as possible, or even say he'd thrown them out. "How about we go old school, sew prawns into the hem of his curtains, that's what they always do on TV? You know I never leave the house without a sewing kit."

"Do you carry shellfish too?" Kate muttered, approaching one of the cupboards. "No sabotage. It's still Alice's home, remember?" She didn't love not having room for her daughter to come and stay with her, but she'd been trying to be the bigger person about things for her daughter's sake.

She checked several identical tall cupboards before hitting the jackpot. Richard had moved things around to group anything belonging to Kate in one place—that over-organized streak of his actually useful for once. Hats and scarves, old handbags, and bits of jewelry. She looked at them all with a feeling of disconnection, like an exhibition of someone else's possessions. She hadn't missed any of them.

"This is it," she said, hauling a brown box from the back of the bottom shelf. Flipping the lid to check, she saw banded bundles of paper and her old laptop. It didn't work anymore, but she'd hung on to it in case there was salvageable stuff on the hard drive.

"Can I cut holes in the pockets of all his trousers? Liv said. "Or the ends off his socks?"

Kate laughed, juggling the weight of the box in her arms. "We're meant to be invisible," she said.

"Moths can be so destructive."

Kate shook her head and nodded at the wardrobe. "Close that door, would you?"

One final scan of the room and they headed back downstairs.

"Liv, come on," Kate whispered, anxious when her sister veered off into the kitchen.

"Just one minute."

Kate followed her sister and found her frowning into the open fridge.

"I thought there might be some champagne knocking around I could nick but there's nothing. Maybe he's on a health kick."

The contents of the fridge were both scant and orderly, nothing to go off in his absence, an unopened carton of milk in readiness for his return and—"Fucking bloody revolting hummus," Kate said, surprising both of them.

"Please tell me I can do something to it," Liv said. "Lace it with arsenic or something?"

"Do you happen to have that in your pocket too, along with the prawns and the sewing kit?" Kate said. She wanted to get going, but a small, unwise part of her also wanted to release a little hummus-related rage. Opening the freezer, she rummaged through and came up with a bag of prawns.

"Must be Belinda's, Richard hates them," she said, unzipping the bag.

Liv looked delighted. "Are we actually going to sew them into the curtains?"

Kate peeled the lid on the hummus. "Nothing so drastic," she said, tipping a good handful of prawns in and mixing them around to hide them. "Just this."

As she put the rest of the prawns away and made sure to put the hummus back where she'd found it, Liv reached out and grabbed her arm. "Did you hear a car?"

They stood statue still and heard a car door slam on the drive.

"Shit!" Kate panicked, grabbing the brown box from the work surface. "Back door, quick."

Thankfully, the key was in the lock, and they heard the front door open just as they slipped outside into the back garden.

"Now what?" Liv whispered, pressing herself flat against the wall.

Kate's heart was banging behind her ribs. "Um, shed?"

They shuffled around the edge of the house, ducking beneath the kitchen window, and made a dash across the perfectly striped lawn.

"It's the cleaners," Kate breathed, once the shed door was safely closed. "We could just wait it out in here, they'll be gone in a couple of hours."

Liv's face made it clear that wasn't an option. "Isn't there a back gate?"

"There is, but we'd have to leave it unlocked if we go through it. I don't want to be responsible if he gets broken into or something."

"I don't know why you even care," Liv said. "I'd stick a sign on the gate saying 'Empty house, help yourself.'"

"Still Alice's home, remember?" Kate put the box down on the floor. "Right, so we either stay in the shed until they leave, or risk cutting through the house while they clean upstairs. They're methodical, top to bottom."

Liv checked the time on her phone. "Much as I'd love to spend the day in a spidery shed with you, I've a silk delivery coming this afternoon, so I vote option B. Plus, it's more exciting."

Kate thought she might say that. Liv's spirit of adventure had landed her in trouble more than once over the years.

"Also," Liv said, "they might lock the kitchen door, then we'd be stuck out here and have to climb the gate or something. I'd be all right but I don't fancy your chances."

"One of us was on the gymnastics team at school, and it wasn't you," Kate shot back, a snarky whisper even though there wasn't anyone in the garden to hear them.

"And one of us has done Pilates for the last twenty years," Liv said.

"You can carry that box, then." Kate nudged it toward her sister with her foot as she quietly unlatched the door and listened. "Come on, let's make a run for it."

She led and Liv followed, pausing at the kitchen window to check the coast was clear. They moved in unison, a cartoon tip-toed dash from kitchen to hallway, breathless as they made it out of the front door undetected, breaking into a run for the safety of the car.

"God, I feel sick." Kate gasped, breathing hard.

"I loved it." Liv laughed. "Same time next week?"

"I'm never doing that again."

They pulled away and Kate's shoulders slowly lowered from around her ears with every passing mile. She wasn't kidding. That was the last time she was ever going to set foot in her old home. Being in there just now had made her realize how much her life had changed in a relatively short amount of time. Everything had imploded the day she'd walked in on Richard and Belinda, the ground around her littered with what felt like a series of emotional land mines. Her stability blown, her marriage in bits, her home a shell. She'd had her identity wiped clean, and it had taken a fair while to gather up what was left behind in the aftermath and piece herself back together. Not the same woman, though. The old Kate would never have found herself in the middle of a publishing industry experiment or put revenge prawns in her husband's hummus. The old Kate had been shoehorned into a box, and only now was she starting to feel like a jack-in-the-box released.

She turned to Liv, laughter bubbling up her windpipe. "That was mad."

"You've got your manuscripts, though."

Kate nodded. She wasn't even sure why she wanted them yet. A nebulous, unformed thought, a vague possibility. She was going to be a ghost author; was there any possibility she could finally become an *actual* author too?

8

IF THERE WAS A MORE GLAMOROUS, SELF-ASSURED TABLE OF PEOPLE ANY-
where in London that afternoon, Kate would have been surprised to
see it.

She'd been welcomed at the publishing house like the bride at
a wedding, hugged and double air-kissed by a reception line of
faces, apart from Rachel from PR, who Kate had *actually* kissed by
accident. Now she wasn't sure how to tell her she had Ruby Slippers lipstick on the side of her jaw.

She'd been a bag of nerves about the meeting for days, her
first official step into Kate Dalloway's shoes, which that day happened to be nude heels to go with the forest-green jumpsuit Liv
had helped her pick out.

Prue, the lead editor, whom Kate had chatted to briefly once or
twice over the last couple of weeks by email, got to her feet and
opened her mouth, then closed it again when Fiona raised her hand
and started speaking without invitation.

"If I could just kick things off with a reminder that the actual
author of the book must remain completely anonymous to everyone throughout the publication process, which includes most of
the people in this meeting." Fiona looked pointedly at Kate, who

kept her bright red smile firmly in place despite the first shot. She was getting used to deflecting Fiona's arrows.

Prue gazed at Fiona over the rim of her oversized patent-red glasses until she was sure the other woman had finished, then drew a breath and started again, probably equally accustomed to Fiona Fox's abrasive agenting style.

"We're all so thrilled to have you with us today, Kate, it's great to put a face to a name. Speaking of which . . ." She paused to click a PowerPoint presentation into life on the wall with a wave of her arm. "Welcome to your new name!"

KATE DARROWBY appeared in large print on the wall.

"So we heard your suggestion of Dalloway, which was a great kick-off point, and we took a straw poll around the team and Darrowby came out as the unanimous winner. It's fresh yet timeless with the right commercial feel, and I hope you'll agree it looks terrific in print."

Kate had practiced signing Dalloway numerous times over the last few weeks and become quite fond of it. Beneath the table she wrote "Darrowby" on her thigh with her fingertip and didn't find it such a natural fit, but nodded anyway as she glanced nervously at Charlie, sitting suited and booted beside her, looking at home here in a way she couldn't hope to emulate.

"Biscuit?" Rachel, the PR representative, pushed a plate toward her and Kate realized they'd been iced with her new name, looping turquoise letters against a white background.

"Oh my word," she said, staring at them with a nervous laugh. "They look amazing."

"So, we thought it might be helpful to go round the table and talk you through the plans we already have in place," Prue said. "I know this will all be brand-new to you, Kate, so please do feel able to speak up if there's anything that doesn't make sense. For the record, authoring a book in quite this way isn't something we've

done before either, so we're all feeling our way through this exciting new experience together."

Everyone around the table nodded earnestly except Fiona.

"Oh, come on, we're hardly reinventing the wheel here," she
barked. "Half the books on the *Sunday Times* list haven't been written by the name on the cover."

Not a hair ruffled around the board table. Prue tucked her
half-black, half-blood-red bob behind her ears as she paused to
allow Fiona's remark to hang in the air uncommented on, then
clicked through to the next screen.

"And now . . . are you ready for a first look at your cover?"
She added a flourish to the end of her sentence like a magician
pulling a rabbit from a hat.

Kate's breath caught in her throat. She already knew the
book had been titled *The Power of Love*, a micro-reference to
the love song mentioned in the story and neatly encapsulating the
overarching theme of the book. Back when she'd been quietly trying to write manuscripts herself, seeing her book cover for the first
time was one of the standout moments she'd dreamed about.

And there it was, her cover, huge and beautiful, projected
onto the boardroom wall, and the experience was every bit as
pinch-me as she'd imagined it would be, even if she hadn't actually written the book.

"Oh my God, I absolutely love it," she breathed, staring at
the intricate design of rose petals falling around the title against
an inky, midnight sky. Things had felt abstract up to that moment,
an unusual acting job, but seeing the cover with her new name
emblazoned across the front brought things home on a whole new
level. She might not have written the book, but right now she felt
every inch the proud adoptive mother.

"Really strong," Charlie said, beside her.

The fact that Fiona didn't object counted as an endorsement.

"Cake?" Rachel lifted the lid on a box of cupcakes, pearl-pink frosting with a tiny perfect rendition of the cover perched jauntily on top.

"I honestly don't know what to say," Kate laughed, blown away. "Can I steal one for my sister?"

Liv would never believe all of this unless she saw it with her own eyes.

"Take the box," Rachel said.

"So, your author bio," Prue said, clicking forward to the next slide. "We took the suggestions you sent over and ran with them, as you'll see here."

Kate Darrowby lives in London with a Bengal cat called Clive, and when she's not writing she loves West End shows, photography, and crochet—she's currently crocheting a mouse orchestra. *The Power of Love* is her first novel.

The room fell silent while they all digested the information, rain drumming against the boardroom windows.

"Clive's a tortoise and, strictly speaking, he lives with my sister's family," Kate said, wondering how all of the crossed wires had happened. "And I can't crochet. I actually think I'm missing a coordination gene—I'm really bad at following anything that requires remembering repetitive steps. I can't thread a sewing machine, yet my sister is a complete whizz at it. Isn't that a weird thing? Dancing too—I break out in a cold sweat if I'm expected to follow a sequence of steps, my brain just goes into panic mode. It's as if balls of tumbleweed blow through my brain when people try to teach me stuff like that . . ."

She mimed scrunched-up balls scurrying across the table with her hands and then looked up to find all eyes on her, perplexed expressions around the table. Except Fiona, who rolled her shoulders as if she was gearing up to give her a dressing-down.

"I mean, we can totally change it to a tortoise, but we collectively thought a cat seemed more accessible," Prue said. "We've gone with a mix of info that seamlessly blends girl-next-door with just a splash of kooky, and crochet is so of the moment."

"She'll learn to crochet," Fiona said. "It's mice. How hard can it be?"

Mice playing trumpets sounded quite difficult indeed, Kate thought, glancing at Charlie.

"You really don't need to worry," he said mildly, and everyone around the table nodded eager agreement.

"Honestly, it'll never come up," Rachel assured her. "You should see some of the other author bios, this is mild."

Prue moved the conversation briskly along with a click of her button, bringing up a map of the world with several chunks shaded the same midnight blue as the cover. "Joel, would you lead with where we're up to with foreign rights?"

A guy in a striped waistcoat with statement glasses and an impressively high quiff sprang to his feet, a transatlantic twang apparent when he spoke.

"Okay, so as you all know, our sister German publishing house is excited to come on board, with other European arms of the business expected to follow suit."

He pointed to the corresponding shaded areas on the map in the manner of a hipster geography teacher.

"Additionally, I know Fiona has been having conversations with the U.S. too, so watch that space for news soon. We're aiming to create a domino effect with the launch, spreading a tidal wave of love for the book around the world."

Kate felt her heartbeat ratchet with anxiety at the sound of

such grand plans. She was certain no one had mentioned international publication. Charlie shot Fiona a sharp look and earned a
nonchalant shrug in reply.

"Surprise," she said, deadpan, adding lackluster jazz hands.

"Not all debuts get this level of buy-in," Joel said, failing to
read the room. "We're all super excited to see how far *The Power
of Love* can go."

He sat, pleased to have imparted his update, and Kate found
herself touching her silver bangles in an effort to remain professional.

"I won't need to actually go to all those places, though, right?"
she said.

"Oh no, don't worry, nothing like that," Rachel smiled, chirpy,
as the next slide appeared detailing a planned blog tour and a list
of podcasts. "We've gone big on the blog tour so there'll be quite a
few written pieces to do, which is perfect as it'll give you time to
plan out what to say. You can play around with things to develop
your author persona more deeply. Podcasts obviously you can't
plan ahead for so easily, but I've prepped a question list for you of
the type of things we anticipate might come up, everything from
inspiration for the story to favorite lovers in literature to quick-fire
questions about your favorite writing snacks. My biggest advice is
to keep notes, be consistent, and be as succinct as possible."

Fiona laughed, then held both hands up as if the derisory
noise had escaped by mistake.

"I can handle that," Kate said, determined not to be rattled.
"Would I be able to have a copy of this presentation to study
again later, please?"

"Already done, emailed across to Charlie just before the meeting," Prue said. "Keep in mind that every territory handles their
own PR, so you'll get separate requests from the U.S. for blog
pieces, interviews, etc."

The meeting whirled on around Kate for a little while longer, positive feedback from the sales team about conversations with the supermarkets and bookstores, plus news of competitions and a couple of potential well-known company tie-ins from marketing.

"I expect this has been rather a lot to take in," Prue said, her hand on Kate's shoulder when the meeting finally broke up. "I'd suggest you just work methodically through everything step-by-step—it'll all start to feel natural in no time."

"Thanks, Prue," Kate said. "I do feel a bit like I need to go and lie down in a dark room, but believe me when I say I'm determined to make a great job of this. For the original author, and for everyone here who's obviously working so hard to make a success of it behind the scenes, and for myself of course, but most of all for the story itself. I've read it so many times now I almost know it by heart. I relate to Leanora in ways I can't even put into words. Whoever the author is, it's as if they looked inside my soul when they wrote it, and I'm sure I won't be the only person who connects to it so strongly. It feels like a story that needs to be out there in readers' hands and enriching their lives, so to be a part of the team making that happen is exciting, it really is."

Kate looked up and caught Fiona's eye, and for a fleeting second thought she saw something akin to approval. Well, it wasn't blatant disapproval, anyway. Baby steps.

KATE MASSAGED HER JAW, SMALL circles just below her ears to relieve the fixed-smile tension.

"You did great back there, everyone loved you," Charlie said.

They'd taken refuge from the rain in a coffee shop just around the corner from the publishing house. It had a vague fifties theme that had seen smarter days, a Wurlitzer jukebox bubbling with faded neon in one corner, peeling chrome strips on the chairbacks. Charlie looked somehow too big for the spindled wooden seat, the way adults do when they sit on kids' furniture at parents' evening.

"Except Fiona," Kate said, reliving the snarky remarks.

"Fiona doesn't love anyone, except Roulade."

Kate rolled her eyes. "Okay, I'll play. Who's Roulade?"

Charlie ripped the top from a tube of brown sugar and up-ended it into his coffee. "Fiona's cat. Haughty-looking thing, high maintenance. Bites people."

"They do say people choose animals that reflect their person-ality," Kate said, watching the guy from behind the counter saun-ter across to the jukebox, unhurried as he made his selection. They were the only customers; it didn't seem the kind of place to anticipate a lunchtime rush.

"I think it chose her, from what I remember. Sat on her step and refused to leave."

"Ballsy move." The thought of Fiona taking in a stray didn't sit well with the two-dimensional Cruella image she worked hard to project.

The jukebox crackled to life, the old-school sound of needle on vinyl, the schmaltzy intro to "In the Still of the Night," famil-iar to everyone thanks to *Dirty Dancing*. It felt suddenly too sultry for a rainy lunchtime in London.

Charlie noticed the mood shift too, raising his eyebrows over his coffee cup. "Did we inadvertently walk through a time warp?"

Given the unreal experience of her first publishing meeting, it felt quite fitting to find herself here in this further interlude of otherworldliness. "If we did, can we hang around for a while? We might see Elvis."

They fell silent as the guy from behind the counter ap-proached their table and placed a plate of pink wafer biscuits down with a knowing look before disappearing behind the counter again, as if he'd read their minds and provided without being asked. He was dressed, inexplicably, as a fifties sailor, white hat perched on his head.

"If I don't make it out of here alive, tell my sister I love her," Kate whispered, silently vowing to bring Liv here one day. She'd probably wear a netted skirt and dance on the tables.

"What does she think about you taking the job on?"

Kate decided against sharing Liv's hotline to his previous world and the caution she'd offered about getting close to him. "She's fine as long as I'm fine."

"And are you fine, after everything you've just heard back there?"

She reached for a pink wafer, thinking. "I'll admit it was a lot. Especially the overseas stuff, I hadn't imagined any of that, but I think I'm okay? Nervous, but okay." She paused. "The mouse orchestra was a bit wild, though."

"I thought it was very you," he said, raising his coffee cup.

She rolled her eyes and shook her head slowly, unwilling to rise to the bait.

"I'd be more worried if you weren't nervous," he said, back in professional mode. "It just means you want to do a good job. And, remember, you won't be doing it alone, you have the whole publishing team around you to hold your hand." He shrugged one shoulder. "And me."

Maybe it was the retro movie music, maybe it was the heartbreaker half smile that lifted one corner of his mouth, but she found herself looking at Charlie's tanned, capable hands around his coffee mug and wondering how they'd feel sliding down her spine. She pulled herself up sharp. There was a whole code of ethics about this stuff. Not to mention the personal stuff she knew about him. Not that it was relevant or any of her business, but it was more than enough to route her thoughts back on track.

Glancing up and finding him watching her, she shoved the pink biscuit into her mouth whole in panic and instantly regretted it.

"Would you like me to look away so you can, you know"—he gestured toward her mouth, not helping the situation at all—"remove it?"

She shook her head and tried to style it out, breathing through her nose as she dislodged it with the dregs of her coffee.

"Try one," she said, surreptitiously wiping away a tear when she could speak again. "They're not as bad as you think."

"I'll take your word for it," he said, still smirking.

She held his gaze, feeling the need to regain ground. "Just so you know, you can take my word when I say I won't let everyone down. It might seem like I sometimes use a hundred words when ten would do, but when the time comes for me to step up and play my part, I won't fluff my lines."

He didn't make a smart reply or glance away. "And just so *you* know, I won't let you down either."

Did he know she'd heard the L.A. rumors? Liv told her he'd pretty much been run out of town, that his ex-wife's family were industry movers and shakers, his script-writing career dead in the water.

"I'll get these," she said, picking up their empty cups to pay, needing some space.

"No need, already done," he said.

It was a simple enough gesture, but somehow it sat badly with her.

She put the mugs on the counter and offered to pay for the biscuits, but the guy waved her away, making an exaggerated heart sign with his hands as if they were in a silent movie. Thrown, she made one back, and found Charlie shaking his head in despair when she looked over her shoulder. Shrugging, she walked out into the now thankfully dry afternoon.

9

UNLIKE FIONA, CHARLIE HAD THE DECENCY TO KNOCK ON HIS BUSINESS partner's door before entering. The look she gave him was pure theater, perfected over the years to win deals and terrify the opposition.

"Charlie," she said, lowering her glasses on their golden chain.

"Fi, I realize this deal is an unusual setup, but to be clear, I'm Kate's agent, not you."

"We've been over this. I represent the author, you represent the actor," she said in the same tone she'd used when he was fourteen years old and hanging around his dad's office. "The book doing well is a win for both of us."

"I know that, but it wasn't fair of you to withhold the information about the overseas deals. You really dropped Kate in the deep end there, and me by default."

"Intentionally so," Fiona said, unruffled. "We needed to see if she cracked under pressure."

"Would you have pulled a stunt like that with my father?"

Fi opened her mouth and closed it again.

"Because I'm never going to be him."

"You can say that again," she shot back.

He sighed. "If this thing is ever going to work long term, we have to be transparent and able to trust each other."

"You've spent too much time in therapy." She rolled her eyes. "*Transparent.*"

"And you've spent too much time sitting up here in your ivory tower, not giving a damn how you treat the people around you," he said, because she knew enough about what had happened in L.A. to not be so judgmental.

They eyeballed each other across the expanse of her desk.

It was on the tip of Charlie's tongue to apologize. It wasn't his way to be so direct with Fiona, but the words stilled in his throat. Something in her shifting expression almost resembled respect.

"Close the door on your way out," she said, perching her glasses back on her nose.

He contemplated leaving it ajar, but he'd done and said enough, and he wasn't fourteen anymore. He'd lost his mother when he was barely old enough to remember her, just abstract catches of perfume and the warmth of her hug. Fiona had never tried to step into her shoes, but as the only constant female in Jojo's life, she'd always been there on the peripheries. Over the years his father had mostly referred to her as "that bloody woman," but their business partnership had been long and fruitful. The jury was out on how things were going to work between Charlie and Fi, but one thing was for sure: it would never be easy.

10

"WHAT'S YOUR FAVORITE SNACK WHILE WRITING?" LIV PICKED A RANDOM question from Kate's list.

"Er, cheese?" Kate said, working her way through a huge bowl of pavlova.

Nish wrinkled his nose. "Too sweaty."

Kate paused to think. "Mint Imperials?"

"Too old lady's handbag," Liv said.

Kate sighed. "How am I ever going to get the big stuff right if I can't even answer a basic question?"

"They're just sound bites," Liv said. "Stop stressing over them so much."

"Say biscuits," Nish said. "Everyone loves biscuits. Or cookies, if it's a U.S. interview."

"Just not pink wafers," Liv said, giving her the side-eye.

Hearing about the international publication plans had changed the game a little for Kate, upped the stakes. She'd already received her signing-on payment and used some of it to clear her credit card, so backing out wasn't an option, and in truth, she didn't want to. This was the most exciting thing to happen to her in as long as she could remember, a step back toward a creatively fulfilling life. Whether it was a good idea or not remained to be seen, but she was moving into the spotlight and hoping like hell she didn't die of stage fright.

"This one's trickier," Liv said, scanning the list. "What inspired you to write the story?"

"Money?" Nish said, gathering up their empty dessert plates.

They both shot him a look and he shrugged, laughing to himself as he loaded the dishwasher.

"I think I'm going to relate my answers to my actual life as much as possible."

"Isn't the book about a playwright who falls so madly in love with a beautiful actress that he can only ever write lines for her, and ultimately her star eclipses his, then she dies an untimely death?"

"Well, obviously I'm not saying the story relates *directly* to my life," Kate said. "But the essence of the love story, the emotions, the sudden loss. I mean, I won't say Richard died or anything, but you know what I mean."

"He will the next time I see him," Liv said.

Kate let her sister's threat go. "I just mean I'm going to draw on what's happened to me for authenticity."

"Is there really no way you can ask the original author some of this stuff?" Nish said, spritzing cleaner onto the kitchen counters.

Kate shook her head. "No contact, that's the deal."

"Have you tried to guess who she is?" Liv said. "I've started scanning the books in the supermarket."

"The only thing I know for sure is they don't usually write love stories," Kate said.

"I'm dying to find out," Liv said. "What even made her write a book she never wanted to publish?"

"You both seem sure it's a woman," Nish said. "Could be a bloke."

"You think?" Kate was unsure how she felt about the idea of it being a male writer. She'd related to the story from a feminine perspective; did it make a difference if it came from a male heart? Did they break the same way? "I'd not really considered it could be a guy," she said. Not beyond Charlie, anyway. Liv had dismissed the idea, sure no guy capable of cheating could write so fluently on the subject of true love.

"Why, because we're all Neanderthals, incapable of feeling emotion as deeply as women?" Nish's cheeky smile took the sting from his words.

"Umm, no," she said. "I guess it's because I related so closely to the story, I just assumed."

"And because they've hired a woman to represent the book," Liv reasoned.

"Classic subterfuge," Nish said, rubbing his hands together.

"No, it's a woman." Kate shook the idea loose before it stuck. "One hundred percent."

Liv slid her finger down the list on the table.

"Favorite drink when you're writing?"

"None," Kate said. "Remember that time when Alice was little and she knocked that glass of squash all over my laptop? The P key never worked again, and trust me, you need that letter more than you could imagine."

"When you need a P, you need a P," Nish said, making both of them roll their eyes. "I'm here all week," he said. "Coffee anyone?"

Kate nodded, relaxing on her chair and turning her face up to the late-afternoon sun slanting through the kitchen skylight. Liv and Nish's kitchen was always cluttered and warm, a place of safety and sanctuary. Thinking back, her own pristine kitchen had never felt this enveloping, a place of industry rather than comfort. She felt a pang of worry that Alice hadn't grown up in a home like this, but then pushed it aside. She was fine. Alice always knew she was loved—Richard might have decided he didn't love Kate anymore, but he adored his daughter.

"I better go, actually," she said, glancing at her watch. "I might try and catch Alice before she turns in for the night. I still haven't found the right time to tell her about all of this book stuff."

Nish boxed up the rest of the pavlova. "Take this with you. No one here appreciates my cooking the way you do."

"You're my favorite brother-in-law," Kate said. "Even if I had a dozen of them, you'd still be the best one."

"Yeah, you're right there," he said, scruffing her hair as he placed the leftovers in front of her.

She laughed, but she wasn't lying. She couldn't remember the last time she'd heard Nish raise his voice; he had an abundance of patience and was a lionheart when it came to his family. If she had to field any questions about relationship goals and inspirations, she wouldn't need to look any further than this kitchen.

11

Morning Kate,

Something's just arrived in the office you're going to want to see. I'll bring it to the photo shoot tomorrow.

C

Hi Charlie,

I hope it's what I think it is!
    Cab booked for St. Dunstan in the East. I WON'T BE LATE.

Kate

"LEAN BACK A BIT, KATE, THAT'S IT, NOW GAZE MOODILY INTO THE DIS-tance for me."

Kate braced herself against the stone church window frame and scowled. She'd spent the last hour gamely trying to follow the photographer's theatrical directions, even though she was never a fan of having her photograph taken. She couldn't argue with the venue choice, though; the church of St. Dunstan in the East's Gothic ruins had taken her breath away, a secret garden sanctu-ary hidden in plain sight among London's hustle and bustle. Tori, the photographer, had insisted on a sunset shoot to capture the golden-hour magic, and beautiful though the backdrop was, her dramatic demands were doing nothing to enhance the magic. So far she'd had Kate pose precariously on stone steps, on a wooden bench with her knees tucked under her chin, and with her back pressed against stone columns covered in creepers.

"Too moody, too moody!" Tori shouted. "Try to think enigmatic rather than murderous."

"I'm trying my best," Kate said through gritted teeth.

On Tori's instruction she'd brought several outfit options and she'd had to try them all, wriggling in and out of her clothes behind a makeshift screen of silver light reflectors. Thankfully, the later hour meant the place was pretty deserted, but all the same, flashing her knickers in public wasn't Kate's favorite pastime. It didn't help that Charlie was there too. He'd ditched his suit jacket and turned back the cuffs of his sleeves, his tie loosened enough to pop the top button of his shirt, aviators on. He was in end-of-the-working-day mode, as if he'd just strolled off the cover of *GQ* to lean against the wall and observe proceedings.

"Now perch beside the ledge there with your chin cupped in your hands," Tori said, sweeping her waist-length silver hair over one shoulder. Model turned photographer, she had the look of someone who'd summered on Ibiza for the last forty years, bohemian and barefoot, her sandals kicked off beside her camera gear.

Kate looked down. "There's a headstone in the way," she said, pretty sure romance authors weren't the type to trample over graves for the sake of a good photo.

Tori lowered the camera. "It all adds to the sense of place," she said. "Trust me, just swing your legs either side of it and bend forward, elbows on your knees."

It wasn't easy, and it didn't feel natural. Kate gave it a go, but it was never going to be the shot that made the cut. It was on the edge of her tongue to say as much when Charlie moved to stand beside Tori.

"The light is especially nice right now over there by the palm tree," he suggested, nodding toward a far corner.

Tori glanced across, her head on one side. "It could work." Pointing both index fingers in that direction as a signal to Kate to haul ass, she skipped across the cobbles, the tiny mirrors scattered over her floor-length skirt shooting light refractions around her as she moved.

"Fun as this is to watch, I don't think it's what the publisher is looking for," Charlie said, as they followed a little behind.

"You don't say," Kate said. "I feel as if I'm at an advanced yoga class."

"I'll make some calls, get them to add contortionist into your author bio."

"Funny," she snarked, as Tori beckoned her over to stand in a Gothic archway, her arms crossed and her shoulder leaning against the warm, mottled stone.

"That's good," Tori said, peering through a viewing rectangle of her own fingers. Kate studied the intricate mandala tattoo covering the back of one of Tori's hands and found herself wondering if body ink was something she might consider. Maybe she would, now that she didn't have anyone else's opinion to take into account.

Tori fired off a volley of shots and then paused. "Show the camera a little love, Kate," she said. "Smolder."

Kate instantly frowned, making Tori shake her head. "Okay, so who do you love? Think of them."

"My daughter?" Kate said, uncertain.

Tori all but growled. "Your husband, your lover, your fantasy. Someone who makes your heart race."

Kate's gaze auto-flickered to Charlie and then back to the camera, flustered.

"Better," Tori said, camera flashing. "Much better. Whoever you're thinking of, it's working."

Rolling the stiffness from her tense shoulders, Kate sat on the low wall beside Tori when she was finally done. Charlie perched on the photographer's other side as they took a first glance through the shots. The earliest ones of the shoot were definitely no use.

"You look as if you're in the dentist's waiting room," Tori sighed. "Shoulders around your ears, too tense."

Kate was grateful when she skipped right through the poses with the headstone in shot, no doubt realizing she'd made the wrong call.

"These final ones, though . . . whoever you're thinking about is a lucky guy."

Tori glanced at Charlie. Kate did the same and found him studying the camera screen over the top of his sunnies. Much as she didn't enjoy having her photo taken, the last handful of shots were undeniably excellent. The late-evening sun had picked up the green in her eyes, and her expression had shifted from uncomfortable to confident, a boldness that wasn't generally there.

"Definitely less teenage," Charlie said, clearing his throat. "Job done."

Tori packed her equipment away with the speed of someone who could do it in their sleep, loading it all into a huge carpetbag with a blown kiss and a promise to send the images over in the next couple of days.

"SO THAT WAS UP THERE among the worst hours of my life," Kate said when they were alone.

"You hid it well," he said, side-eyeing her behind his aviators.

"I'm just amazed she got anything decent."

He looked away. "Draped over a headstone is definitely an under-used angle for a romance writer."

"Hilarious." Kate pushed her hands under her thighs on the low wall and looked up at the blue sky, stark against the soaring granite-gray walls of the church, the birdsong louder than the low hum of the city. "This place is something else."

He nodded, his eyes on the church tower. "Bombed in the Blitz, lost its roof."

"It's like a film set, a jungle oasis or something."

"Is that who you thought about for the photo? Tarzan?"

She laughed, despite herself. "You got me."

He reached down into his slim black-leather backpack. "You might want to close your eyes for this."

"Oh," she breathed. She'd forgotten he'd said he had something for her. Nervous awareness rendered her vulnerable when she closed her eyes, chewing the inside of her lip.

"Hold your hands out."

He drew the moment out just long enough to make her consider peeping through her lashes, then placed the unmistakable solidity of a hardback book in her upturned hands.

Her eyes flew open and her heart quickened as her fingers curled around its gilt edges, a sigh of pure pleasure as she took in the full glory of the book for the first time.

"Oh my God, will you look at that," she said, tracing her finger over the golden slopes and loops of her name. She didn't even care that it wasn't Dalloway anymore. "Isn't it the most beautiful thing you've ever seen in your life?"

She didn't overthink it, just let herself feel the moment of realization that this crazy, unexpected adventure was actually happening. Clutching the book against her chest, she could feel her heart pounding against the backboard.

"What do you think?" he said, his eyes on the novel, and then her face.

"Do you even need to ask?" she said. "I know I didn't write it, but honestly, I feel incredibly protective about it already, if that makes any sense?"

"You have every right to feel proud," he said. "You and the author are a team on this, the public face and the private face." He pulled his mobile from his pocket. "At the risk of you draping yourself over the nearest headstone, shall I capture the moment?"

She turned to him and grinned, still pressing the book to her chest like a proud mama. This was one photo she didn't mind posing for.

"Can I keep this?" she said, turning the book over in her hands. It was an advance copy, missing the back-cover blurb and author photo as yet, but peppered with early author endorsements from names that made her swoon.

"Of course, it's yours," he said. "There's something else too. I chatted with the author a few days ago. They're open to anonymous email contact with you, if it would help?"

"Really?" Kate said, taken aback, thinking of the numerous occasions when Fiona had reiterated the no-contact clause.

"Really. I can pass on your email if you're open to it."

"God, yes. I'd love that, I have a million questions."

"I'm not saying you'll get all the answers," he cautioned.

"Anything is a help," she said. "Did you see Rachel's email this morning?"

The publishing team always copied Charlie and Fiona into emails they sent her, and this morning's PR update had been particularly startling.

Charlie nodded. "How do you feel about it?"

Rachel's exclamation-mark-laden message had filled her with

the kind of fear usually reserved for leaning backward over a sheer drop.

"Oh, you know, full-on terrified," she said.

"If it helps, I've talked to Glynn a couple of times, he'll put you at ease as soon as you meet him. It's one of those things that sounds more frightening than it is."

"Like root canal, or a math exam?" she said, unconvinced. She'd read Rachel's email aloud to Liv when it pinged in that morning and they'd both gone wide-eyed with panic at the sight of such a household name.

"Just think of it like a chat with an old friend," he said.

"Sure, if my old friend happens to be a national treasure on live radio," Kate said. Rachel from PR had been bursting about landing her a spot on the nation's most-listened-to Sunday-morning show. It was a complete scoop on her part and no doubt earned her a good old pat on the back in the weekly meeting.

"I can meet you there if it would help?"

She shook her head. "I'm actually better on my own in terrifying situations," she said. "I've been working on my author Q&A list with Liv, trying to practice my answers so they come naturally." She sighed. "It feels like trying to learn lines without a script."

Charlie didn't quite meet her gaze. "I might not be the authority on agenting my father was, but script writing I do know a thing or two about," he said. "And my unsolicited advice would be to keep things as simple and honest as possible. Draw on your own experiences of love and heartbreak rather than someone else's—even the author's, if they decide to tell you their story. Grief and love are universal. However lightly you press on that bruise, people are going to feel it and relate."

Kate took a few moments to digest his unexpectedly insightful reply.

"There's a line in the book about life being a series of uncon-nected scenes," she said. "How sometimes things happen outside of the expected timeline of events, and they only ever exist in in-visible ink. Then there's an intentionally blank page for the reader to imagine or interpret."

"It's my favorite part of the book," he said.

She looked at him, surprised, because it was hers too. "I love the way the author has trusted the reader to decide what's written there."

"You're better at this than you think you are," he said quietly.

She swallowed, absorbing the compliment. "I've probably spent too much time worrying about the small stuff."

"Like your favorite flavor of cake, you mean?" he said.

"Always chocolate."

"Solid choice," he said. "If you're five."

She rolled her eyes.

"Favorite genre to read when you're not writing?" he said.

She frowned. "You see, that's exactly it. You say 'when you're not writing' and straightaway I feel like a fraud again."

He slid his aviators off, hooked them over his shirt pocket and turned and looked her directly in the eyes. "Isn't all acting about inhabiting the skin of the character you're playing, believing the lines rather than just delivering them?"

She nodded.

"So be you. Be the you who didn't give up on writing manu-scripts twenty years ago. Be the you who got a publishing deal, the you who writes love stories."

Kate thought of the box of unfinished manuscripts. "She doesn't exist."

"She does now. She's Kate Darrowby, and I'm looking at her. Write your name over and over like lines in a schoolbook, order the drink Kate Darrowby would choose, buy the outfit she'd pick out for an interview with a national radio host. Step into her shoes, Kate, you'll find they're just your size."

"You're better at this than you think you are," she said after a beat.

It was his turn to look conflicted. "I hope so, because it's all I've got."

"Do you miss it? Script writing?"

His eyelashes swept down, covering his eyes, and she thought about what he'd said earlier about pressing on a bruise and regretted her question. Reading the book for the first time had felt a lot like that: the black-and-blue pain of remembering, the slow, inevitable watercolor fade toward sunrise yellows. "You don't have to answer if you don't want to," she said.

He still didn't meet her gaze. "The short answer is yes, I miss it. And the long answer is I guess script writing was kind of tangled up with who I was when I was in L.A., and now I'm here and all I've got is blank pages."

She remembered what Liv had said about his scandalous marriage breakup and hasty return to London. Was he alluding to writer's block, or had the words never been his in the first place?

The thought was enough to make her stash the book carefully in among the outfit changes in her bag. She'd let her guard down too much, strayed too close to personal. They'd achieved a fragile working truce; keeping some of the pages intentionally blank felt like the only way to make sure it held.

"I should get back," she said, standing up. "Thanks for the pep talk."

He slid his glasses back on, hiding his eyes.

12

"STAND STILL OR THIS HEM WILL BE ALL OVER THE PLACE."

"I'm trying my best," Kate said, glancing down at Liv. "This crate doesn't feel very secure. You can tell Fiona if I go through it and twist my ankle two weeks before the book comes out."

"It won't break, I've used it loads of times," Liv said, kneeling beside the wooden crate to adjust the length on the midnight silk skirt of Kate's dress. "That's got it, I think," she said, wincing as she straightened up to inspect the result. "Perfect. Hop down."

Kate took her sister's outstretched hand and stepped down, then turned to look in the full-length mirror in the changing room.

"What do you think?" Liv asked, behind her.

Kate turned to the side and then back again, admiring her sister's handiwork.

"I love it," she said, skimming her hands down the strapless bodice to the flare of the calf-length skirt. Liv had carefully matched the colors from the book cover, ink-blue silk scattered with blush-pink petals, as if a rose in full bloom had shed its petals as she brushed past.

Liv handed her a copy of the book from the box that had arrived a few days ago, prompting a flurry of excitement and nervous tears when she'd opened the seal.

Kate held the book in her hands and turned back to the mirror to see the whole look come together.

"You're so clever," she said. "I need a fancy launch party to wear it to now."

Liv reached for her phone and took snaps from every angle.

"For your social media," she said.

Kate Darrowby was now set up on all social media platforms, her official author photo at the top, a scattering of posts from the last few weeks filling out her new persona. A selfie in the cab on the way to lunch with the publishing team, the book cover reveal using the photo Charlie had taken of her clutching it at the Gothic ruins, a mini unboxing video of the finished copies, a vase of pink roses she'd bought because they were the exact color of the petals on the book. It felt a little like painting a picture, adding background colors to enhance the main focus—the book. She'd been hired to give this beautiful story oxygen through social media collages and online interviews, and so far it was all going to plan. The dress was Liv's idea, a gift from sister to sister, a just-in-case-you-need-to-go-somewhere-fabulous dress.

"Not sure which shoes," Kate said, stepping into one strappy sandal and one patent heel.

"Go with the one on the left, it makes your ankle look slimmer."

Kate and Liv turned in unison at the sound of the unsolicited male advice and found Richard lounging in the open doorway.

"Her ankles are none of your business," Liv snapped, then pointed at the step. "No farther."

"It's fine," Kate said, even though the sight of her ex-husband had tarnished what had so far been an excellent day. "What are you doing here?"

"I was passing," he said, earning himself a derisory snort

from them both. "You were in my house," he said. "And you." He shot daggers at Liv, who lifted her chin in challenge.

There had always been a veiled underscore of tension between Liv and Richard, an unspoken sense of "I'm watching you" that had burst out in the open since the divorce.

"Lois told me," he said.

Kate rolled her eyes internally. Of course Lois told him. Her old neighbor had no doubt studied her spy cameras and zoomed in to take photos as evidence to present her case to Richard, probably with a bottle of Chablis and a cheese board to share while she filled him in.

"And?" she said, choosing not to deny it.

"I could have you arrested for breaking and entering," he said.

Kate started to sweat inside the silk dress, imagining how bad the optics would be for Kate Darrowby, how loud Fiona's rage would be.

"And I could have you arrested for being the biggest twat in England," Liv said. It made no actual sense, but Richard's cheek twitched all the same.

Kate watched him, seeing Alice in his blue eyes, remembering better days. They'd been happy once upon a time. Or so she'd thought, anyway.

"I just wanted a few things I'd left behind," she said.

"You could have asked," he said.

"You were out of the country," she said.

"And you'd have said no anyway, because you can't help being a massive dick," Liv said.

"Liv," Kate said. "Can you give us a minute?"

Liv shrugged as she glared at Richard and wandered away toward the back of the shop. "I'll go and sort the Roman costume stand out."

Richard waited until she was out of earshot and then turned to Kate.

"Have you heard from Alice lately?"

Kate narrowed her eyes. "Of course, why?" In truth she'd been having trouble catching Alice for a proper chat in recent weeks, she was always off somewhere or between lectures. Kate had become all too familiar with Alice's voicemail message, and usually received a flurry of chatty texts as a reply rather than an actual call. She missed hearing her daughter's voice, but had tried to tell herself it was all part and parcel of letting Alice grow up and find her feet away from home.

"Just something she said to Bel last night," he said.

Kate frowned. "What something?"

"She's met an Australian guy up there."

How could Richard possibly know this first? And why would Alice choose to confide in Belinda rather than her own mother? It wounded her, as Richard no doubt knew it would.

"Is it serious?"

"Serious enough for her to want to spend the summer in Australia with his family."

"What? She's not coming home?"

Kate's voice skittered up an octave and her heart missed a beat, her mind skipping straight to the thought of Alice emigrating and barely seeing her apart from on FaceTime.

"I'll talk to her," she sighed. No doubt that was the purpose of Richard's visit, to let her play bad cop to his good cop, the one who didn't bounce with sunshine at the news.

Liv moved stealthily behind him with a Roman sword held aloft and mimed plunging it between his shoulder blades, then lowered it behind her back when he turned to leave.

"You've always been strange," he muttered.

"And you've never been good enough for my sister," she shot back, following him to the door to make sure he actually left.

Kate watched from behind the counter, nursing a lukewarm cup of coffee, her mind miles away with Alice. She'd call her later, get to the bottom of things.

13

"HEY, ALICE, IT'S MUM."

It had taken three straight-to-voicemail calls before Alice finally picked up, and Kate heard her daughter's half laugh, half sigh rattle around the kitchen. She'd spent the afternoon wondering how best to get Alice to confide in her about the Australian guy without coming straight out and saying Richard had already filled her in. Parenting 101—don't back them into a corner, it never ends well.

"I know it's you, Mum, your name came up on my screen."

"I just wanted to hear your voice," Kate said. "I've got you on speakerphone. Tell me your news while I make spaghetti."

Alice groaned. "You're making spaghetti? I wish I was there."

"I wish you were too," Kate said, staring longingly at her phone as she chopped onions. "Not long now though, Al, summer break soon. I'll make spaghetti for your welcome home dinner."

So far, so good. She heard her daughter's small intake of breath and nervous silence and she waited, fighting the urge to jump in.

"Um, I need to talk to you about that actually, Mum." Another pregnant pause, and Kate pressed her fingers to her lips to stop herself from saying the wrong thing.

"Oh?"

She could picture Alice on the other end of the line, screwing her nose up as she always did when she was trying to talk her way out of something.

"I've been asked to go to Australia! Mum, I've been holding back on telling you this because I didn't want you to start, but I've met this boy, Flynn. He's Australian, and he's finished studying now so he's going home, and he's asked me if I'll go with him, and—"

"Whoa, whoa! Hang on, let me catch up." Kate forced a laugh, trying to sound lighthearted when she felt anything but. "Tell me all about him, then, what's he like?"

Alice let out a rom-com-worthy sigh. "Oh, Mum, he's so cool, he looks like one of the Hemsworth brothers and he makes me laugh all the time. We only met a couple of months ago but it feels as if I've known him forever, do you know what I mean? He's been doing business studies here, and now he's going home to open his own surf shack on the beach in Queensland. I know it probably sounds crazy to you because you haven't met him yet, but he's asked me to go with him, and I was thinking I could maybe defer my studies for a year, see how it goes? You know I always said I wanted to go traveling . . ."

"But it's hardly the same thing, is it? You've made such a great start at uni and made some good friends on your course too, I really don't think it's a wise move right now."

"I knew you'd be like this," Alice sighed, the bubbles gone from her voice. "I'm nineteen now, Mum, old enough to make my own decisions."

Kate laid the onion knife down and sat at the kitchen table, staring at her mobile in front of her. She was desperate to find the right words.

"Look, Al, I'm not saying I don't understand. I do, more than you can imagine, actually. I was about the same age when I married your dad and moved to Germany, remember?"

"Exactly! Mum, you can't really criticize my decisions when you made the same ones yourself, can you?"

Kate screwed her eyes closed, willing herself not to say something that painted Richard in a bad light.

"With the benefit of hindsight, I made some unwise decisions," she said. "I should have focused on my own career and dated your dad long distance rather than given up my dreams for his. You have such ambition, Al, and you love your new life in Leeds."

Alice went quiet. "But I love him more, Mum."

"Long distance can be romantic," Kate tried, hearing the creep of desperation in her own voice. "Please, Alice, just say you'll think about it some more. Don't do anything rash without talking to me and Dad?"

The answering huff was more teenage than grown-up, reminding Kate how young her daughter still was, how impressionable. She could only hope that they still had some sway over her now that she didn't live at home anymore, and that she wasn't as headstrong as her mother at the same age.

14

Dear Kate,

(I'm not sure if Kate is your actual name or your pen name. Don't tell me if you don't want to.)

I wanted to let you know how grateful I am to you for taking on this assignment. I realize it's out of the ordinary, but I hear you're a very out of the ordinary kind of person, so hopefully you and the book are a good match.

I have to confess to not reading the final edit. It's so intensely personal to me, I cannot imagine I'll ever crack the spine.

If I can be of any assistance to you in a general sense, just ask—I'll help if I can.

Yours in gratitude,

H

(I hit a random key on the keyboard with my eyes closed. H is as good as any, isn't it?)

Hello H,

I cannot tell you how glad I am to be in touch!

Firstly, it's me that needs to thank YOU, not the other way around.

The Power of Love is the most extraordinary love story, I cry every time I read it. I so wanted Leanora and William to get their happy ever after, but then it wouldn't have felt so raw and real and human if they had, would it?

How I wish I had the talent to write something so pure and poignant, it's unforgettable. I hope you will still feel a glow of pride when it's published, even though your name won't be on the cover.

Thanks for offering to answer some questions for me, I've attached a list here so as not to clutter up your email. I haven't sent too many, there's plenty more if you're in the mood! I just thought it would be cool to embroider some of your (unidentifiable!) truths into interviews and things for authenticity.

All my best,

Kate

(I am a Kate, just not Darrowby)

Dear Kate,

As promised, the answers to your questions...

What would I be if I wasn't a writer?

Six feet under, probably. Writing has been both my joy and my salvation, my way of making sense of the world. I've written my way through my best days and my darkest nights, my celebrations and my solitude. I confess to wondering of late what it's all for. Words for words' sake.

My favorite writing snack (REALLY?)

I used to have licorice every now and then, the proper kind, not those hideous multicolored kids' things. These days I tend to write late at night in my study, so just black coffee and the occasional Scotch.

My inspiration for writing the book?

If there was a "prefer not to say" box, I'd tick it. As there isn't...the unexpected end of my love story.

Music, coffee-shop hubbub, or silence when writing?

Definitely not coffee shop, in fact not anywhere but my office usually. I find noise in general to be distracting, certainly no radio. I used to enjoy having music on.

Cat or dog person?

Do I have to nail my colors to one mast or the other? A rescue cat once decided she lived with me, deaf and yowled like a banshee. I haven't had a dog since I was a kid, a mutt who hated everyone except me.

What song do you sing in the shower?

I don't sing in the shower or anywhere else.
And now a couple of questions of my own, it seems only fair...

Why did you take the job?

Who is Clive?

Sincerely,

H

Dear H,

You don't sing, ever? Not even when you're on your own and your favorite song in the world comes on the radio? I'll readily admit to being the world's worst singer, but I still belt out "Someone Like You" as if I am actually Adele, especially in the car.

I like what you said about writing being your joy and salvation. From reading the book, it feels as if you spill your DNA onto the page—it must be a very exposing and vulnerable experience. You said you've been wondering what it's all for, of late. For what it's worth, reading is my sanctuary and escape, never more so than in the last year when my life basically went to hell in a handcart. So maybe that's what it's all for—for you, the catharsis of writing, and for your readers, safe harbor.

Have ordered licorice. Am not convinced but willing to give it a try. I've been saying Jelly Tots in some of the written interviews. Jelly Tots! What was I thinking? I haven't had them since my daughter, Alice, was about five! I don't know if they even have them in the U.S., I'm probably saying something gross. Have been doing lots of online interviews and blog posts ready for the publication blog tour (I've had a crash course in publishing world lingo from Charlie and Prue).

And now to answer your questions. (Feel free to ask me anything, I'm an open book. See what I did there?! I should be on the stage.)

Why did I take the job?

Well, my life fell apart last year when I discovered my (now ex-) husband was having an affair with his secretary—cliché, I know. I felt as if I was starring in my own straight-to-TV movie, walking in on them in a VERY compromising position, him saying it's not what it looks like when there's very little else he could have been doing with his trousers around his ankles! It's all very sordid, sorry.

Long story short—I'd signed a pre-nup, and I found myself living above my sister's fancy-dress shop in what used to be her storeroom. A lady of reduced circumstances. Our daughter stayed in the family home for a while but is off at uni now, probably glad to get away from us!

It's not as bad as it sounds, the studio flat is really quite pretty in a tiny homes sort of way and I get to spend a lot of time in the shop with my sister, who's basically Rebecca from *Ted Lasso* crossed with Villanelle from *Killing Eve*.

So anyway, I wrote to Jojo, who used to be my agent before I got married and disappeared off the face of the earth for twenty years, and Charlie picked up the letter at just the right moment. It felt like one of those puzzles where one missing piece turns up and they all fall into place. I'm one of the pieces. I guess that makes you one of the pieces too. You're a bigger piece than me, though, obviously. You're a corner, I'm a random piece of the sky.

Clive is a tortoise I co-own with my sister, Liv. He was given to us by a neighbor when we were kids; imagine, a 6- and an 8-year-old girl in charge of a 54-year-old male tortoise! We were clueless but thrilled to have a pet, he was our one and only. He lives like a reptile king with my sister and her family these days. I don't think boarding-house life would be for him, somehow.

(Note to self: never use personal email address for book-related things! I promise I've set an official one up, it just felt more appropriate to speak to you as the real me, unfiltered.)

Can I ask you a couple more questions that have cropped up a few times?

Do you write longhand or on PC/laptop?

Have you ever broken any bones?

Favorite holiday destination?

Speak soon,

Kate

Dear Kate,

Your ex-husband sounds like an arsehole and your sister should run the country.

Longhand or typed?

Both. PC mostly for getting the words down, but I sometimes switch to longhand if I need to chew over a few different scenarios—more satisfying to cross out than delete. I have a 1952 Hermes Baby typewriter, a beloved gift that's far too beautiful to use. Plus a mechanical keyboard for an alternative sound—writing is a long, old job, it can feel monotonous. Having options to switch things up is useful when you're flagging. That's where the licorice comes into play too. Can't say I've ever eaten a Jelly Tot, possibly because I don't have children to buy them for, so feel unqualified to comment.

Have I ever broken any bones? (Have you?)

I broke a bone in my back twenty years ago, came off a bike. A tandem, ridiculously, the one and only time I'll ever get on such a contraption. While on deadline, of course. Someone gifted me some bizarre telescopic glasses to use the laptop while lying flat, which worked at a push but caused so much hilarity they proved more of a hindrance than a help.

Favorite holiday destination?

Some of my most carefree days have been spent on Formentera, an island off the coast of Ibiza. A place so beautiful it hurts your eyes, as if a rogue tornado scurried a tiny Caribbean jewel across the world and deposited it in the Med. Don't mention it publicly—it's one of those places people in the know don't talk about in case everyone discovers it.

India was fascinating, L.A. all-consuming, New Zealand breathtaking. Those aside, put me in a remote cabin on a Welsh hillside, sea view non-negotiable. Perhaps that's the key. I need to be near the coast.

Where makes your list?

Best,

H

Hi H,

Am replying from my sparkly new official Kate Darrowby email—Clive has been jettisoned at last! (Have given myself an awful image of him being unceremoniously fired from a cannon. Rest assured, no tortoises were harmed in the creation of this email account.)

A tandem? I can't think of another human I'd trust enough to get on one of those with. Whoever invented them should be fired from that cannon instead of poor old Clive!

I've never broken any bones at all. I do have a crooked little finger, though. Liv slammed her foot into it sliding down the banisters at our grandmother's house. I was at the bottom with my hand on the rail and she smacked straight into me then fell off and twisted her ankle. We conducted the entire grisly scene in strangled silence, because we had the kind of grandmother who really detested having children in her house.

I've looked Formentera up and I'm officially OBSESSED. I'll keep the secret, but it's gone straight to the top of my bucket list.

Where makes my list?

I'm really not well traveled—I'm ashamed to say I've barely ventured outside Europe. Florence made my heart sing, Sardinia too. I find myself drawn to Italy for the pasta, pizza, and passion!

I love Cornwall best of all, though. If I ever have enough money, I'll buy a tiny shuttered house overlooking a harbor and spend every morning drinking good coffee and watching the boats come in. They'll be so used to me they'll look up at my open windows and I'll shout down to see what they've caught, and they'll save me the best for my dinner. Community, I guess. Belonging. I lived a long time in a place where it was severely lacking, despite the regular dinner parties and garden gatherings.

Do you get nervous before a book comes out?

Because I feel as sick as a parrot about this one and I didn't even write it! I guess some of my nerves stem from the possibility that people might realize they're not my words, but mostly I just want people to love the story as much as I do. It really matters to me.

Do you have any publication-week rituals or tips?

What do you like to do when you're not writing? As in, what lights you up, besides books?

This is a random one, but someone asked for my favorite smells. Anything come to mind?

Until next time,

Kate x

15

"H HASN'T REPLIED, IT'S BEEN ALMOST A WEEK," KATE SAID, BITING THE edge of her nail. They'd decamped up to her flat for a cold glass of wine after a long, sticky day in the shop.

"Stop doing that, you'll make it bleed," Liv said. "Your hands need to be perfect for all the pics I'm going to take of you holding the book in various bookshops and supermarkets."

"You don't need to come with me to shelf-spot, it's fine." Kate had seen enough authors posting shelfies to know the publication-day drill.

Liv ripped the bag of licorice open on the coffee table. "I do. Would I let you go to prenatal classes alone if you were pregnant? No. No, I would not." She picked up a piece of licorice and sniffed it, then placed it down again, unimpressed. "You're about to give birth to this book, and I'm gonna be there to wipe your sweaty brow and take proud-sister pics of you cradling it in your unbitten hands."

"I'm not planning on being sweaty. Thank God supermarkets have air-conditioning." Kate flapped her T-shirt, too hot. The windows in the flat didn't open fully, and there wasn't a breath of cool air. "Why hasn't H replied? Did I say something wrong, do you think? Was it the x at the end? I typed it, deleted it, then typed it again—it just felt as if we were on those familiar kind of terms. It's a reflex after I type my name, I do it all the time."

She turned her laptop screen to her sister beside her on the sofa.

"Stop over-thinking everything. You haven't done anything wrong." Liv scanned the emails Kate had already read aloud twice. "Tell you something, though. Scotch and licorice? This is a guy."

Kate chewed her lip and shrugged. She wasn't certain, but she'd increasingly been of the same mind. Not so much from the breadcrumb trail Liv had pointed out, more the general turn of phrase and opinions.

"Unless they're deliberately saying things to throw you off the scent, of course," Liv said, warming to her theme. "Oh my God!" Liv's eyes rounded. "Work with me here . . . Could it be Fiona?"

Kate's double take was movie-worthy. "What? Why would you think that?"

Liv shrugged. "I don't know, just throwing it out there. Maybe she has a secret soft side."

"You wouldn't think so if you'd met her." Kate frowned. There was no way Fiona could be the mystery author, surely? The exposing vulnerability of the story just didn't fit with Fiona's iron-lady persona, it was unfathomable.

"Someone else then, someone younger. They might actually hate licorice and be addicted to watching makeup tutorials on TikTok."

Kate frowned, closing her laptop. "I really hope not."

The idea that H might be fabricating their answers hadn't occurred to her. She reached for the G&T Liv had mixed her, despondent at the idea. The connection she'd built with H felt genuine and had bolstered her confidence about the whole project in a way she hadn't realized she needed—as if they were a team, in this thing together. It didn't sit easy to think it might be yet more smoke and mirrors.

Liv flopped back against the sofa, shoulder to shoulder with Kate.

"Forget I said anything. He, or she, is probably in a hut somewhere on a wild Welsh hillside, no reception to reply. You'll hear from them tomorrow."

"You reckon?"

Liv nodded. "They said Richard was an arsehole, so they must be genuine."

"And that you should run the country," Kate said.

"I'll only do it if my cabinet can wear fancy dress," Liv said.

Kate laughed into her gin, her mood lightened by her sister, as usual. "What would they be?"

"Stormtroopers on Mondays, cats on Tuesdays," Liv said. "Wednesday, they all have to come as Harry Styles tributes, and on Thursdays they don't get into number ten unless they turn up in full *Bridgerton* regalia."

"Oh, I like that one best. Can I be in the cabinet on Thursdays?"

Liv clinked her glass against Kate's. "You can be the minister for Thursdays."

"What about Fridays?"

Liv took a second to think. "They all come in as Muppets."

"Business as usual, then," Kate said.

"Guess so." Liv leaned her head on her sister's shoulder. "You're not a random piece of sky, Kate. Not to me."

Kate relaxed and closed her eyes, exhausted.

"Have you heard anything else from Alice?"

"Nothing of consequence. She's avoiding talking to me again, mostly just texts telling me to stop panicking and let her be, and that she hasn't made any rash decisions." Kate huffed. "Bloody

Flynn from bloody Australia. What kind of guy encourages his girlfriend to give up everything she's worked for on a whim for him?"

Liv's cough of derision was sharp and instant. "Richard?"

"Exactly. I don't want her with a Richard, someone who clips her wings rather than helps her fly."

"Have you told her about the book yet?"

Kate shrugged. "Not yet. I don't think she's in the mood to listen anyway, it's all Flynn this, Flynn that, Flynn the other. I hate the name more every time I say it."

"Don't mention that to Alice," Liv cautioned.

"Oh, I know. I won't." Kate sighed. "She's lucky I have the book keeping me busy or I'd be on the next train up there."

"Which would make things a million times worse," Liv said. "Show her you trust her, she'll come through."

"You think so?"

"Well, I tried to talk sense into you all those years ago, if you remember, and look where that got me."

It had been the closest they'd come to falling out as adults, awful for them both until Liv held out the olive branch. At the time Kate had felt as if everyone in her life wanted to stick their oar in because they didn't know Richard the way she did. She'd been determined to prove them all wrong.

"I know you're right, but it's so hard not to wade in and bring her home for the summer, make her see sense over endless plates of spaghetti."

"Spaghetti or a surfer that looks like a Hemsworth brother and lives on the beach?" Liv said.

Kate screwed her eyes closed and burrowed into her sister's shoulder, defeated.

16

KATE LAY IN BED, WATCHING THE CLOCK COUNT DOWN TO MIDNIGHT. She'd spent the day getting book-prepped and polished, staying busy to keep her nerves in check.

Her social media pages were awash with glowing excitement from reviewers who'd already read the book, teasers and competitions to build anticipation, shots of her fingernails painted to match the cover, and the towering stack of books other publishers had sent her to read and review in the hope of a cover quote. It was all about building the buzz, and right now she felt as if she lived inside a beehive, curled into a fetal position around the book to protect it at all costs.

"Eleven fifty-seven," she whispered into the darkness.

It had been ten days now and H still hadn't replied, which troubled her greatly. She'd agonized over what she might have said to cause offense, whether to send a follow-up email, if she should seek advice from Charlie. She hadn't done any of those things so far, cautioned by Liv to just hold her nerve. Why wasn't there a handbook for all of this debut author stuff? The pressure of waiting to see how the world would treat the book sat like an elephant on her chest.

Eleven fifty-nine. Sudden surety that she should never have taken the job pinned her against the mattress, cold sweat on her forehead. She wasn't up to the grade. She wasn't good enough for the book. She was going to say the wrong thing, post the wrong image, offend someone crucial, alienate the actual author. She kicked the quilt away and sat up, too hot, queasy.

Midnight. Zero hundred hours. She clutched her mobile in the dark room as a message popped in from Liv.

Here we go! Congrats sis,
love you lots. Tomorrow,
champagne! Xxx

She read it twice over, allowing her sister's excitement to seep in and become her own. It wasn't publication eve anymore, any final chance to back out was officially gone. Rehearsals were over. It was opening night.

SHE SLEPT IN FITS AND starts, a combination of sickly nerves and mixed-up dreams of Alice. They were together under the shade of a palm umbrella in an Aussie beach café, sand warm under the soles of her bare feet. Alice ordered for them; the owners seemed to know her, they shared a familiarity and inside jokes Kate didn't understand. A guy appeared. She didn't get a clear look at his face but when Alice stood to greet him, Kate belatedly realized her daughter was heavily pregnant. Sun-streaked gold had lightened her hair and sand clung to the back of her tanned legs beneath her denim cut-offs. A slim wreath of tattooed flowers circled her ankle, and she laughed as she cradled her bump and stood on tiptoe to kiss the guy. She didn't turn to introduce him to Kate, and she didn't glance back as they wandered away toward the sea.

Kate rose through the layers of sleep, fighting to stay under to call her daughter back. She didn't need a psychologist to decipher that particular dream; it may as well have flashed up "Talk to Alice" in huge neon letters.

Her phone burst into frantic life when she flicked it off night mode: a barrage of messages from various members of the publishing team; separate ones from Liv and Nish because he was away on a work trip. An avalanche of social media notifications too, well wishes from readers all clamoring to let her know they finally had their hands on the book and couldn't wait to read it.

"Kate, you decent? Let me in regardless."

Liv's voice carried up the stairwell, and by the time Kate opened the door her sister was waiting outside it, slightly breathless with her hands full.

"Celebratory breakfast." She held a brown paper bag up as she came in. "Fancy pastries from that new shop down the road and coffee strong enough to wake the dead."

"I just made one," Kate said.

"Instant is *so* not the vibe for today, Katie." Liv laughed as she took the lid off her cup and blew on it.

No one except Liv called her "Katie," and rarely now they were all grown up.

"Will you take my coffee lid off too? I'm terrified of damaging my nails," Kate said, holding them out in front of her. Liv's nail technician friend had based the arty design on the book cover to ensure her publication-day hands were on point for photos.

"Cinnamon roll as big as my head." She pulled it from the bag and held it up beside her face for comparison.

Liv snapped a photo. "First one for your publication-day reel," she said, breaking the outside edge from one of the pastries.

"Is this going to be an everyday thing now I'm a published author?" Kate said, nodding toward the breakfast.

"Only if you're paying," Liv said. "I had to take a small mortgage out for these. Nish would have a heart attack, he keeps sending me fake-away take-away posts so the kids won't want to order food."

"I won't breathe a word," Kate said. "God, they're good, though. I feel as if I'm in Paris."

"You might be, when the book goes big! Imagine, a world tour. Can I come? You absolutely cannot do New York without me."

"I think you might be getting just a tiny bit ahead of yourself," Kate laughed, distracted as more messages flew in on her mobile. "Oh, Liv, look," she whispered, putting her coffee down. "H has just emailed. I'm scared to open it."

"Well, they better not rain on your parade, not today of all days," Liv said. "Want me to check it first?"

Kate shook her head. "I'll do it."

Dear Kate,

Publication day at last, enjoy every moment. I'm sorry not to have replied sooner.

To answer your question regarding publication-day rituals, the truth is I always left those plans to someone else. I was lucky enough to live with a born planner, everything an opportunity for a party or a surprise dinner.

I'd suggest setting your expectations low, that way you can't be disappointed. It can feel something of an anticlimax after all of the build-up and anticipation, even more so when you've seen the process through from blank page to publication.

I have come to think of it as release day rather than publication day. The book is released from you, a flock of birds taking flight and settling on shelves and bedside tables, migrating across oceans to places you may never visit in person. But a piece of you has—your book has been to beach bars in Bali and hospital wards in Germany, kept insomniacs company in L.A.

So that's what publication/release day means to me. A toast, and a wish for a safe journey for all of those migrating birds.

Thank you for being the release vessel for those birds, Kate.

I'm sure you're aware I never intended this book for publication. I turned to writing as somewhere to channel love that suddenly had nowhere to go. I don't expect that makes much sense, but it was my escape from utter desolation.

It's taken a fair amount of detachment to come to terms with the idea of publication, but in the end I think the person who inspired the story would get a kick out of seeing it out there in the world. They were fearless, undaunted by anything, curious and kind, mercury in human form.

Thank you for being the book's guardian angel.

Enjoy today,

H x

Kate finished reading it aloud and then sat for a quiet moment at her small dining table.

"Definitely a guy," Liv said.

"It could still be a woman," Kate said. "But yeah, I think it's a guy too. A very lonely, heartbroken one."

Liv nodded, sipping her coffee. "At least you don't have to worry that you've pissed him off now," she said.

"True," Kate said. It was a relief to hear from H, but heartaching to hear about his reasons for writing the story.

"I like what he said about being the book's guardian angel," she said.

Try as she might, she hadn't been able to fully shake her lingering sense of unease. On the one hand, it was a fairly straightforward job—she'd been offered the position as a working actor with the terms and conditions clearly laid out. Charlie and Prue had explained the behind-the-scenes mechanics of the publishing industry, how pulling the right levers at the right time would get this once-in-a-generation love story into readers' hands. But it was only now, reading H's side of things, that she truly relaxed. The guardian angel of the book. She could work with that.

"I better get downstairs and open the shop," Liv said, screwing up the empty pastries bag as she drained the last of her coffee.

"I'll be down in a while. I need to reply to a few emails and do, you know, social media–type author things," Kate said, wide-eyed and overstimulated by coffee and relief and the sudden Christmas-morning elation of it all.

HEADING DOWNSTAIRS A COUPLE OF hours later, Kate found herself faced with a wall of flowers on Liv's small counter.

"Ms. Darrowby is popular this morning," her sister said. "Not one but two monster flower deliveries."

Kate plucked the card from a burst of bright summer roses in a glass fishbowl. "From the publishing house," she said, reading Prue's congratulatory note. "Don't they smell beautiful?"

The second arrangement was less formal, hand-tied cream peonies flushed peach on their outer frills, lavender snapdragons, baby-pink anemones, as if someone had wandered through the watercolored countryside and gathered them by the armful.

"This arrived with them," Liv said, producing a bottle of champagne and a card.

Dear Kate, something to celebrate this momentous occasion in style! My father would have been very proud, as am I. Fiona is too, although she'll never say it. You're an indispensable part of something very special.

Charlie x

"Charlie," Kate said, touching a velvet peony petal.

"Thought so," Liv said. "Probably lifted straight from one of his rom-com scripts. This is seriously good champagne, though."

Kate wasn't sure what to say. Liv was her sister and her best friend rolled into one, yet still she hadn't found the words to explain her conflicted feelings toward Charlie. If she had to what-three-words him, she'd choose charismatic-confusing-unsettling. And every now and then she'd choose *Top Gun*–hot, quietly inside her own head, after a couple of G&Ts. It was the aviators and the broad shoulders and the suntan—she couldn't explain it and she'd never say it aloud, even if she was the only person in the room. Her agent–client relationship with Jojo Francisco had been clear-cut, but her relationship with Charlie was far more difficult to define. The undercurrent whenever they were in the same space was undeniable

As if she'd summoned him, his name appeared on her screen.

"Hello, Charlie," she said. He was in L.A. for a few days at meetings with one of his clients; she hadn't expected him to call.

"Happy publication day, Kate." She could hear the smile in his delayed voice when he spoke.

"Thank you." She laughed. "What time is it for you? Crazy early or crazy late?"

"It's an unfashionably early three A.M."

Unbidden images of rumpled white sheets against suntanned

skin blew through Kate's mind, and she shook them hastily away. "You didn't wake up just to call me, did you? The flowers came by the way, they're gorgeous. Liv's trying to steal the champagne but there's no chance."

"Drink it, you've earned it. Any big plans for the day?"

Kate looked at her painted nails. "Liv's closing the shop in a bit so we can head out to spot the book on the shelves," she said. "And then champagne, now I have some."

"Are you still feeling okay about Sunday?"

Her stomach turned. She was feeling anything but okay about the radio interview, but that wasn't the right answer.

"Well, I'll be glad when it's over," she said. "But I'll be fine."

"I could ask Fiona if she's free to come and meet you there?" Charlie said.

"God, no," Kate said, emphatic. "Honestly, I've got it."

She could well imagine Fiona eyeballing her through the glass booth, drawing her finger slowly across her throat.

"I'll tune in from here," he said.

The thought of him listening from L.A. didn't help her nerves one bit.

"How's L.A.?"

The expected delay on the line was definitely a few seconds longer than necessary.

"Hot. Relentless. I don't know how I lived here for so long."

"You'll be home soon," she said. She wondered how he'd found being thrust back into the movie-making community he'd been a part of; if he'd run into his ex-wife, even.

"I'll raise a glass to you later." He sounded tired, reminding her it was the middle of the night for him.

"Liv's locking up, I think that's my cue to go book-spotting," she said. "Night, Charlie."

"Morning, Kate," he murmured, ringing off.

Thoughts of a bedside lamp being clicked out, a middle-of-the-night hotel room thrown into darkness, spooning into comfort and sleep.

Liv danced across from the other side of the shop, tapping her watch. "Come on, then, Kate Darrowby. Let's go find your book in the wild."

17

"CAN YOU SEE IT?"

Kate and Liv stood in front of the wall of paperbacks in the supermarket, scanning.

"It should definitely be in here today," Kate said. "Prue said so."

"Maybe they've already sold out," Liv suggested, frowning.

"Surely not." Kate bent to check the lower shelves. "Why can't I find it, Liv?"

In all of her imaginings of shelf-spotting her first-ever copy of the book, she hadn't considered it just not being there.

"Shall I ask someone?" Liv said, glancing around.

"I'll do it." Kate spotted a guy with a name badge loitering farther down the aisle. Clearing her throat, awkward, she said, "Excuse me, do you have any copies of *The Power of Love* by Kate Darrowby, please?"

The guy put his head to one side, scanning the books. "Have you looked all over?"

She wrinkled her nose and nodded. "It's not there."

"I think we had a delivery this morning." He looked doubtful. "I can go and check if you want?"

She nodded, giving him a grateful smile.

"What was the name again?"

"Darrowby. *The Power of Love* by Kate Darrowby."

He wandered away, and Liv elbowed her, laughing. "How did you resist telling him you're Kate Darrowby?"

"Because I'm not a complete nob?" Kate said, looking at the myriad of book covers in front of her. "I know I'm biased, but my cover is the prettiest, don't you reckon?"

Liv nodded. "I'm just going to go and grab some milk," she said. "Be right back."

She disappeared around one end of the aisle just as the guy ambled back around the other holding a couple of books in his hands. Kate's heart banged as he drew nearer. So this is what it felt like. Her palms were actually clammy, but she wasn't about to wipe them on the beautiful launch-day dress Liv had made her.

"Is this it?" He handed her a thriller by someone called Kate, but with a totally different surname and title.

"No," she mumbled. "Sorry."

"Yeah, didn't think it would be. Sorry." He passed her the other book in his hands, the latest Jojo Moyes. "In that case, try this one, my missus loved it."

"Thanks," she sighed, downcast and feeling like a fool. "I'll, umm, I'll have a read of the back."

"That Kate Davison one might come in at some point, you never know." He shrugged. "Just a case of keep checking, really."

He walked away, leaving her holding his book recommendations, and she stood in the deserted aisle and looked from side to side, deflated and embarrassed in her fancy new dress. She should have taken H's advice to set her expectations low more seriously.

"Did he find it?" Liv said, returning with milk.

"Not exactly." Kate showed her the books he'd left her with. "Gave me these instead."

"What?" Liv's annoyance was instant. "Where did he go? I'll ask him to look again, it must be here somewhere."

Kate put a hand on her sister's arm. "Can we just leave?" Her voice threatened tears, startling them both.

"But —"

"I know," Kate said. "Let's just try somewhere else. Please?"

Liv scowled, ready for battle, then dumped the milk on a random shelf and stalked away, shooting daggers at the guy's back as he filled the magazine rack, oblivious.

THEY WERE LUCKIER SECOND TIME around. Copies weren't on the shelf yet but a girl working on the display produced several from a pull-out drawer beneath the book stand.

"This one, you mean?" she said.

Kate pressed a hand against her heart. "Yes, that's it," she breathed, taking all three copies. "Thank you."

"I was just about to put them out, actually," the assistant said. "It's change-over day."

"Someone should tell that to the guy at the last store," Liv muttered.

Kate handed the books back. "For the shelf," she said.

"Can I film you putting them out?" Liv said.

The wary look in the assistant's eyes reminded them they hadn't made a great job of explaining themselves.

"She's the author." Liv nodded toward Kate.

The assistant looked down at the cover then up at Kate, unconvinced. "You're Kate Darrowby?"

Kate was starting to feel awkward again. "I am, yes. Look, we'll go and do a bit of shopping, come back when you're done."

Liv shot her an incredulous let-me-take-this-from-here look.

"It'd be cool to film them going on the shelf for Kate's social media, if you don't mind?" She checked the girl's name badge. "Claire?"

Claire's silence had Liv flipping her phone around to show her Kate's official author page and headshot. The assistant narrowed her eyes and zoomed in on Kate's picture with two fingers, then clocked Kate's cover-themed dress. Strapless silk really was too much for the supermarket run, but this was Kate's one and only chance for a debut author shelfie and she'd gone all out.

"My nails match too," Kate said, holding her hands out as evidence. It was enough to tip the balance.

"Yeah okay, go on then, if you'll tag me in the pics. I run a book blog so it'll be cool for my Insta." Claire dug a lip gloss out of her trouser pocket and slicked some on. "Shall I say something first or just shelve them?"

"Just do whatever you'd normally do," Liv said. "Pretend we're not here."

They stood back and watched Claire change the ticket on the shelf where the books needed to go, then fill the slot with beautiful, pristine copies. She turned to the camera at the end with a cheesy smile and double thumbs-up, then walked out of shot.

"Perfect, thank you," Kate laughed.

"So are you famous, then?" Claire said. "Can I grab a photo together for my followers?"

"God, no, I'm definitely not famous," Kate said.

"It's her debut, though, she will be," Liv said, brisk as she pushed them together. "Cozy up, gals, I'll take the shot."

Footage in the bag and Insta handles swapped, Claire went off on her break, leaving Kate and Liv gazing at the book sitting pretty among all the others.

"You came on like Fiona a bit back there, you know," Kate said. "I thought you were going to start doing a breathy voiceover, like David Attenborough."

"And here we see Claire in her natural habitat," Liv whispered into an invisible microphone on her lapel. "About to shelve copies of debut author Kate Darrowby's heart-wrenching new blockbuster, *The Power of Love.*"

They took a few more shots under Liv's strict direction: Kate pointing at the books with a goofy grin; Kate holding a copy in front of the display, her perfectly matched nails gripping the cover so as not to hide her name or the title.

"That was exhausting," Kate said with a laugh afterward. "Let's go and drink that champagne."

She walked away, then turned back to see Liv rearranging the shelves to spread the book around more of the slots.

"No," Kate said, gathering them back into their rightful place again. "Don't."

"But it looked so good," Liv wheedled.

"Think of Claire," Kate said. "She might get fired and her children would starve."

"It's survival of the fittest on those nature shows," Liv said. "I think Claire would understand."

"We're leaving now, before we're caught on camera and I go viral for the wrong reasons. Fiona would come after us with pitchforks."

"I could take her down," Liv said.

"Honestly, Liv, I'd very rarely bet against you, but when it comes to Fiona, you'd lose."

Kate linked her arm through her sister's so she couldn't run back and rearrange the shelf again, then marched her out of the store in search of champagne.

Dear H,

It was so lovely to hear from you, today of all days!

God, publication day is a bit of a whirlwind, isn't it? I've typed my fingertips sore replying to social media messages and emails, resisted chewing my fancily painted nails when the first reviews appeared online. I've cried, I've laughed, and I've drunk champagne! Not my average Thursday! Sorry for so many!!!!!s, it's been that kind of day!

Thank you for sharing such personal details with me, you can absolutely trust me to keep those things private. It's helped me understand where the story came from—I'm so sorry you've been through so much. That you've found the strength to articulate and translate your pain into something so heartrendingly beautiful is impossibly romantic. I can almost see the real story woven into the blank spaces between the lines now and my admiration for your talent has grown exponentially.

Thank you, H, for allowing me this taste of how being an author feels.

Confession—I started to write myself years ago when my daughter was a baby, but life took over and it fell by the wayside. I had this same conversation with Charlie and he suggested that the distinction between writers and non-writers might be the will to persevere, regardless? And the ability to touch people's souls, of course.

Just so you know, being the guardian angel of your story is something I'll never take for granted. You've trusted me with something precious—it's safe in my hands.

Kate x

18

"SO FIRST-CLASS TRAIN TRAVEL IS MY NEW FAVORITE THING," KATE MUR-mured into her mobile even though there was only one other person in the quiet, sun-warmed carriage.

"Only the best for Kate Darrowby," Liv said. "Wish I was with you instead of making this giant bloody birthday cake. Coffee flavor as well, which I hate, with peanut-butter icing, which I hate even more. I've got the radio on ready to listen, though, can't wait."

Kate's stomach rolled at the mention of the impending Glynn Weston radio interview. She'd woken to a "good luck" voicemail from Charlie, his voice tense and far away, and a "don't stuff this up" voicemail from Fiona, shouty as if she was in the next room. An email from Rachel, the chirpy PR girl too, assuring her she'd be brilliant and Glynn was a sweetie and here was her number, just in case. In case of what, Kate had wondered, saving it to her phone anyway. Rachel had been over the moon when she'd called last week to confirm the interview had got the final go-ahead—a real scoop, she'd said, "Such amazing coverage for a debut book in its publication week. Just be yourself and everything will be marvelous!" Kate had hung up and stroked the wine bottle in the door of the fridge before reaching for the milk for her morning coffee.

She'd heard a trailer for the weekend show while she was driving on Friday morning and Glynn had name-checked Kate Darrowby as his upcoming guest. She'd yelped and slammed her fingers over the radio buttons to stop him speaking before she almost threw up, thoroughly panicked.

And now here she was, London-bound, her color-coded character notes all laid out on the train table for a last minute reread.

Kate breathed a sigh of relief when the train lurched forward out of the station bang on time. She'd double- and triple-checked to make sure she'd built in long enough to get across London to the radio station without looking bedraggled and rushed, aware she was expected to get a photograph with Glynn for her socials without Liv at her side to direct any necessary extra shots.

Closing her eyes for a steadying couple of minutes, she jolted upright when the train came to a sudden and unexpected stop.

"What's happening?" she said, even though there was no one but the dozing elderly guy at the other end to hear her, and he was out for the count.

"Apologies for the pause, folks, some engineering works on the line. Shouldn't be long before we're moving again."

Kate stared at the carriage doors, hoping a real human might appear to reassure her rather than the announcement.

Fifteen minutes passed. That was her bookstore-browsing time gone, then.

"Oi, oi!"

The doors slid open and about twenty men in soccer shirts flooded the carriage, settling around her.

"Mornin'," a red-faced guy said, hovering near her table. "Mind if we sit down? The boss said it'd be all right if we spill in here, what with the delays and everything." He jerked his head toward the adjoining carriages. "Standing room only through there."

She swallowed and gathered her notes up as three men in gold soccer shirts piled into the empty seats around her table.

"Going to the Wolves match?" the one opposite asked her.

She shook her head.

Another nodded at her notes. "Exam?"

She shook her head again. "Interview."

"Job interviews, the pits." The first guy grimaced as he opened a can of beer. It was like a starting whistle—all around the carriage cans were hauled from pockets and bags and cracked open.

"Want one to steady your nerves?"

Kate half laughed, slightly hysterical. It wasn't even nine-thirty in the morning. "Umm, no thank you, better not."

"Thanks for your patience, folks." The carriage fell quiet to listen to the train manager over the loudspeaker. Not much we can do about the delay, I'm afraid, it's looking like another twenty minutes or so before we'll get moving again. I'll keep you updated as soon as we hear anything. Now might be a good time to grab coffee from the buffet in carriage J if you're thirsty. I'm afraid there won't be any first-class trolley service today due to staff shortages, apologies for any inconvenience caused."

A collective groan went around the carriage.

"Bloody trains," someone muttered. "Thought we were in for a treat."

Kate felt her hairline start to prickle with sweat. The pleasant warmth of the carriage had fast become overheated in the full glare of the morning sun, exacerbated by the pub-at-closing-time smell of lager and the dialed-up noise level on the now-packed train. She could feel all of her well-rehearsed lines blustering out of her head. No browsing in the bookstore, no leisurely coffee, but she should still be just about okay.

The guy opposite nodded at her notes. "What's the interview for, then?"

She pinched the bridge of her nose, glancing at her phone for the time again. "It's live on the radio," she said quietly.

"On the radio?" he said, really quite loud. "Which show?"

She nodded, jangling the bangle Liv had slid around her wrist last night. "Glynn Weston," she said, almost heaving.

"No bullshit?"

People all around the carriage were listening in now.

"No bullshit," she said, half wishing she'd accepted that beer.

"How come?"

Kate closed her eyes for a brief second. This was it, the job she'd been hired for. "I'm an author." She could only hope the words didn't sound as alien as they felt in her mouth.

"Blimey," the guy next to her said. "What sort of books do you write?"

"Love stories," she said. It didn't feel too difficult to say, because the abandoned manuscripts she'd recovered from her old home were romances.

"And you're going on Glynn Weston's show today? They better hurry this bloody train up, then," someone said.

On that, the train manager stuck her head in. "Sorry, guys," she said, shrugging. "It's just one of those things, it happens. We'll get another update soon, hang in there."

She backed out as quickly as she'd arrived, non-message delivered.

Kate excused herself to the loo, locking herself in and calling Liv.

"Liv, help! The sodding train has stopped five minutes outside of the station, God knows why, something wrong on the line is all they're saying. Can you google it? I don't know why I'm even asking that, sorry—I know you're busy with the cake from hell. I'm on the train with an entire carriage full of soccer supporters who've all had a three-course breakfast of beer, beer, and beer, and I swear I'm a whisker away from having one myself! Oh God, Liv, what if I'm late? You can't be late for live radio! What will Glynn say? And shitting Nora, what will Fiona say? This is a total disaster. I'm going to be fired for sure."

It was only when she stopped to draw breath that she realized she wasn't speaking to her sister at all, just voicemail, which informed her she'd run out of space for her message and she needed to start again. She hung up without bothering and sat on the loo with her head in her hands, listening to the stupid recorded train message about not flushing your hopes and dreams down the toilet with your tampons and loo paper. She tried not to let it register, dreading the thought of it tumbling out of her head on live radio, if she ever made it there on time.

"Another twenty minutes," her beer neighbor informed her as soon as she returned to her seat. "We might be able to reclaim our ticket costs if it goes on much longer, though, so cross your fingers."

Kate slid into her seat and tried to work out what to do, because she was now running frighteningly close to the wire. All of her built-in extra time had evaporated, and at this rate she might even be a no-show.

She messaged Rachel on the number she'd saved just in case, and then spent the next eight minutes obsessively checking to see if she'd replied. Nothing. It was Sunday morning; if the girl had any sense she'd still be in bed. Or more likely at hot yoga. Either way, she wasn't answering her phone. Liv was making her awful cake for her mother-in-law's birthday and Charlie was still stateside. She reread her emails from Rachel, suddenly remembering mention of a contact at the radio station. She had a number! *Thank everything*, she thought, clicking on the number and then screwing up the nerve to talk to whoever answered it. She pressed the mobile to her ear, sticking one finger in her other ear, and waited.

"Hello?"

"Umm, hi, I'm Kate Darrowby, is this the right number to speak to someone from Glynn Weston's show? Only I'm due on there this morning as a guest and I'm so sorry, but my train has stopped. Just stopped! I should still make it as long as we get moving in the next few minutes, but I thought I ought to warn you, just in case."

"Okay, Kate, don't panic," the guy on the other end said, soothing and serene. "I'm Glynn's producer. I can juggle things around a little this end, just do what you can and keep me up to speed so we can stay fluid, okay? Call me back in fifteen with an update."

Kate hung up and slumped in her seat.

"Will they wait for you?" one of her new table friends asked.

"I have no idea," she said. "If we get moving soon, they might?"

"Sure you don't want that beer?"

She shook her head and leaned her forehead against the window, miserable. How could she still be sitting just ten minutes from home? Why had she relied on Sunday trains? Why couldn't she just get out and get a bloody cab? It was ridiculous. She did the math again. She was due at the radio station by ten-thirty, and it was already half past nine. She closed her eyes and wished Charlie wasn't so far away—he'd know what to do. She thought back to their conversation after her photo shoot. What was it he'd said? Be Kate Darrowby. Buy the outfit, walk the walk, inhabit the skin of the character. Okay. So maybe the question wasn't what should Kate Elliott do, it was what would Kate Darrowby do?

Kate Darrowby would look for the silver lining, she'd be storing this up as a scene for her next novel. Opening her eyes, she looked down at the expensive denim dress she'd bought for the interview and mentally slid herself into her alter ego's shoes. Looking up again, she spread her hands wide and forced a laugh.

"Guys, I need a really big favor . . ."

FINALLY, AT JUST BEFORE TEN o'clock, the train lumbered into action to a collective cheer from all the hot-and-bothered passengers, most of their journeys sweetened by the thought of a free ride thanks to being able to claim their tickets back. Not Kate's, though; she'd been regularly updating Glynn's show producer, who'd started to consider the idea of rescheduling if she completely missed the slot. The soccer fans ushered her out of the doors in front of them as soon as they pulled into the station, yelling "You can do this, Kate!" as she ran along the platform as fast as her too-high sandals would permit, waving her notes over her head as a thank-you to her now fully invested new friends. Hurling herself into a taxi, she collapsed on the back seat, breathing as if she was about to give birth. She knew there wasn't a prayer she'd make it for the allotted time, but the producer had said he would see what could be done. Anything was better than nothing.

"Where to, love?"

She took a deep breath. "The News Building, please, London Bridge."

The driver nodded and pulled into the traffic.

"How long does it take to get there?" she said, just as a "send latest update" text appeared on her phone from Glynn's producer.

"About twenty-five minutes, I'd say? Busy this morning, a fun run's closed half the bloody roads."

"Oh no," Kate groaned, sinking into the seat.

"All right, love? Still want to go?"

She nodded, holding his gaze in the mirror. "I need to try," she said. "I'm due on the Glynn Weston show this morning, and I'm running horribly late."

He narrowed his eyes, clearly trying to decide whether she was having him on. He'd probably been told a few tall tales in his time.

"Famous, then, are you?" he said, and she could hear it in his voice, the creep of disbelief. He wasn't to blame. Her hair was clinging to her sweaty forehead and she was probably purple in the face with panic.

"No," she said. "I'm not famous. I'm an author. A new one."

On that, her phone rang. The producer, of course. She clicked it on to speaker. "Where are you now, Kate?"

"I'm in a cab on the way over," she said, trying to sound calm.

"Good, good. We can shift things around a tiny bit more, but it's tight. Glynn's show finishes in twenty minutes. Where are you precisely?"

She stared wide-eyed at the cab driver for the answer, who'd heard every word and suddenly fired the cab off down a side street at alarming speed, clearly on board with this now he'd heard it from someone other than Kate.

"Hang on to your hat," he half shouted. "I'll get you there as fast as I can."

Her mobile went again. Liv this time, in a fit of laughter.

"Kate, what's happening? I've got Glynn's show on in the kitchen, he's mentioned you're having transport issues getting to the studio? He's talked about the book already, and now he's giving the nation live updates on your whereabouts. It's become a whole thing, you're not going to believe it when you listen back to the show."

"Oh my God," Kate groaned, swiping her hair off her damp

forehead. "Everything that could go wrong has gone wrong, Liv, I'll tell you later."

"Hang on, he's just dedicating a track to you." Liv paused for a second, then started laughing again. "It's 'She Moves in Her Own Way,' by The Kooks."

Hanging up, Kate could barely swallow, her mouth sandpaper dry.

A voice message buzzed in, from the producer again. "Kate, if you can get here in the next few minutes you can do the interview from your phone in the lobby. There isn't going to be time to get you miked up and upstairs to the studio."

"Bloody joggers," the taxi driver yelled out of his window, running red lights and swerving bikes, fully into it now. "I've not read your book but I have read Glynn's, cracking they are," he said, and Kate could only agree. The radio producer called constantly for location updates, the cab driver shouting out street names as he hurled the car around corners, scattering runners everywhere.

"That's the building we're trying to get to," he said, gesticulating over the bridge.

"I can see your building," Kate told the producer. "I'm almost there."

The driver took a final detour and screeched to a halt.

"Get out, you can do it!" he yelled, shooing her with both hands.

"Get in here, you can do it!" a tall guy with ear cans and a clipboard yelled from the revolving door, waving her into the building.

There was no time for introductions, just the nearest bench seat to fling her bag on and sit down to talk directly to Glynn, who was ten floors up.

"Kate Darrowby, you've made it at last, we hear you've had

quite the journey." Glynn's Irish voice landed familiar and warm in her ear. The producer stepped away and threw her an encouraging double thumbs-up, mouthing "You're live," most probably as a reminder not to swear, despite the morning she'd had.

"Oh, Glynn, I'm so sorry," she gasped. "It was genuinely the journey from hell, my train just stopped moving. Stopped dead on the tracks! A whole hour just sitting there in a carriage full of soccer fans drinking lager for breakfast, and then there's some kind of fun run in London, joggers everywhere. All of the streets are blocked. I seriously considered getting out of the cab and running with them, except I didn't know where I was going and I'd never have made it in these heels. Honestly, I was a fireman's pole away from complete disaster!"

"I get the feeling you and Bridget Jones might have been very good friends," Glynn laughed, thoroughly enjoying her nightmare.

"One of the soccer fans offered me a can of lager for my nerves—I didn't have one but it was a close-run thing, Glynn, I felt like it."

He laughed down the line. "Oh, I would have so taken that beer."

"The strangest thing happened while we were stuck there, though," she said. "I was sitting there in a panic, and I looked across the table at the guy opposite me, and you know when you get that feeling you know someone, but can't place where from? We both got that."

Glynn gasped, always front of the queue for the gossip. "Oh, do tell!"

"Well, we got talking, and after a few minutes we realized we *did* know each other. More than that—we were at school together."

"Is this going where I hope it's going?"

"If you're hoping he was my first crush—well, my first kiss, actually—then yes! I couldn't believe it, I'd never have recognized him if we hadn't been stuck opposite each other for an hour on the train. It was so bizarre."

Glynn clapped his hands. "You do know the entire nation needs this meet-cute to be the beginning of your own real-life love story, right?"

She laughed, giddy with relief to have made it to the radio station and salvaged the situation. "How funny would that be? They do say you never forget your first love. We said we'd catch up over coffee, so watch this space."

"I'll buy my hat!"

Glynn's good humor was balm to Kate's tattered nerves, and when he smoothly steered the conversation on to the book, she ignored all of her color-coded notes and spoke for a few off-the-cuff minutes about the story. It was over before she had time to worry whether she'd said the wrong thing, and she couldn't recollect a word of the conversation afterward, but she'd done it. Placing her mobile down on her abandoned notes, she dropped her head into her hands and pressed her fingers into her eye sockets. Oh good God. She'd talked about lager and first kisses and fireman's poles. On balance, Fiona would probably have preferred it if she hadn't turned up at all.

19

IT WAS A MARK OF HOW STRESSFUL THE MORNING HAD BEEN THAT KATE trudged up the stairs to her flat, locked the door and crawled straight into bed. She didn't want food or wine or conversation, just the oblivion of sleep, preferably dreamless. The sun had slipped behind the building by the time she roused again, curling herself into a grumbling ball under the quilt when she remembered the series of unfortunate events. Why was she always like this? It would never happen to Jojo Moyes, she thought, remembering the book recommendation from the guy in the supermarket. She'd followed many of her favorite authors on social media to get an insight into the kind of life she needed to attempt to emulate as Kate Darrowby, and from what she could see, none of them lived the haphazard, pressure-cooker kind of existence she did. She really needed to get her shit together.

Mug of tea in hand, she fired up her laptop, hesitating to open her emails in case Fiona's name loomed large and furious. Turning to social media instead, she squinted at the number of new followers she'd gained since she'd last looked. Did these things glitch? Not if the bombardment of posts and messages was anything to go by. She was inundated with empathy and sympathy from people who couldn't get enough of that morning's drama, new followers who'd ordered the book on the strength of

shared clips of the interview, because if her book was half as en-
tertaining as she was, they wanted in.

A message alert from Rachel in PR slid across the top of her
screen.

> Kate! I'm so sorry I wasn't around to
> help you this morning, but I'm also kind
> of #NotSorry, because no run-of-the-mill
> interview could ever have created this
> much coverage! Well done, you! I can't
> believe you bumped into your first love
> on the train too, how fabulously random,
> you couldn't make this stuff up!
> Excellent for promo purposes!
> Speak tomorrow, R x

Kate stared at the message, putting her mug down slowly. Yes,
Rachel, you could make this stuff up, actually. She hadn't had
time to think through the bigger picture when she'd thrown Kate
Darrowby's first crush anecdote into the mix that morning. The
soccer guys on the train had been well up for going along with the
subterfuge, amused to be part of a story on national radio. Should
she tell the publishing team it wasn't true? Her first instinct was
yes, absolutely, but then . . . what would they think of her? Sure, the
whole job was based on fabrication, but the lines were being fed
to her and now she'd veered off script. Was that allowed? She
really didn't want to tell them that she'd outright lied, it made her
feel shoddy and about seven years old. Would it shake H's faith in
her? And then, of course, there was Charlie. However much he'd
urged her to walk in Kate Darrowby's shoes, he probably hadn't
been suggesting she invent star-crossed meetings with ex-loves.

Prue was next up on the message chain, letting her know the

"Darrowby effect" had sent the ebook rocketing up the online charts. Kate clicked over to check, doing a double take at the way it had bobbed up the numbers like a champagne cork fired from a shaken bottle. It seemed there really was no such thing as bad publicity.

She closed her laptop, rattled by the whole thing. Wrapping her arms around her knees, she slumped into the corner of the sofa, feeling blue without being able to put her finger on exactly why. The fiasco of the morning had taken its emotional toll, but it was more than that. If *The Power of Love* were truly her own book, she wouldn't have felt the need to pepper the truth with an attention-grabbing lie, and all of those reassuring messages would probably have lifted her flagging spirits. As it was, though, they added to her ominous sense of unease. A copy of the book lay on the coffee table, and she picked it up and folded her arms around it, trying to summon her inner guardian angel, when her mobile buzzed yet again.

Free for a quick video call?

Speaking of guardian angels. Charlie.

That'd be really good actually, thanks.

Within seconds, her phone was buzzing again with his incoming call. Pushing her hair behind her ears and pinching color into her cheeks, she clicked "Join."

"Hey," he said, his face filling her screen. He was at the desk in his sunlit hotel suite, making her wish she could climb into the phone screen to escape.

"Hey, you," she said, flat. "How's L.A.?"

"Manic, but I'm on the home run now. I fly back this evening.

So . . ." The pause on the line was definitely more than the usual long-distance lag. "It sounded like you had a stressful morning."

"You heard it, then," she sighed.

"I did. You okay?"

She was grateful he wasn't making light of it, and she curled deeper into the corner of the sofa, miserable enough for a rogue tear to slide down her cheek.

"Hey, don't cry, there's no need. Everyone over at the publishing house is thrilled," he said, concern thickening his voice.

"I'm all right really," she said, swiping it away. "Rachel and Prue have both been in touch about their plans to maximize on what happened, but I just feel like such an idiot, Charlie. I'd planned everything so carefully, and then it all went out the window in a sea of soccer shirts and joggers."

"Don't beat yourself up," he said. "You're putting too much pressure on yourself."

"The book deserves better," she said.

"The book is damn lucky to have you," he countered right back. "And look at it this way . . . at least you didn't join the fun run."

"There's that." She half laughed despite herself. "No need for ice baths or blisters."

He smiled, but his eyes were serious.

"Things didn't go to plan, but you adapted. You were funny and people were invested, and it's all worked out for the best as far as the book is concerned. Prue is over the moon . . ." He paused, and she micro-cringed because she could sense what was coming. "Especially about the train meet-cute with your first love."

This was the moment. If she was going to confess to the casual lie, now was the time.

"Even Fiona is impressed," he said, filling the awkward pause before she could. "Trust me, Kate, today was a good thing, not a bad one. You made lemonade out of lemons, it's all anyone can ask of you."

Murky fear that Charlie's opinion of her would diminish kept her from blurting the truth, and the part of Kate that would be forever seventeen basked in Fiona's approval. It was such a small, insignificant untruth. How bad could it be to let it lie?

She pressed the phone against her heart after Charlie disappeared, and then closed her eyes and saw herself running down the train platform, waving her notes over her head at the crowd of soccer fans behind her. Hauling her backside off the sofa, she went in search of wine.

Hey Alice,

I can almost hear your eyes rolling at me for emailing, but I've called you again a few times just now and I feel like I'm in a one-sided relationship with your voicemail. Please don't avoid me. I'm always on your side, even if I don't always say what you want to hear. I love you and I want what's best for you, in the long term as much as right now. Anyway, this isn't supposed to be a lecture—I've got some news to tell you.

I've taken on an acting job over the last couple of months. Don't panic, you're not about to spot me in the next *Avengers* movie or anything! I should be so lucky.

I won't bore you with all the background details, but a while ago I was asked to represent a book as its official author, because the book couldn't be published otherwise. So it has my name on the front (Kate Darrowby, not my actual surname!) and my face on the inside cover, and I answer any public questions as if I actually wrote it, which of course I didn't. I don't know who the real author is, but we've chatted by email and they seem really lovely, so I'm glad to be able to do it for them, as well as it being quite exciting for me.

It was small scale in the beginning but it seems to be suddenly gathering popularity, so I'm letting you know just in case you hear or see

anything and wonder what the hell is going on. You won't, I'm sure—
I mean, it's hardly like I've gone viral or anything!

No one knows about this apart from you, Liv, and Nish. Please don't
breathe a word to anyone else, especially not Dad or Belinda. I know you
won't, but mum's the word. Literally, in this case! I've had to sign a
non-disclosure contract, I might actually get sued or something, so eat
this email after reading.

Call me soon, I miss you.

Love Mum xx

20

"SO, WELCOME, WELCOME, WELCOME!" RACHEL FROM PR GOT TO HER feet to kick the meeting off, clapping her hands with what could accurately be described as pure, unadulterated elation.

Kate had attended her first publishing meeting full of nerves about the unknown. This time around she was anxious about the chaos of Sunday, but she'd been greeted with a full body hug from Prue and a double high five from Rachel, plus an actual kiss on the cheek from Joel in sales. Not an air-kiss kind of day, then.

She glanced at Charlie beside her, aware of his familiar cologne, glad of his quiet confidence. They were a team within a team here. No Fiona today, which Kate was relieved about.

"So, Kate. Sunday!" Rachel said, directing her generalized clapping to focus in on Kate in particular, which everyone else at the table joined in with enthusiastically. Kate looked around, then shrugged her shoulders and pressed her hands over her face.

"Don't," she said. "I've made a mental note to never rely on Sunday trains again. Or trains at all, if it's something important."

"Hey, we're not complaining," Prue said, tucking her bob— now half-emerald-green, half-jet-black—behind her ears and gazing at Kate over thick-rimmed green glasses. She really had this hair and glasses combo down. "It was unconventional, for sure, but it created a golden opportunity, which is where Rachel and the marketing team have been concentrating their efforts ever since." She smiled across the table at Rachel, who was pretty much bouncing in her chair.

"You've hopefully seen some of the reels and posts we've put together appearing across social media," Rachel said. "We've gone for a huge push to amplify the message as quickly as possible."

Kate smiled, unsure where this was headed. "The message?"

Rachel nodded. "So far we've directed all of our marketing toward the actual book, but over the last couple of days we've pivoted the focus toward you personally, Kate, because your relatability factor is off the scale."

"It is?" Kate's gaze flickered around the publishing team and found them all gazing at her intently.

"The iron is hot right now, like, scorching, and it's our job to turn that heat up even more, especially as we're still in the all-important launch week. We want that book finding its way into as many shopping baskets as possible over the next couple of days, and that's where you come in."

"What are you thinking?" Charlie said, sitting straighter in his chair.

"Well, what's so great is the way people have reacted to Kate, and to the first love meet-cute angle specifically, so we've made sure the story has been picked up by newspaper entertainment pages, online showbiz columns, those type of outlets. The fact that it happened on Glynn's show adds the necessary star power to guarantee the clicks, and"—Rachel paused to look around at them all, shiny-eyed with drama, to ramp up the tension—"I've managed to land you a spot on the sofa on the *Good Morning Show!*"

Kate gasped. "As in the show that's been on TV every morning for the last twenty years?" She'd watched it intermittently, mostly when Alice was a baby and she was flopped, exhausted, on the sofa between feeds. "I honestly don't think I can do it," she rushed on, too freaked out to maintain a professional face. "What if I say the wrong thing and they see right through me? I haven't properly acted in front of a camera in years, let alone been on live TV."

Anxious eyes swiveled around the table, everyone unsure who should speak next.

"Kate, it's okay," Charlie said. "If you're not comfortable with it, you can absolutely say no." He locked eyes with her and everything in his stance and tone told her he'd have her back on this. She didn't need to do anything she didn't want to do. Relief watered down her alarm to a manageable level, a cooling sprinkler so she didn't need to get up and leave the room.

"But for the record," he continued, "you absolutely could do this. Your natural ability to communicate is extraordinary, people will sit up and listen to whatever you have to say. There's no better spokesperson for the book than you, and a spot like this is promotional gold dust. Everyone around this table knows you can do it. I have faith in you, and the author themself thinks you're pretty damn special too." He paused, choosing his next words carefully. "You're better at this than you think you are, Kate."

He held her gaze steadily, and she felt his words settle into her brain and make themselves at home. She could do it. She could sit her guardian angel backside on that famous red sofa and tell the world all about *The Power of Love*.

"It's tomorrow," Prue said.

"Tomorrow?" Charlie and Kate said in startled unison.

"Not going to be a problem?" Rachel said, crossing her fingers in the air on both hands as she fired them her most winning smile.

Charlie looked only at Kate. "We can go grab a coffee downstairs and have a chat about it if you'd like?"

She appreciated his offer to escape for a breather, but she'd made her mind up.

"It's okay," she said, consciously forcing her shoulders down from her ears. "I'll do it."

The relief around the table was palpable; Rachel looked as if she could do with a double brandy.

Charlie's intent gaze silently double-checked she was okay with it, and she nodded.

"I'll make sure I get an early enough train this time."

Rachel sat down. "No need. They want you on site by eight in the morning at the latest so they'll send a car for you at six."

Kate looked at Charlie. "What do you think?"

What she was really asking was *Will you come with me?*, but she didn't want to sound needy in front of the whole team.

"I think it's a terrific opportunity, as long as you're comfortable with it. You could always stay over in London tonight if you'd prefer, be on hand in the morning without worrying about the early start?"

He was right, of course. In a previous life, she'd have had to juggle childcare and organize meals in advance to have a night away, which was vanishingly rare. There was something liberating about being able to say yes without the need to consult anyone else.

"I need to go home first and throw all of my clothes around in a panic while I decide what to wear, but staying nearby definitely sounds less stressful," she said, raising a knowing laugh around the table.

"At least you won't have too long to panic about things," Prue said, checking the time on her mobile. "In less than twenty-four hours, you'll be on the sofa with Ruby and Niall."

21

SPENDING A NIGHT ALONE IN A HOTEL WAS A FIRST FOR KATE, AND SHE'D been impressed by the publisher's upscale choice of venue. She'd hung her dress ready to go in the morning, and set her makeup out ready to apply even though they'd most likely do it again when she got to the studio.

Charlie had said he'd swing by for a drink in the bar, probably concerned she'd work herself up into a ball of anxiety if left to her own devices.

He was there already when she headed downstairs. She'd expected he would be. He'd told her at their first meeting that he'd be beside her every step of the way, and as long as he wasn't on a different continent, he'd been a man of his word.

She spotted him sitting at a table with what looked like a Scotch in one hand, his head dipped to read paperwork. It was a quiet midweek night in the hotel, a sparse scattering of patrons, a table of women over on the far side. Straight from the office, Charlie had laid his jacket on the empty chair beside him, no tie, dark hair falling forward as he studied the papers. Were they something to do with the book, or did they concern someone else entirely? He always managed to make her feel as if she was his only focus; it was easy to forget he had a roster.

"Fancy seeing you here," she said as she drew close.

"And now I feel underdressed," he said, putting his paperwork away as he took in her short pink summer dress and heels.

"And I feel overdressed, so we're even," she said, smoothing her skirt over her thighs. The dress had seemed longer the last time she'd worn it; she was glad to at least have the benefit of some summer color.

"Pink looks good on you," he said.

She'd think nothing of the compliment coming from Liv, but from Charlie it was enough to send a matching flush up her neck.

"Thank you," she said, then waved a hand in the vague direction of his shirt. "And, umm, black suits you."

"Drink?"

"Please," she said, glad of the chance to give herself a mental slap.

She watched him cross the room, noticing the way people's eyes followed him, the subtle movement of his shoulders beneath his shirt as he leaned forward to speak to the woman behind the bar. Was it unwise to meet him tonight? He was Charlie Francisco, her agent, but he was also someone she was coming to rely on. She knew the rumors about the end of his marriage and what sort of man he might be in his private life, and she wasn't in the romance market after the shocking end of her own relationship, but if she spoke purely as she found, Charlie was damn good company and he had never let her down. Not to mention he looked like he could have starred in Hollywood rom-coms rather than written them. If he'd written them at all, that was. Throw in a moodily lit bar, a hotel room upstairs, and a large glass of wine to steady her nerves, and she really needed to be careful what left her mouth and what stayed inside her head.

"Have you eaten?" he asked, placing the chilled glass of white in front of her as he sat down.

"Room service," she said. "Living the high life. It was good of them to book such a nice place, I expected a budget hotel or something."

"You're helping them make a lot of money, Kate, a good night's rest isn't exactly a luxury."

"So I don't balls things up again?"

"You didn't balls things up with Glynn, and you won't balls up tomorrow." He sipped his drink, something short on the rocks again. "Rachel called earlier," he said. "She wondered if they'd be able to track down your crush from the train."

"Oh God," she said. "Charlie, I—"

"It's fine," he said. "They'll always try to maximize on any angle that presents itself. The story is already out there doing its thing so don't feel obliged to hand over names and numbers."

Kate swallowed a cooling mouthful of wine, completely split over whether to come clean. She'd really just prefer it if no one ever mentioned it again. "I don't really want to . . . you know, go down that road if we can avoid it," she said in the end, feeling lame.

"We can avoid it," he said. "I'm sure neither of you want to be paraded on TV before you even decide whether to go for that coffee."

"I wanted to ask you something," she said, changing the subject. "Earlier, in the meeting, you said something about the author being pleased with how things are going."

He watched her steadily over his glass. "What I actually said is that he thinks you're pretty damn special."

She nodded, thrown because Charlie had inadvertently referred to the author as "he" rather than "they." So she and Liv had been right with their hunch it was a guy.

"Was it true, or were you trying to bolster my confidence? It's fine if you were."

"I wouldn't lie to you," he said. "You remind them of some-one who isn't in their life anymore."

"I do?" She frowned, surprised by the detail. "How so?"

He sighed into his glass. "Things you've said on email and on the radio, I expect." He shrugged a shoulder. "You're the right person for the job, Kate, and tomorrow will be no exception. They might press you about your guy-on-the-train encounter, but only say as much as you want to and steer the conversation back toward the book."

Kate didn't miss the way he'd subtly steered the conversation away from the author and back to the book either, and admired his skill. She listened as he ran over some basics about the day, timings and pitfalls to watch for. The bartender wandered across to offer them a refill; she hesitated and then accepted, and he checked the time, then did the same.

"Can we not talk about tomorrow anymore?" she said. "I'm as ready as I'll ever be."

Her knee brushed his as she reached for her glass. "You re-minded me of your father earlier," she said. "In the meeting. Jojo had a way of making me feel I could do anything I wanted to. You did that same thing today."

Charlie's half smile lacked his usual confidence. "I hope so. It's a lot to live up to. Today was a moment for me too—I thought you were going to walk out of there, but I should have known better."

"Not really. I seriously thought about it."

He drank a mouthful of his drink. "My father was fond of you, from looking at his notes in your file."

Jojo blustered straight through Kate's head, always in a crumpled linen jacket and one of his florid collection of bow ties.

"I was fond of him too," she said. "Telling him I was leaving was worse than telling my own father." She remembered walking up the stairs to deliver the news, full of dread. "He told me to commute to Germany, that I was barely out of nappies let alone old enough to get married, and that if any child of his tried to pull a stunt like that he'd lock them up till they saw sense." She laughed softly. "I guess he must have been talking about you."

Charlie huffed under his breath. "I wouldn't have put it past him. He was the best father in the world in most ways, but God, could he be stubborn. I'm surprised he didn't handcuff you to his desk." He swirled his drink in his glass. "He wrote that you were a rising star, and that you'd come back one day."

"Oh my God, that breaks my heart," she said. "He was right about me coming back and he never got the joy of *I told you so*."

"At least Fiona is there to see it," Charlie said.

Kate took a gulp of wine. "She terrifies me as much now as she did back then. Although saying that, she once gave me a squirt of her perfume and straightened my collar before I went up for a part. It shocked me so much that I forgot my lines."

He laughed then. "She is what she is."

"I feel like a teenager again every time she's in the room. I have this crazy need to impress her." She decided to ask a question she probably wouldn't have without two glasses of wine under her belt. "Were she and your father ever together?"

"In a romantic way?" Charlie said. "No. Great friends, but Bob was the big love of Fi's life. He's been gone a good ten years now, maybe even fifteen. She and my dad were too alike, and when they rowed, *they rowed*."

She could imagine, they were both such huge personalities. "You must miss him."

"Every day." Charlie drained his drink. "I should hit the road, let you get some rest for tomorrow."

"I'll walk out with you," she said. "Grab some fresh air before I head up. You need a degree in engineering to operate the air con."

He swallowed. "Need a hand with it?"

Kate so nearly said yes. "I'll be okay, I can always call reception if I get desperate." He nodded, and she followed him across the quiet bar. Her heels clicked against the marble reception floor as they headed outside into the warm evening.

"It's quite some view, isn't it?"

The hotel perched on the South Bank, lit-up London spread out in front of them, the glitter of lights reflected in the river.

"Best city in the world," he said.

"Different from L.A., I should imagine," she said, leaning against the hotel wall.

"Another planet."

"Do you miss it?"

He shook his head, his eyes on the river. "Being back there recently reminded me exactly how much I don't miss it. It feels as if the sun bleached its soul out. I'd be happy to never see the Hollywood Hills again."

"Tricky for a screen agent," she said.

"Yes," he said. "My father was a fish out of water over there too—too honest and direct for the slippery smiles and handshakes. It's a big old machine, the wheels keep turning with or without you. There's things I miss about it for sure, and people, but not the life I lived there—" He broke off. "It got complicated."

She wrapped her arms around herself, aware they'd strayed into uncharted waters. "Love does that."

His dark eyes met hers, a shared moment of acknowledgment that they weren't kids, that they'd both been around the block.

"Will you go for coffee with the guy from the train?"

She glanced away, not wanting to talk about it. "Would you go for coffee with the first girl you ever kissed?"

He laughed then. "Jenna Jackson. I was twelve, she was fourteen."

"Scandalous," she said. "First kisses are best left to teenagers."

He side-eyed her. "Don't say that on TV tomorrow. You're a romance writer now, remember? You need to believe in the magic moments."

"The magic moments?" She knew what he meant from the movies, but magic had been sorely lacking from her own love life, even when she was nineteen and Richard proposed in a packed restaurant. He'd had the chef bury the ring in her dessert— summer pudding. It had ended up being a bit macabre, like fishing the diamond out of a bowl of blood and guts. Her fingertips were purple for a week.

"You know," Charlie said. "The part in the story when one person does or says something unexpected, and the other person looks at them with new eyes."

"Whiskey and cola," she said.

He looked at her, quizzical.

"Your eyes," she said. "They're whiskey and cola."

"Yeah . . . that kind of unexpected," he said after a surprised pause. "And then something like this might happen"—he braced one hand flat on the wall beside her head and brushed the back of his fingers down her cheek—"and he might say he'd never met anyone quite like her in his whole life."

The warmth of his breath fanned her lips, and Kate's breath caught in her throat.

"Maybe you did write those rom-coms after all," she said, unguarded.

He was close enough for her to see the micro-expression of hurt flicker through his eyes before he caught it. They hadn't really talked about his previous career, what she knew or didn't know. He stepped away, and she floundered for the right thing to say.

"I'm sorry, I didn't mean to—"

"Forget it. I'll go, let you get some rest," he said, lifting one shoulder as he backed away. "I'll see you at the studio."

She nodded, not trusting herself to speak, unsure what she'd say anyway.

22

BREATHING EXERCISES. SQUARE BREATHS, TRIANGULAR BREATHS, ALL
the breaths. Count five things you can see, hear, touch, smell, and
taste. Kate's answer to all of those questions at that precise moment
would be fear, fear, fear, fear, and fear, because she was seated on the
familiar red *Good Morning Show* sofa waiting for Ruby and Niall to introduce her. It felt weirdly like a fever dream, as if she'd fallen asleep
and woken up inside the TV. She'd rehearsed with Charlie for this
kind of thing, and filled out countless online interviews over the last
few months where she'd honed her answers to the mostly similar
questions: *red licorice; two thousand words a day, mostly early morning or late at
night; she'd been writing for some years, although this was her first published book.*
The answers jostled around in her head—she just hoped she could
find them when she needed them, because there was no editing live
television. She could feel herself spiraling and had to fight the instinct
to bolt, but then Ruby gave her a jiggly little thumbs-up and they
were live to the nation in five, four, three, two, one.

Something inside clicked under the lights and cameras, an
awakening of old memory-muscles. She could do this. She knew
the answers to any question they might throw at her, and she was
going to represent the hell out of this book.

SHE WAS DOING IT. ANSWERING their questions, smiling, and gosh the sofa was actually quite comfortable when you relaxed into it! This really wasn't so bad, she had to be at least halfway through her six-minute slot. She'd managed to talk eloquently about the book with what felt like ease and relevance, a copy of it on her lap with the cover angled toward the camera. At this rate, Fiona was going to be raising her martini at the TV.

"So as a romance writer, I'm guessing you must be a born romantic in your personal life too?" Ruby said, warm and smiley and exactly how she looked on the television.

"Well, I guess so," she said, trying not to think about the night before as she glanced over at Charlie standing behind the camera operator. "Flowers on Valentine's Day, dinners on wedding anniversaries, those kinds of things, you know."

"I sure do," Niall said. "My lovely wife and I have been married ten years on Sunday. Any top tips on how to keep the romance alive?"

Kate laughed. "Oh, I'm probably not the one to offer advice on that score, I've done some spectacularly stupid things over the years. I even tried to shave my pubic hair into a love heart for my ex-husband's fortieth, only I slipped with the razor and put a jagged line straight down the middle. Broke my own heart, so to speak, then a few years later my husband did the same thing." She stopped speaking and cleared her throat. "Broke my heart, I mean, not shaved his pubic hair. God, I'm sorry, can I even say pubic hair on morning telly?"

Niall was trying hard not to laugh and looked at his co-host to reply.

"The things we do for love," Ruby said, brushing over it.

"Speaking of which, tell us more about getting stranded on a train with your first love over the weekend—you had the nation enthralled!"

Deer-in-the-headlights fear crept up Kate's body. She looked down at the book on her knees, at her name in gold. What would Kate Darrowby, romance writer, say next?

"It was just one of those random things," she said. "One of life's magic moments." She didn't dare glance at Charlie as the words left her mouth.

"I love that so much," Ruby said. "And you said you didn't recognize each other straightaway. What made it click into place?"

Had she said that? "Well, I hadn't seen him for over twenty-five years. We both looked pretty different. Eyes don't change, though, do they? His are a distinctive shade of . . . blue. Pale blue. Like a husky."

Ruby's eyes rounded a little, but she ran with it. "It feels like fate threw you two back together at just the right moment. Is it too soon to ask if you've met up again?"

"Um . . . no, not yet," Kate said, seeing disappointment freeze Ruby's smile. "We're going for a drink later, actually. Dinner, maybe, see how it goes."

"Exciting stuff. Promise to come back and update us, won't you?" Niall said, finally letting her off the hook, then pulling her straight back onto a different one. "So, a little bird tells us you love to crochet in your spare time. Tell us more about this mouse orchestra you're making?"

Fresh panic snaked through Kate's veins. Why the hell had the publishing team written that mouse orchestra into her bio? It was so weirdly specific. She half nodded and half shook her head; anyone with knowledge of body language would have a field day with her.

"Well, I'm trying," she said, with a slow laugh. "My sister got the sewing gene to be honest, she runs a fancy-dress shop and makes all her own costumes. I can't even thread a sewing machine. I just wanted something I could do with my brain and my hands to relax. There's only so much *Bridgerton* one woman can watch, you know?"

She realized she was veering off message and tried to bring things back in line again.

"So yeah, I make little mice." She showed them the size between her index finger and thumb. "With trumpets and violins and, er, tambourines."

Niall didn't look as if he believed a word she was saying. "These we *have* to see, Kate."

"Oh, I couldn't possibly." She forced a laugh. "I mean, they're not great. One only has three legs and another one is half-purple because I ran out of wool. They're pretty wonky and unlovable to anyone but me. I enjoy doing it, though, so that's the main thing."

"Well, one thing you *do* do exceptionally well is write, Kate, the book is an absolute triumph," Ruby said, picking up her copy of *The Power of Love* to hold for the camera, wrapping things up at last.

"Available in all the usual places now, folks, this one has 'bestseller' written all over it," Niall said, bringing the interview to a close. "It's been a genuine pleasure, Kate, lots of luck."

"WELL, I'M GLAD THAT'S OVER," Kate said as they emerged into the glare of the summer morning. "Even if I did just embarrass myself on national telly."

"It went well," Charlie said, neutral as he slid his aviators on. "I'm sure the team will be pleased."

There was a new coolness between them, an overhang from the night before, as he hailed them a cab.

"I'm sorry if I offended you last night," she said, once they were in the quietness of the car.

He shook his head. "You didn't."

"It's really none of my business what happened in L.A.," she said. "I didn't mean to come off judgy."

He drew in a slow breath. "I overstepped last night, I won't let it happen again. Let's just keep the focus where it needs to be: on the book and you. It's all good PR."

"You told me to walk in Kate Darrowby's shoes," she said. "I'm doing my best."

"I did, and you are. You're doing exactly what's been asked of you, Kate, and it's working. Prue sent across half-week sales figures just now, they're even better than they'd hoped," he said. "Rachel wants to look for available spots at book festivals and signing events, if you're comfortable with the idea?" He looked her way, his eyes hidden behind his sunglasses.

"Kate Darrowby would be," she said, unsure, because it was turning out to be much more hands-on than the team had initially led her to expect.

"And Kate Elliott?" he said.

"Thinks it's snowballed more than she anticipated."

"More than anyone anticipated," he acknowledged. "Which is as much down to you as the book. The 'Darrowby effect,' as Prue calls it."

Kate leaned back in her seat, drained after the stress of the morning. "H said he thinks of me as the book's guardian angel," she said.

Charlie frowned. "H?"

"The author," she said. "He signs his emails as 'H,' a random letter because it's better than not having anything to call him."

"Him?"

Kate backtracked. "I'm just guessing based on our conversations. I could be totally wrong."

The cab pulled into the pavement outside the green door of Francisco & Fox.

"It's booked to drop you at the station," he said, opening the door. "Good luck tonight."

She stared at him, unsure what he meant. "Tonight?"

"Dinner with your husky-eyed first love," he said.

"Oh, that," she sighed, hating the whole invented thing. "It's just a glass of wine."

He nodded, touching his fingers to his brow in salute as he slammed the door.

23

Hey Mum,

So that's BIG news, a book! You always said you had one in you, even if this one only has your name on the front. Does that mean I can call myself Alice Darrowby from now on, then? And there I was thinking I'm the one who wants an adventure!

About that … Mum, I know you disapprove, but you'll get it once you meet Flynn. He's so cool and SO into me, no one's ever made me feel like this before. I'll bring him down to meet you and Dad soon, you'll change your mind then, I know it.

Sorry about emailing, I just can't cope with a row. My voicemail sends you its love! 🌀

A xx

Hi Kate,

Congrats on the show this morning, you were excellent! Loving the husky-eyed man detail, keep those tidbits coming.

How are you fixed for the weekend? Crossing my fingers and hoping you're free, because I have some terrific news! There's a huge romance festival in Cornwall on Saturday and I've managed to wrangle a last-minute table. It's basically a meet-and-greet: readers will come by to get their books signed, have a quick chat, nothing too difficult, I promise.

Let me know and I'll make all the arrangements.

Rachel

Dear Kate,

So how have you found publication week? I caught the TV show, you handled it well. Those things are never easy, even if you're used to them. Writing is by necessity a rather solitary existence, and by and large that has always suited me.

My love was the opposite, brightened any room just by being in it. Even if she was sitting in silence reading a script, or writing, or painting still life. She'd paint food, mostly, buy odd fruits and colorful tins of fish and go crazy if I ate them without realizing.

People are like that, aren't they? Human dimmer switches. Some people throw light, others cast shadows. You asked me what lights me up, apart from books. She did.

I hear the book is selling gangbusters, to use Fiona's favorite phrase. The best thing I've ever written, as she delighted in telling me!

Is there anything you need from me? Besides my real name, any form of human connection beyond email, or any acknowledgment of my involvement with the book?

You asked a while back about favorite smells. It's strange how the question seems innocuous at first glance. I think of my wife's perfume and the buttermilk pancakes she perfected over the years. Other scents too, childhood associations I can almost recall if I close my eyes and concentrate. My grandmother kept a small shop, which always smelled of sugar from the sweet jars mixed with newsprint ink from the morning papers. My grandfather's silver-walled greenhouse was always sun-warm and redolent with the green-leaf scent of tomato plants. Comforting memories more than scents, lost connections to simpler days.

Probably best to play it safe and just say freshly cut grass and babies' heads, they seem to be the internet stock answers. Readers are savvy, though—always be as honest and specific as you're able.

I've told you mine, you tell me yours?

Speak again soon,

H x

24

"THIS IS YOU." THE TAXI RUMBLED TO A HALT PARTWAY DOWN A STEEP hill winding toward the harbor. "I'll grab your case."

Kate unfolded herself from the back of the car, grateful to stretch her legs. It had been a hot, sticky day of upheaval and last-minute changes, traveling solo rather than with Liv as she'd hoped.

They'd had everything meticulously planned out. Nish would mind the shop and the kids were sleeping over with his parents while Liv and Kate headed to Cornwall for a girls' trip, which had gone a long way toward keeping Kate's nerves in check. And then Nish's father had fallen from a stepladder while pruning a climbing rose in his garden and ended up in the ER with a broken hip, and Liv had been left with the shop and the kids and a head full of uncharitable thoughts about her father-in-law needing to be more bloody careful at his age. She'd handed Kate a box wrapped in brown paper before she left and told her to open it in Cornwall.

"Oh," Kate said, more a sigh of pleasure than a formed word as she took in the postcard-worthy scene laid out before her. "Would you look at that."

"I do, every damn day," the driver muttered, dropping her case on the cobbles beside a sun-bleached garden gate. He looked like someone who should have retired ten years ago and still wasn't over the fact he hadn't.

"Lucky," she said.

"Some might say," he groused, not looking as if he was one of the people who might. "Key's under the pot."

He jumped back in his car and drove away, leaving her to look around for the plant pot. It was easy; too easy in Kate's view, coming as she did from busier places with higher crime rates.

She'd had no idea what to expect of the accommodation Rachel had arranged for her; everything had been so last-minute they'd only confirmed the address that morning. She'd expected a hotel room or a local B&B, but it seemed she was in a tiny petal-pink cottage overlooking the glittering harbor.

"It's like a movie set," she typed, almost sending the image to Liv and then changing her mind and sending it to Charlie instead. Liv didn't need to see what she was missing in all its beautiful, ivory-shuttered glory.

The cottage-core interior more than held its own against the outside: whitewashed stone walls, a low, inviting linen sofa, natural sheepskin rugs, a splash of color from a jug of fresh wildflowers on the kitchen table. Steep wooden stairs led to the bathroom and only bedroom, where she found a huge carved wooden bedstead with billowing white linen and a vintage rose-velvet throw. Flinging the shutters open, Kate stood in the sun-drenched room and sighed with pure joy. It was as if someone had studied the mood board in her head and built this magical cottage especially for her. Her commuter-belt new house with Richard had been show-home worthy, but it had always been his dream rather than hers. This tiny, aged cottage with its uneven wooden floors and simple, unfussy décor made her feel as if her lungs had actually expanded in her chest. She could breathe more deeply; her bones felt at ease inside her body. It took awhile to identify the sensations washing over her as she watched the industry of the harbor. Peace. Freedom. No one to please but herself. No one to feed, no one to put first, just an overwhelm of serenity, a moment of full stop. She watched the fishing boats come and go for a while, then lay down on the bed and slept.

SHE WOKE EARLY THE NEXT morning in what was officially the world's most comfortable bed, basking in the already light-filled bedroom. The cottage had worked its magic on her the night before: a simple dinner from the supplies left for her in the fridge, a glass of wine as she'd read the festival itinerary Rachel had sent across. A table had been reserved for Kate Darrowby, stocks of the book would be available for sale, and she just needed to greet readers, chat, and sign copies of the book. Totally doable.

Nerves had kicked in when she poured a second glass of wine and googled the event. It was larger scale than she'd anticipated, the online buzz among romance readers through the roof. Charlie had messaged last thing to make sure she had everything she needed, and she'd cracked and confided she had everything except her sister.

And now it was Saturday morning. She'd gone with a striped sundress shot through with metallic thread to elevate it beyond the beach, and light makeup that wasn't likely to melt down her face in the heat of the festival tent.

Reaching for her phone, she found her social media jumping with reader messages, people making their way down to the festival, others wishing they could be there. She'd gotten into the habit of spending the first couple of hours of the day replying to reader messages and posting candid pictures of her adventures in publishing, striking up conversations and friendships with people who'd read the book and were helping to spread the word far and wide.

She'd never had a big circle of female friends and the book world sisterhood was a revelation.

The brown-paper-wrapped box Liv had given her as she left the shop sat on the kitchen work surface. Kate had been planning to save it for after the signing, but she was ready early and yearned for the boost of her sister's company. Reaching for it, she carried it through to the table by the window and sat down, taking her time. Liv had tacked a note to the lid of the box.

> *I was going to wait for your birthday because this was a SHIT TON of work, but I wanted to give you something special to celebrate the book coming out.*
>
> *L xxx*

Easing the lid off and carefully folding back layers of blush-peach tissue paper, Kate peeped inside, then she started to laugh and swallow tears at the same time. Reaching into the box, she removed the crocheted mouse orchestra one piece at a time. They were wonky, and one had three legs, and another was half-purple. And there were violins and trumpets and tambourines. An intricate twelve-piece mouse orchestra, each individually styled, including a conductor with his arms flung wide and the most theatrical whiskers of them all.

"I bloody love you, Liv," she whispered, arranging the orchestra on the table.

Reaching for her mobile, she took a photo.

You're the most iconic sister on the entire planet

she typed, and pressed "send." And then added

and the most talented x

Liv replied instantly.

You forgot best-looking. Break a leg, Katie xxx

Bang on time, the same cab driver as the day before rolled to a halt outside Pink Cottage, where Kate stood nervously jiggling from foot to foot.

"Me again," he grumped, arm resting on his open window.

"Me again," she grinned and clambered into the back, noticing a copy of her book waiting on the seat beside her.

"The wife wants you to sign that," he said, catching her eye in the mirror.

She looked at the book, and then at him, as she pulled one of her signing pens from her bag and opened the book flat on her knees. "Is it really for you?"

"June. Her name's June. J U N E." He spelled it out, testy. "Like the month."

"Pretty," she said as she clicked the end of the pen. "Anything special you'd like me to write?"

"Yes. *Dear June, get your head out the clouds and read something more useful instead.*"

She held his glare in the mirror.

"This is the first time I've ever signed a book for someone in person," she said, writing June a much less offensive message. "Thanks for making it so memorable."

She earned herself a twitched gray eyebrow in response.

"The women's books festival at the showground, then," he muttered, flinging the car into gear and juddering down the hill.

Kate sat on her hands for a second, then couldn't keep her

mouth shut. "Love stories are for everyone, not just women," she said.

He didn't even pretend to consider it. "Give me the newspaper and I'm done."

"War, pestilence, and indigestion with your breakfast it is, then," she said, fixing her smile in place. It was as well that Liv wasn't there, she'd have enjoyed a rumble with this guy. Kate didn't have the appetite for it; she needed to stay calm, slide Kate Darrowby on for size, and hope she didn't do or say anything unnecessary this time around. If she could make it back to the sanctuary of the pink cottage unscathed, she'd count today as a win.

"Just don't see the point," the driver said, catching her eye in the rearview mirror again. "Romance books. Pie in the sky."

Kate let out a slow, measured breath. Why was he baiting her, today of all days?

"No?" She felt her guardian angel wings shudder, desperate to unfurl and curl around the book balanced on her lap. Or to jab the driver in the eye with the sharp end of an iridescent feather. One or the other.

He shrugged, and his face told her he was pleased to have made his point. She had two choices. Stay quiet and stay cool, or rise to the bait. Calm. Cool. Quiet. Oh no . . .

"Have you honestly never read a single love story?"

"I have not," he said, resolute.

"I think it was quite romantic of you to bring the book for me to sign."

"It wasn't." He scowled. "Better than being nagged, that's all."

"Okay." She smiled as she glanced away out of the window at the beautiful Cornish countryside, her stomach turning over with nerves when she spotted signs for the festival. "Well, tell June I hope she loves it. Tell her I wish her the best."

She added "of luck" in her head, and the look he gave her in the mirror suggested he'd heard her unspoken words loud and clear.

"I grow poppies in the garden because they're her favorite," he said, managing to make it sound like an act of sufferance rather than love as he pulled into the festival entrance and followed the signs for author arrivals.

Kate nodded. "There we are, then, I knew you were a romantic at heart."

He didn't smile, exactly, it was more of a resigned huff as he eased the cab to a stop. "This'll be you."

"Thanks." She glanced at the busy scene outside her window, working up the nerve to get out. This was her first time among so many readers, but also among other authors too. Would they sniff her out as a cuckoo in their nest?

"Meter's running," the driver said, not unkindly. "They're just normal folk. Everyone farts, even the king."

She laughed, breaking her fear. "Everyone farts. That's my new mantra."

"Get out of my car."

"I'm going, I'm going," she said, knowing better than to ask if she could take his photo for her inevitable social media post later.

25

/

"FIVE MINUTES EVERYONE, FIVE MINUTES, SHARPIES AT THE READY!"

The PA announcement had Kate straightening her already neatly lined-up signing pens and glancing over the table that had been set up for her. Copies of the book arranged in artful piles, a banner behind her with her name on it—Rachel had arranged all the trappings and staging to make sure she blended in seamlessly among the other authors. She glanced to her right and found the next table empty, the author yet to arrive. Two minutes before opening time, an impossibly glamorous blonde with her husband in tow strolled over with water, sweets, and all of the things Kate hadn't thought to bring.

"Spot the signing rookie," Kate said, watching wide-eyed as her table neighbors arranged their display and stashed their belongings in thirty seconds flat. "I wish I'd recorded that to study later and copy you move for move."

The author, dazzling and fresh as a daisy, winked a perfectly made-up eye, then skipped over and dropped a bag of gums and a bottle of water on Kate's table. "Trust me, you're gonna need sugar. Shout if you need anything else, it can be a lot if you're new to it. Or even if you're not. Make sure someone closes your line for lunch."

"Got it. Close the line," Kate nodded. She'd be lucky to have a line, and no idea how to close it if she did, but she was relieved all the same to have such a welcoming neighbor.

"Curtain up," the announcer said, sending a ripple of anticipation around the huge tent as people streamed in.

"Oh God," Kate whispered. "Please come to me, please don't come to me."

A couple of large table plans stood near the entrance, explaining the layout in IKEA-level detail. The biggest-name authors were on a roped-off stage area to one side with a ticketing system and queue managers, while everyone else had been spaced around the edge of the tent. Kate had read the list and found herself starstruck, hoping to grab time to get around the tent herself later for a few social media selfies. Liv would be so proud. *Liv.* What she wouldn't give for her sister's company and confidence right now. Pretty much every other author had someone with them; she put a brave face on it, but she felt very alone. She reached for her water and sent her pens flying with her elbow, bending to gather them up from the grass.

"Kate?"

She banged her head on the underside of the table as she pulled up sharp, pink-cheeked, and found a couple of women looking at her expectantly with copies of the book clutched in their hands.

Everybody farts, everybody farts . . .

"Hi," she said, painting on a wide smile.

The younger of the two women held her book out. "Can you sign it to me, please? My name's Ruby. I read it on the train before work last week, had to go in the loo and wipe my ruined mascara before I went to my desk."

"Ah, I'm sorry," Kate said, unsure how to react.

"Oh no, don't be," Ruby said. "I love it when a book rips my heart out and stamps all over it."

Her friend nodded. "Me too. If I haven't had a complete breakdown, I want my money back."

Someone else appeared behind them, and then someone else. Kate spotted her author neighbor posing for a photo with one of her readers, her arm around their shoulders. Did she need to do that? Ruby passed her phone to her friend and stood beside Kate's banner, expectant. That would be a yes, then.

"Don't tell anyone, but this is my first signing event," Kate laughed as she posed in front of her banner, noticing someone else join the back of her line. Her line! "Thanks for showing me the ropes."

And so it began, her line growing, everyone chatting and unhurried when it was finally their turn at the table. She stored the bookish compliments away to share with H later, grabbing gulps of water between readers. A glance around neighboring authors showed their helpers smoothing things along in their queues, opening books to the signing pages, handing out sweets and anecdotes. *Oh Liv, how I wish you were here*, she thought, unable to see how many people deep her queue was, jumping up every couple of minutes to pose for pictures. By the time it had turned one in the afternoon, she'd run out of water and had no idea how to close her queue to even go to the loo, let alone for lunch.

"Sign my book, Miss Darrowby?"

A reassuring hand landed on her shoulder, and she looked up to find Charlie beside her.

"Charlie, what are you doing here?" she breathed, her cheeks flushing at his unexpected presence.

"Thought you might need a hand."

"More than you know," she said, feeling the tension drain from her bones.

He took one look at the situation and slid straight into ultimate host mode, effortlessly charming her queue, working his way to the back and roping it off so she could take a much-needed break.

"Seriously, how are you even here?" she said, once they'd made their way out the back to the hospitality area.

"I was passing," he said.

She wasn't buying it. "We're two hundred miles from London."

He shrugged. "I promised not to leave you alone in this. Liv couldn't make it."

"You didn't have to," she said. "But I'm really glad you did. I'm so desperate for a wee it's not even funny."

She made a dash for the Porta Potty and caught sight of herself in the mirror as she washed her hands. Pink cheeks, sun-activated freckles, lip gloss long gone but an undeniable shine in her eyes. She'd been so daunted by the idea of the festival, then so swept along by the tidal wave of bookish joy that she'd all but forgotten her nerves. Charlie's arrival had lifted her onto surer ground; she had someone in her corner now, a sense of being a double act rather than flying solo.

They helped themselves to the buffet in the hospitality tent and found a quiet bench under the shade of a patio umbrella.

"Storm's coming," Charlie said, glancing out over the rolling hills.

Kate frowned at the clear blue skies. "How can you possibly tell?"

He opened a bottle of sparkling water, then grinned. "Heard it on the radio in the cab."

"They must have it wrong," she said. "It's clear as a bell."

"Hi, Kate," someone said, a thin voice behind her.

She twisted and found herself face-to-face with Sally Rose, the starriest superstar author at the entire event, and one of Kate's all-time favorite writers. She shot up out of her seat and practically curtsied, making Sally laugh and place her suntanned, liver-spotted hand on Kate's arm.

"I read an advance copy of your book on holiday in Portugal a few weeks ago," Sally rasped, in a voice Kate would have recognized in her sleep. "You've got a dazzling future ahead of you, my darling."

And then she was gone, clutching the arm of her assistant. Sally's books were myth and legend among the romance community, her inimitable heroes and ballsy heroines the bedrock of the genre for the last thirty years.

"Oh my God, I love Sally Rose with my whole heart," she said, watching her retreating figure. "I should have said something, anything. Did I even say thank you? Oh shit, I didn't, did I? I was dumbstruck by the sight of her. She's going to think I'm a monster."

"You curtsied, I think she got the message. Prue will be straight on the phone to get a cover quote for the next print run," Charlie said. "Speaking of which, I bring news."

"Go on?"

He put his plate down and gave her his undivided attention, sending heat prickling up her neck.

"It's made tomorrow's *Sunday Times* list, Kate. Straight in at number three."

She gasped, wide-eyed, and he put a cautionary finger against his lips. "You can't breathe a word until it's out in print."

She stared at him, her fingertips pressed against her mouth to stop any noise escaping. He nodded, triumph in his whiskey-cola eyes, enjoying being the one to deliver the news every author dreams of, even pseudo ones.

"I can't believe it, Charlie," she whispered, euphoric. "They won't change their minds?"

He turned his mobile around to show her Prue's confirmation email, the flurry of out-of-character exclamation marks and whoops.

"Wow," she murmured. "This is really special, isn't it?"

He whistled low under his breath. "It sure is. Everyone's excited."

She sat for a few quiet seconds thinking about Sally Rose, and the readers she'd met in the tent, and the impending *Sunday Times* listing. It was all such terrific news, validation that the book was knocking it out of the park.

"Okay?" Charlie said, watching her carefully.

She nodded, then shrugged. "It's . . . I don't know. I'm being selfish, really. I just wonder how it would feel if it was genuinely mine, you know? If I'd *actually* written the *Sunday Times* bestseller that Sally Rose loves." She stopped, then started again. "I feel like a fraud among all these people."

"Right." He drummed his fingers on the table. "Kate, how many people have told you just today how much they love the book? The woman who said it took her mind off her husband's illness, or the girl who'd read it to her neighbor who can't see to read anymore? None of those things would have happened without you."

She took a cooling drink of water, trying to let Charlie's conviction shore up her own. Her face must have told him she wasn't quite there yet, and she really needed to get over this attack of nerves before she went back inside the tent.

"You've seen Russian Matryoshka dolls?" he said.

She frowned. "Liv had a set when we were kids."

"Right," he said, his knees skimming hers as he turned to look her straight in the eyes. "See the book as the smallest doll in the center." He bunched her hand into a fist on the bench between them. "Then there's the author," he said, blanketing her fist with his own hand. He nodded for her to add her other hand to the top of the pile.

"That one is you," he said, and then he placed his bigger, warm hand over hers like a protective cap. "This is me, then the publisher. We're one team, all working together to protect the book and get it out there into the hands of the people who matter the most. The people queuing in that tent."

She looked at his fingers, strong and capable over hers, and then she looked up into his dark, deadly serious eyes and believed him.

"It's a good thing," she said, letting out a long, slow breath.

"A really good thing," he said. "Now come on. Kate Darrowby's public awaits."

26

AND BOY, DID THEY AWAIT. HER AFTER-LUNCH QUEUE SNAKED ITS WAY among her neighbors, made up of avid readers hauling trollies full of books, bloggers with prizes for her to sign, handmade albums with beloved quotes pulled from the story. She was hugged, she held someone's baby, she video-called with someone's best friend on the phone in France, and she signed, signed, and signed. Her face ached from smiling and her back ached from being constantly up and down, but she loved every last second.

"What's that noise?" she said, toward the end of the afternoon.

Charlie handed her a fresh bottle of water. "Rain. I did say it was on the way."

The woman at the front of the queue grumbled about the weather and handed her book over, then narrowed her eyes as she studied Charlie for a long second.

"I was hoping he was going to have husky-blue eyes," she leaned in and stage-whispered, more than loud enough for Charlie to hear too.

Kate froze, even as her internal voice told her to laugh it off.

"Oh, right," she managed. "No, this is—it isn't him."

"Maybe next time. Can you make it out to Melanie, please?

It's a gift for my best friend, she's been telling everyone they have to read this book."

Kate looked down, thrown off her stride, and signed the book *To Stephanie, with love.*

"It's Melanie," Charlie said, glancing over her shoulder.

Kate bit her lip, unsure what to do, and he just shrugged and handed her a fresh copy off the pile.

"Any Stephanies in the queue?" he called, raising a laugh as he held the mis-signed book up in the air.

Overhead, the weather had taken an abrupt turn for the worse, rain drumming on the tent roof.

"Sounds like a good old Cornish storm is blowing in," someone in the line said, as the crowd thinned with end-of-day weariness and the sudden desire to beat the weather home.

The festival clear-down crew moved in with an efficiency that had tables folded before Kate could even gather her belongings up to leave. Authors milled around chatting, many coming to see how Kate's first signing event had gone, some even snagging a signed copy of the book. She felt included, part of something special, and more than a little out of her depth.

"Ready to go?" Charlie said, looking out of the tent at the pouring rain. Kate was in her sundress and Charlie in jeans and a T-shirt, not a jacket between them. "We're gonna get wet."

She threw her bag across her body and shrugged. "I don't mind the rain. I already look like I've been dragged through a hedge backward and that was the most exhausting day ever. A cold shower is kind of welcome right now."

"All right, then . . ." he said, as if he wasn't convinced she wouldn't change her mind. "There's a pub down the lane we can call a cab from."

"No need," she said. "Rachel's already booked one to pick me up there, let's make a dash for it."

Turned out it didn't matter whether they dashed or dawdled. The rain fell in solid sheets from the slate-gray skies, forks of lightning ripping through the clouds toward the sea in the distance.

"Oh my God!" she shouted, catching hold of Charlie's hand when he reached out to pull her along beside him. Thunder cracked overhead and they picked their pace up to a run, water streaming down their faces, the road a river when they reached it.

"Just keep going," he yelled. She was glad of his hand—she could barely see through the rain clinging to her lashes.

By the time they reached the pub they were drenched to the skin, hair plastered to their heads, clothes clinging to their bodies, gasping at the ferocity of the sudden summer storm. A familiar car flashed its headlights from the gloom of the car park.

"God bless my miserable cab driver," she said.

They tumbled into the back seat, apologizing for the state of themselves as they landed in a sodden heap.

"Am I glad to see you," she said to the driver. "You're my hero for coming out in this."

"A pre-booking is as good as a promise," he grouched, navigating his way carefully along the rain-flooded road.

"Where are you staying?" she said, looking at Charlie.

He paused, looking at the weather. "I'm getting the train back."

"Londoners," the cab driver barked with pleasurable derision. "Line won't be running till morning after this lot. Station floods at the drop of a hat, some smartarse built it in a dip. I'll drop you both where I've been paid to and then I'm away home." He glanced up into the gray sky. "June doesn't do well with thunder."

Kate softened into silence, managing not to comment on the everyday romance of him racing back for his anxious wife.

"Pink Cottage." The driver stated the obvious when he came to an abrupt stop beside the gate.

They splashed out into the still-sheeting rain, Kate digging around in the bottom of her soggy bag for the front-door key.

"Sorry, I should have found it in the cab," she said.

"We couldn't be wetter," Charlie said, unfazed. "At least it's warm rain."

Kate's fingers finally closed around the key. If this had happened with Richard, she'd have been on tenterhooks and felt somehow responsible for the weather, and he wouldn't have made any attempt to lighten her load. Over their years together they'd fallen into a pattern where she facilitated and made his life as easy as possible, and anything that played against that narrative always left her feeling as if she'd somehow planned inadequately. Even something as uncontrollable as the weather.

"Got it," she said, throwing the front door wide. "Come in."

Pink Cottage didn't have a hallway; they were straight into the living room, dripping onto the old oak floorboards.

"I'll grab towels," she said, kicking her sandals off and running barefoot up to the bathroom. She'd used the biggest of the towels for her shower that morning, and there was only a small extra supply piled on a driftwood shelf. Not nearly enough for two unexpectedly drenched adults. Her eyes landed on the chunky white terry-toweling robes hanging on the back of the door as she stepped out of her soaked dress, and she wrapped one around herself, cocooned.

A glance in the mirror told her she looked as much like a drowned rat as she felt, makeup washed away, hair coiling heavy around her neck. She could use a hot shower, but was too aware of Charlie waiting downstairs so wrapped a towel around her hair and headed back down.

"There's another of these robes on the bathroom door," she said. "Have a shower if you like, I'll put your clothes in the tumble dryer."

He was back within ten minutes, his clothes and her sundress jumbled together in his hands. She ignored the shiver down her spine and grabbed them from him.

"So, there isn't a tumble dryer," she said, having investigated while he was upstairs and found only a collapsible clothes drying rack in a cleaning cupboard. It was far too warm to light a fire, so they were left with no option but to hang their clothes to dry slowly over the rack in the kitchen.

"I feel as if we've joined a cult," she said, gesturing between their matching outfits as she filled the kettle.

"Sorry, it's a bit weird," he said. "Definitely not in the agent handbook."

She started to laugh as she added tea bags to the pot. "I just had an image of how much Fiona would hate being caught in this situation. Or worse, your dad! I definitely wouldn't have wanted to be in bathrobes with your father."

The thought of Jojo charging around Pink Cottage in a bath-robe didn't work at all. He was considerably shorter and less rangy than his son, yet somehow he'd seemed to take up more space.

"He'd have been like a small, trapped bull," Charlie said, standing close to the window to study the steel-gray skies. "I'll walk into town when it blows over and sort a hotel."

"You're very welcome to the sofa," she said, aware they were being awkward around each other and not sure how to make things less weird, because in truth he looked as if he'd just wan-dered down for breakfast in his Amalfi villa and it was massively distracting. He was just naturally luxurious on the eye and it had her on edge. "I can't vouch for it, though, it might be lumpy as hell." She opened the fridge. "And the establishment would like to make it known that it can only supply egg-based meals, and"— she picked up a bottle of red that had been left for her and in-spected the label—"Pinot Noir."

He accepted the mug of tea she passed him. "Let me make a few calls," he said. "It's a tourist hotspot, somewhere nearby will have a room."

They didn't. Not available places, in any case, being the height of summer, a heat wave, and romance festival weekend.

"Looks like I'll have to take you up on the sofa, if the offer still stands?" he said, pushing his hand through his hair.

"Honestly, it's fine, we're adults. You came all this way, I'm not about to chuck you out in a storm." She twisted her hair around her fingers, nervous.

"I'll cook."

"No arguments here," she said, holding her hands up. "I can't remember the last time someone except Liv made me dinner, and I'd never tell her but she's a pretty terrible cook. Her kids are always glad when Nish is on weekend cooking duty."

He opened the fridge, and she clutched her mug of tea, suddenly overwhelmed with the forced intimacy of the situation.

"I might go and grab a shower," she said, turning away. In the bathroom, she threw the lock and leaned against the door. So they were spending the night together in Pink Cottage. That was okay, wasn't it?

27

"WHAT THE HELL ARE YOU DOING IN CORNWALL, CHARLIE?" FIONA DIS-
pensed with a greeting and went straight for the throat.

He looked at his mobile, surprised by her sharpness. "Giving
Kate a hand?"

"Putting your hands all over her, more like."

Charlie looked over his shoulder, half expecting Fiona to ma-
terialize in the small kitchen. He was alone, the sound of the running shower upstairs assuring him Kate was out of earshot.

"I have absolutely no idea what you're talking about," he
said, letting a slightly pissed-off tone creep in.

"I'm talking about you two gazing into each other's eyes and
holding hands like lovesick teenagers at the damn festival today,"
she said.

"Still not with you," he said.

"Don't lie to me, Charles, you forget how long I've been in
this industry. What were you thinking of, making eyes at each
other over lunch? Thank God you were at least out of public
sight, but people in this industry talk, and trust me, they are."

He'd been at the center of enough gossip and rumors for her
comment to hit a nerve. "Who is, and what are they saying?"

Her irritated sigh rattled down the line. "I've put the agency's reputation on the line for this book, this isn't the time for your hero complex. Do I need to remind you how much everyone involved has to lose if this thing publicly unravels?"

While she'd been speaking, he'd been thinking. The only thing that could possibly have been misconstrued was the Russian doll moment at lunch; she was way off the mark with her assumptions. He didn't owe her an explanation, though, and he wasn't about to apologize. He tuned back into the tail end of Fiona's rant.

"People love to talk. One photo of the two of you together would be enough to set the internet sleuths on the case."

However much he didn't appreciate Fiona treating him like a teenager, there was an undeniable element of truth to what she'd said. People did love to talk, and clearly already were. He didn't like the idea of someone watching him and reporting back; they would never have treated his father with such disrespect.

He sat at the table for a while after the call ended, bruised by Fiona's words. Had he compromised everything by coming here? He'd fallen into the habit of making his agenting decisions based on what he thought his father would do, and in truth, Jojo probably wouldn't have been in Cornwall right now. He'd made the choice to come here based on his own instinct, not his father's. It had felt right, in the moment, and right in the tent that afternoon, but sitting in a robe in the small, quiet kitchen . . . suddenly not so much. He dropped his head in his hands, weary.

"I THINK YOU WIN THE award for best omelet I've ever had," Kate said, laying her cutlery down on her empty plate. Charlie had managed to create a decent dinner out of very little—simple cheese omelets and a green salad—but cooked well enough to elevate the meal beyond emergency. The view helped: any meal eaten beside the open window overlooking the harbor stood a good chance of being a winner.

"Cooking was makeshift therapy for me when I moved back in with my father," he said. "I don't think he'd ever even used the oven; he had every restaurant in town on speed dial."

"I can imagine he was a challenge to live with," she said, trying for tactful. Jojo had approached life with flourish, someone who gesticulated wildly and made decisions on the hoof.

"That's one way to put it," Charlie said. "I was no picnic myself either, though, in his defense. Moving back into my childhood bedroom with a shattered career and an impending divorce made me pretty sour company for a while." He shrugged. "You play the hand you're dealt. I was lucky to have him as a safety net."

Kate had sensed a shift in Charlie's mood when she came down from the shower. He'd put his clothes back on, even though they must have still been damp, but it wasn't that so much as the dispirited set of his jaw.

"I certainly know how that feels," she said, thinking of Liv as she refilled their wineglasses. "Liv is mine."

Dusk had fallen over the harbor outside the open window, the air heavy with the scent of the ocean after a storm. Lanterns shone in a few of the trawlers and people milled around, emerging after the rain.

"Fiona called while you were in the shower."

Whatever she'd said had clearly knocked Charlie's mood off-center. "Is everything okay?"

The low lamplight cast shadows across his face. "I shouldn't have come here today," he said.

"Did she tell you that? Because I'm glad you did. I was struggling and you saved the day."

"Me and my hero complex," he huffed, shaking his head.

"I didn't mean it like that," she said, unsure how she'd said the wrong thing.

He sighed and rolled his shoulders. "I know. But the last thing either of us needs is people seeing us together and jumping to the wrong conclusion. Or seeing us together at all. I didn't think things through."

Kate had seen confident Charlie and wise-cracking Charlie, but she hadn't encountered unsure Charlie before. Did Fiona even realize the impact she had on him?

"The book is the only thing that matters here. I lost sight of that for a while back there."

"I don't agree," she said, deciding not to hold her opinion in. "Of course the book matters, but you matter too. And I do. You don't have a hero complex, you just saw I needed help and stepped up."

"My father wouldn't have come," he said, unwilling to let himself off the hook.

"You're right, he probably wouldn't," she said. "And to be honest, he wouldn't have been able to do what you did today. Your father was many brilliant things, Charlie, but he'd have caused total chaos in that tent today. I needed you, not Jojo."

He lifted his dark gaze to hers across the table.

"You're better at this stuff than you think you are," she said softly, because his troubled eyes told her he still needed to hear it.

"Everyone loved you there today," he said, deflecting the conversation back to her.

"They loved you more," she countered. "Several of them would have preferred your number to my signature in the front of their books."

"Not once the *Sunday Times* news breaks in the morning," he said. "Those signed books will soar in value."

She still couldn't quite believe the bestseller news, it had really thrown her into a spin. "Thanks for what you said today," she said. "About the Russian dolls. It helped make sense of things."

He scrubbed a hand along the five-o'clock shadow on his jaw. "Someone misconstrued it and told Fiona they'd seen us holding hands," he said.

Kate all but laughed at the absurdity of someone bothering to report back, let alone misreport back. "What are we, school kids?"

He shook his head and shrugged, nonplussed. "I'm pretty accustomed to people spreading shit about me. I'm done justifying or defending myself, but the fact is, innocent things get misconstrued all the time. We know nothing happened today, but that doesn't stop people spinning the truth into something else. What if they'd seen us running in the rain like a scene from the damn *Notebook*, or could see us here right now? Photos could so easily end up splashed around, which could be a disaster for the book. This whole house of cards relies on the secret staying a secret."

Kate saw his bleakness, his weariness. He was a closed book when it came to what happened in L.A., but this was clearly opening up old wounds.

"Then I guess the best we can do is make sure we don't give people anything else to misinterpret," she said, finishing the last of her wine. It was almost midnight and it had been one hell of a long day.

He nodded slowly. "It's probably time you got yourself out of my bedroom."

She stood up. "I'll find you a blanket."

28

"IT'S NOT SO BAD," CHARLIE SAID, TESTING OUT THE MAKESHIFT BED HE'D made up on the sofa a few minutes later.

Kate leaned down to turn the lamp out and jumped back when an electric shock buzzed her fingertips.

"Static from the storm," Charlie murmured.

She paused at the bottom of the stairs. "Night, Charlie," she said into the quiet darkness.

"Goodnight, Darrowby."

KATE STOOD AT HER BEDROOM window watching the quiet harbor beneath the clear, star-studded sky. How could the universe throw them together for one night in this place that was neither his life nor hers and ask them to still play by the rules? She thought of all the years spent doing the right thing as a wife and a mother, and of her makeshift home over the fancy-dress shop. She'd spent her whole life reacting to circumstance rather than directing the action. Sitting on the edge of her bed, she studied her toes, remembering sitting on the edge of her bed on other portentous nights of her life. Her wedding night. The first night in the hospital after giving birth to Alice. Her first night alone in the flat above the shop. All first nights, all scenes written in bold black ink.

Pressing her fingers to her lips, she realized something. She couldn't bring herself to get into bed.

Tiptoeing back across her room, she stood at the top of the stairs, racked by indecision, then moved before she could lose her nerve. She didn't speak as she sat silently beside the sofa on the wooden floor, resting her head on his blanket. He didn't speak either, just smoothed his hand over her hair. Pale shafts of moonlight spilled across the floor, stars hanging in the midnight sky over the harbor.

"You said 'Goodnight, Darrowby,'" she whispered. "I wanted you to call me Kate."

He lifted the edge of his blanket. "Come here."

She climbed up and he settled the blanket over them.

He turned his back against the sofa and shifted her into the crook of his arm, her head tucked beneath his chin.

"It's been a long day," he said. "Get some sleep now, Kate."

She was exhausted to her core, his heartbeat a lullaby against her ear. She curled herself deeper against him, her mouth close to his neck, his arm warm around her shoulders.

"I wrote the scripts," he said, so quietly she wasn't sure if she was dreaming as she fell beneath heavy layers of sleep. "I'm pretty used to ignoring whatever people say about me, but not that."

"I believe you," she breathed.

CHARLIE HAD ALREADY GONE BY the time she woke the next morning. He'd left a brown paper bag of croissants on the kitchen table, beside a bottle of champagne and a copy of that morning's *Sunday Times.*

29

"YOU LOOK TIRED," LIV SAID, HANDING KATE A TIN OF MISMATCHED BUT-tons to sort into a plastic organizer TikTok had convinced her she couldn't live without.

"I am." Kate tipped the buttons out on the counter. "It seems to get crazier every day. More reader messages to reply to, more podcasts and online interviews."

"But look at you handling it all like a pro," Liv said. "Have you thought about what to do when all this ends?"

"Well, Prue is already talking about the idea of more Kate Darrowby books, but there's no set plan."

Liv frowned. "Written by the same author?"

Kate shook her head. "That's the problem really. He's got no interest in writing any more love stories."

"Do you still think it could be Charlie?"

For reasons she couldn't even explain to herself, she hadn't told Liv that Charlie had been in Cornwall. The relationship be-tween them had slid straight back into professional mode on their return to London, just as it needed to. And nothing had happened in Pink Cottage, except for the undeniable intimacy of sharing the sofa, and no one had been there to see and misconstrue it.

"I honestly don't know, but there's not a chance I could write anything up to scratch myself."

"Not even those manuscripts we risked a criminal record for?"

Kate screwed her nose up. "They weren't bad, but they weren't good enough. Not in the same ballpark. Or even the same city. They'd have to hire a ghostwriter."

Liv put her head on one side. "A ghostwriter for a ghost author?"

"Too many ghosts," Kate said, unconvinced. The idea had been floated in one of the many emails between Kate, Charlie, and the publishing team since the *Sunday Times* listing. Prue was understandably keen to brand-build, but Kate had found herself unable to get on board with the team's enthusiasm.

She'd taken the assignment because she wanted to share H's beautiful story with the world. He'd spilled his soul onto the pages of the book, and as Kate Darrowby, she'd become a part of that story too. But Kate Darrowby was only ever supposed to be a once-around-the-sun deal.

"Weird," Liv said, fastening a full-size T-Rex costume onto the display dummy.

"That's actually quite intimidating," Kate said, impressed.

"I got carried away," Liv said. "Nish tried it on last night and scared the kids next door."

Kate laughed at the image of her gentle brother-in-law causing a scene, then reached for her beeping mobile from the back pocket of her jeans. One glance at the messages flying across her lock screen told her something was blowing her phone up, even by Kate Darrowby's standards. A call buzzed in from a number she didn't recognize at the exact same time as a message from Charlie slid across the top of her screen.

Kate, don't answer any calls from the press
or reply to anyone online—I'm on the first train
back from Edinburgh. Am talking to Prue
and the team now. C x

"What the . . . ?" she frowned, letting the call go to voicemail as she read Charlie's message aloud to Liv. He was away at a film premiere with one of his biggest clients in Edinburgh, not due back for a couple of days. "I've no clue what he's talking about."

Liv pulled her mobile out too and clicked on Kate's social media, ominously quiet as her thumbs flew over the screen.

"Oh God . . ." Kate whispered, trying to read her sister's face for clues. "People know I didn't write it, don't they?"

A storm gathered in Liv's blue eyes. "Did you tell Alice about the book by email?"

Kate couldn't fathom the connection between her daughter and whatever was happening right now. "Every conversation we have lately seems to be Flynn-dominated. I just emailed her quickly in case she saw anything in the press."

"And Flynn is the fabulous Aussie boyfriend she's ready to throw her life in with, right?"

"Liv, you're scaring me," Kate said, spiraling. "Has something happened to her, or to them?"

"Not yet, but if Alice has any sense, she'll find a deadly spider and put it in his fucking mouth while he sleeps." Liv laid her mobile screen down and put both hands flat on the counter in front of her sister, a stance that said she was about to rip the bandage off in one swift swoop. "Flynn has sold a screenshot of your email to the press. It's out there for everyone to see. Your real name, your admission that you didn't write the book, the fact that you're a hired actor . . . all of it. Pictures of you and Alice pulled from her social media too."

"Oh my God," Kate breathed, pressing her hands against her hot cheeks. "Oh no, no, no." Fear paralyzed her, Charlie's words ringing in her head. *This whole house of cards relies on the secret staying a secret.*

Her mobile buzzed again.

"Don't get it," Liv said, lunging for it.

"I need to, it's Alice." Kate grabbed it back, clicking to join the video call. Her tearful daughter appeared, full of horror and apologies.

"He's gone, Mum. Left a note telling me he's sorry but the money was too good to turn down. He's using it to set the surf shop up."

"I hope he fucking drowns," Liv said, thumping her fist down on the counter.

"I thought he loved me." Alice crumpled, sounding about five years old.

"I know, darling, I know," Kate said. "I wish I could reach into the screen and give you the most massive hug right now."

"Are you mad at me?"

Alice's broken sob brought a lump to Kate's throat. "Of course I'm not. I'm mad as hell at him, but none of this is your fault."

"I'll get the next train home, tell everyone what he did," Alice said, her voice faltering through fresh tears.

"Darling, you can come home whenever you want to, but you're not talking to the press or anyone else," Kate said, intentionally sharp to cut through Alice's emotion. "You were loving the life you've built up there before Flynn turned up. Is he really worth losing all of that for? I'll tell you the answer to that question—it's no. Absolutely not. Everything will blow over here, you need to concentrate on feeling better right now, tonight. Are you with people? Do you have friends who can stay with you?"

Alice sniffed, nodding. "I'm more worried about you than me," she said. "I've ruined everything."

"And I'm more worried about you than me," Kate said. "The job is pretty much over anyway—the book is out there selling like hotcakes with or without me. Even hotter cakes now, probably." She tried to laugh, to inject a lightness she didn't feel in order to make her daughter feel safe. Default parent mode, smile even while your world falls apart. "Promise me you'll go out tonight? Go and be with your friends, call that absolute twatbag all the names under the sun, dance him out of your system."

Alice nodded, wiping her eyes with the hem of her T-shirt. "I love you, Mum."

"Love you more. I'll call you in the morning." Kate blew a kiss just before the screen went black, then sank down onto the nearest stool and covered her face with her hands. "Fuck. Fuck, fuck, fuck."

Liv's arm snaked around her shoulders. "Let's sit tight and see what Charlie says."

"Oh, what can he say?" Kate said, getting up to pace the shop floor, her mobile in her hand. "It's done. There's no point in trying to deny it. The genie is well and truly out of the bottle."

Liv fell uncharacteristically quiet.

"Christ, people are really going to hate me." Kate started doomscrolling through social media and found it was every bit as awful as she feared. Her pages were swamped with readers wanting to know the truth, long threads on book clubs picking over every sentence of her email confession, snippets of her appearance on the *Good Morning Show*. "She's definitely an actor," someone said, "she had me fooled." "Was everything she said just one big lie?" someone else asked. "If she didn't write it, who did?" Everyone wanted to know and speculation was already rife, names being thrown around like confetti.

"No one hates you," Liv said. "It's just the bloody internet, feeding gossip and fueling the fire unnecessarily. It'll calm down in a few days, it always does."

Kate tipped her head back and stared at the ceiling. "I went on bloody TV, Liv. People have been coming up to me in the street to talk about it, and now they'll want to talk about this instead. I'll be heckled, called a fraud." She sat down hard, shoulders slumped over. "I don't know what to do."

"Wait for Charlie," Liv said, rubbing her back. "And for God's sake get off social media, you're going to drive us both nuts."

30

TWO HOURS AND THREE CUPS OF COFFEE LATER, AND STILL THERE WAS radio silence from Charlie.

"It must be really, really awful news and he doesn't know how to break it to me. Do you think they could sue me for breach of contract? I can't give them the payment back, I've spent half of it," Kate said, thoroughly miserable and full of regrets. Regret that she'd emailed Alice, leaving a paper trail to trip herself up on. Regret that she'd let everyone down, H most of all. Regret that she'd ever fired off the damn begging letter to Jojo.

The shop door flew open, startling them both.

"Christ, she looks like trouble," Liv murmured, as a woman stood framed in the sunlit doorway.

"Oh my God," Kate whispered, staring at the silhouetted power shoulder pads and hair-sprayed helmet of hair. "It's Fiona."

Liv reared up cobra-like and stepped in front of Kate. "Can I help?"

Much as Kate appreciated the protective big sister act, she needed to deal with this herself. Fiona had locked eyes with her the moment she came in. There was no slinking quietly away through the back door.

"Fiona," she said, wishing the tremor in her voice away. She wasn't certain she could take many of Fiona's shots today; the reader reactions online had already kicked her around emotionally.

"Kate." Fi looked as if she was sucking a lemon.

"I'm honestly so sorry about all this, I don't know what to say—" Kate went straight into panicky garble mode, but stopped mid-sentence when the older woman held a hand up.

"No words, please. I have a situation."

"*You* do?" Liv said, one hand on her hip. "Not half as much of a situation as Kate does."

Kate put a hand on her sister's arm, a silent plea to keep her cool.

"I'm not here to advise you in an agent capacity, Kate—Charlie will be in touch with you in due course—but right now I have the actual author, as in the person who wrote the damn book, sitting in his car outside insisting on talking to you, and we both know that's a terrible idea. If I'd arrived five minutes later he'd have barreled in here already and blown the whole thing, but as it is I've managed to hold him off, for now. Trust me when I say I've tried my best to talk him out of this, but he's as stubborn as an ox when he makes his mind up about something. He's given me three minutes to come in here and sort something out before he does it himself." Fiona looked at her watch. "Make that two minutes."

"H is here, right now?" Kate stared at the doorway. Charlie was on a train from Edinburgh . . . if it wasn't him, then who? "Outside?"

"Don't ask for details, it'll take too long to explain." Fiona turned to Liv. "I need a head from one of these"—she batted a hand around the shop—"ridiculous outfits."

"Custom-made costumes," Liv corrected, waspish.

Fiona rolled her eyes. "If I can't stop him coming in, we can at least preserve his anonymity for both your sakes."

"Is it really necessary anymore?" Kate said. "Everyone knows who I am now."

"But they don't know who he is, and neither do you, and that's the way it's going to stay," Fiona said. Kate realized in the moment that Fiona wasn't especially bothered if she was hung out to dry, as long as H wasn't hung out alongside her. And, despite everything, Kate didn't want that to happen either.

"Find him a head, Liv," she said, quietly.

Liv scanned the inventory, drumming her fingernails against her front teeth. "The storm troopers are all out for a stag do and Spider-Man isn't due back in until tomorrow. Even the lobster is at the dry cleaner's . . ." She paused, clicking her tongue. "How tall is he?"

"How should I know?" Fiona snapped, gesticulating wide and high with her arms. "Man-size."

Kate watched Liv fight to keep her temper, and vowed to pour her a large gin when this was over.

"There's the T-Rex," Liv said finally.

Fiona turned to survey the huge costume, stepping away from it as if offended.

"It's a one-piece, though. No detachable head."

"You want my world-renowned author to dress up as a dinosaur?"

"No, *you* want your world-renowned author to dress up as a dinosaur," Liv corrected. "This is your shit show, not mine."

Fiona stared at Liv, who glared straight back. Kate looked between them, unsure which she'd place a bet on, but she thought she saw a flicker of admiration cross Fiona's face.

"So be it," Fiona sighed. "If it's all there is, it's all there is. You two leave the shop while I get him inside that thing. He's not going to like this one bit."

"Leave my own shop?" Liv's arms paused in mid-air as she

removed the costume from the dummy, her face suggesting she wasn't going anywhere.

"We can just go in the storeroom for a few minutes, it's fine." Kate jumped in and gestured at the door behind the counter, desperate not to lose the chance to speak to H, to try to work out what to do for the best. "You can tap the door when you're ready."

Liv draped the costume over the counter then flipped the sign on the door over to closed. "Be careful with my T-Rex," she said. "And my sister."

"Are you always like this?" Fiona lowered her glasses on their golden chain and looked down her nose.

Kate grabbed Liv's arm and steered her bodily toward the storeroom. "Knock when we can come out."

KATE AND LIV STOOD SHOULDER to shoulder in the tiny storeroom. It was more of a cupboard really, a pantry once upon a time when the shop used to be a butcher's in days gone by. Bolts of material lined the shelves along with reels of ribbons and trimmings, plus a rack of wigs at the back.

"It sounds like they're arguing," Liv said, straining to listen as Fiona and H came into the shop.

"He was never going to take the T-Rex idea well," Kate whispered, even though they were unlikely to be heard.

"You should have turned the radio off," Liv muttered, frowning as she practically pressed her ear to the wood. "All I can hear is Lady sodding Gaga."

"They're definitely arguing."

"Is he Welsh?" Liv said. "It sounds like Tom Jones is out there."

"I've no clue, remember?" Kate hadn't imagined H to be Welsh. She hadn't really imagined him to have an accent at all, and nerves kicked in at the thought of going out there to actually talk to him. They'd shared meaningful conversations over email, but she'd always had the benefit of time to write, delete, and rewrite her replies. She'd come to look forward to their exchanges, but everything had changed now, thanks to Alice's feckless ex-boyfriend.

"What am I going to say to him?" she said, pressing her hands against her hot cheeks.

Liv paused. "Please don't eat me?"

Kate side-eyed her sister and found her trying not to laugh.

"Not funny," she said.

"You know it was," Liv grinned, then they both jumped when someone knocked on the door. As Kate reached for the handle, Liv quickly slid her silver bangle from her own wrist to her sister's. They shared a look that didn't need words, then opened the door.

Fiona blocked their exit, lugging Kate out by the arm and maneuvering herself into the storeroom with Liv.

"No way," Liv said, backing into the wall of wigs.

"His rules, not mine. I like it even less than you do," Fiona snapped. "Let's just get this over with, shall we?" She leaned back out and called, "Remember to disguise your accent."

"Christ Almighty, Fiona! I'm not the only Welsh author in the world, just shut the fucking door, will you?" H roared, sending Fiona scuttling inside the storeroom with a slam of the door.

Kate turned around slowly in the small shop and found herself face-to-face with a pacing, seven-foot T-Rex. Her bracelets jangled on her wrist as she wrung her hands in front of her, unsure what to say or do.

"I'm so sorry about all of this, Kate," H said, clutching his massive head with his clawed hands as he moved around the shop, restless. "I should have stuck to my guns. I never agreed with this ridiculous circus in the first place."

"It's not your fault," Kate said. "Taking the job was my choice, and let's face it, it's my family who caused the leak, not you."

He tried to throw his arms up and found himself constricted by the tiny T-Rex arms. "Christ alive, I can't believe I'm dressed as a fucking dinosaur! I need a bloody Scotch," he said, swinging around so hard the weighted tail thrashed behind him. "I'm going to make a public statement." His deep, melodic Welsh accent was entirely at odds with his T-Rex outfit. "Put a stop to this crock of shite once and for all."

He was angry and anguished in turn, and Kate found herself sliding into let-me-help mode, her default for so many years.

"Look, we've come this far. How does you going public now help anyone? People are going to judge me for my choices just the same, so don't do it for me. You don't want this book attached to your name. That was always the deal."

"But I can't let you suffer for me," he yelled, loud and pained, planting his claws on the counter in front of her. He probably didn't realize it but his snout was almost touching her nose. The *Jurassic Park* theme struck up unhelpfully in her head, and much as her rational brain knew she wasn't in any danger, she took a couple of small steps backward toward the storeroom door. Although things would have to get significantly worse for her to squeeze herself in there with Fiona.

"I'm not suffering for you," she said. "If I suffer for this, it's on me. And you know something? I'm not sorry." She was thinking aloud, analyzing how she felt about the day's turn of events as she went along. "I love the book so much. It's sorrowful and raw and hopeful all at the same time. Whoever said being a guardian angel was going to be an easy job?" Kate placed a hand over one of the giant claws. "I've had so many readers tell me they've found real comfort in your words, people who've been through unimaginable things and can relate, who've found solace and comradeship in this story. Sanctuary in your grief. One woman even got herself a rescue dog, just like he did in the book. Can you believe that? You've provided a blueprint for grief, a map of survival." She paused, hoping her words were landing somewhere inside the ridiculous costume. "Dog sanctuaries around the country will be grateful to you," she said, trying to shine a light into the darkness.

Something like a low growl emitted from deep inside the T-Rex.

"What the fuck, Fiona?" he shouted, startlingly loud. "There was no fucking dog in my story!"

"Er, there is a dog," Kate said. "Hamlet, the rescue Jack Russell."

"Fucking Hamlet?" he full-on roared, and Kate backed away again.

Fiona inched the storeroom door open just enough to shout back. "Readers need hope! The ending was too dismal so they made it more upbeat."

"Hamlet? What did you do, get the book of one hundred and one clichéd fucking dogs' names out of the library?" He stomped around the shop in a temper. "And dismal? Grief *is* dismal. That's what you should have called the fucking dog, Dismal." He stopped and stared toward the storeroom door. "I can't believe you did that, Fiona, I really can't."

Fiona still had the door open just enough to shout through. "You didn't want to be involved in the edits, you said so yourself."

"Because I trusted you not to give it a Disney makeover! Christ, this thing just gets worse and worse."

Kate pinched the bridge of her nose and stepped into the breach.

"Don't out yourself. It won't help either of us," she said.

"I don't even know anymore." He hung his massive head. "That dog has floored me. We never had a dog, my wife was allergic to fur. A costumer's nightmare, she always used to say."

Kate let his words, his snapshot recollection, sit between them in the air for a few beats.

"You really don't want to be connected to that clichéd ending," she said softly. "Think of your fan base, it just wouldn't work."

He grumbled and thrashed about, muffled words she couldn't quite catch.

"I need a drink," he said, sudden and loud. "A fucking big one." He swung around and stomped out into the sunny afternoon toward his low black car, too intent on escape to consider the fact he was still dressed as a T-Rex.

Kate followed him to the step and watched him battle to fold himself into the driver's seat as a woman with a small child crossed the road to avoid him. He slammed the door on his tail and let out a full-throated roar as he flung the door open again, dragging the tail into the footwell before he shot off down the road.

Back inside the shop, Fiona and Liv had emerged from the storeroom.

"Where's my T-Rex?" Liv said.

"Heading for the M25," Kate said.

Fiona gathered herself to her full, still-diminutive height.

"Your job right now is to do precisely nothing," she said, eyeballing Kate as she gathered up H's left-behind belongings. "No more wild soliloquies or galivanting around town drawing yet more negative attention." She stood in the doorway to deliver her parting shot. "It's time for this ghost author to be exactly what the name suggests. Invisible."

Liv practically ran to lock the door behind her. "Well, she's hideous."

Kate slumped against the nearest wall and slid down onto her bum.

"What an almighty mess," she said, weary.

Liv dropped onto the floor beside her. "Look on the bright side."

"Is there one?"

Liv cast around for a second. "Alice is okay."

Kate sighed, because that truly was the most important thing. "Yes."

"And you got to meet the author."

"Dressed as bloody Godzilla," Kate said. "I couldn't make this up."

"Godzilla wasn't a T-Rex," Liv said.

Kate shrugged, not willing to argue the toss.

"You missed a call from Charlie," Liv said, handing Kate her mobile, rescued from the storeroom.

Kate took it back, glancing at the stacked-up messages on the screen with trepidation. Clicking to return Charlie's call, she sighed when it went to voicemail.

"Will you be okay if I head upstairs for a while?" she said, giving Liv her bangle back. She needed some time to try to make sense of the chaos. She'd been blindsided by the news and jumped straight in to comfort Alice, then Fiona and H had barreled through the door and taken over the afternoon. She'd automatically assumed her customary role supporting everyone else when, actually, she was the person at the center of the story.

"Promise me you won't go online?" Liv said, hauling her up by both hands. "It's news today and chip paper tomorrow."

Kate nodded and hugged her sister quickly. It probably would be chip paper for everyone else come tomorrow morning, but the fallout was going to reverberate through her life for far longer.

———— ✦ ————

SHE DID GO ONLINE, OF course, and what she found there sent her plummeting into a pit of self-loathing and misery. Readers were understandably up in arms. She'd written her email to Alice in such a way as to deliberately downplay things to her daughter, making it sound like a lighthearted dash of excitement to perk her boring life up. If she could just offer her side of the story she might feel better, but as it was she could only read the endless vitriolic comments and let shame burn her cheeks. People were marveling at her sheer gall to go on the radio and TV, to turn up at events and sign her fake name without a care in the world. Someone even said they might set fire to their signed copy, because they'd queued for an hour to meet Kate and now felt like a complete idiot. They may as well have stayed home and signed the book themselves. They all felt taken in. They all felt fooled.

The more she scrolled, the more desperate she felt, because the fact was there was an element of truth to what people were saying. Without context or nuance, it looked as if she'd mercilessly lied and exploited the reading community for her own financial benefit, laughing behind their backs because she knew something they didn't. She longed to reply, to try to change the narrative, but she'd agreed to wait for Charlie, at least. Besides, what would she say anyway? She'd most likely plunge in headfirst and make things even worse. Kate closed her laptop and pressed her face into her pillow, searching for the oblivion of sleep over the misery of being awake.

31

SHE WAS AWOKEN BY SOMEONE PRESSING HER DOOR BUZZER AND A MESSAGE from Charlie letting her know he was there, at last. She swung herself out of bed and snatched her hair back into a ponytail, swiping her fingertips under her eyes to sweep away any tearful mascara stains.

He looked her over searchingly when she opened the door, as if assessing her for damage.

"Oh, Kate." He dropped his bags to hug her. "I'll make everything okay, I promise."

She shook her head as she stepped back to allow him inside the flat, closing the door behind him with a weary sigh.

"I don't see how it can be okay after this," she said, leading him into the kitchenette.

He took one of the two chairs at the tiny kitchen table as she went through the motions of making coffee.

"Have you seen everything that's being said online?" she said.

He nodded. "Yes."

"Everyone hates me," she said, unscrewing the lid from the milk.

"No, they don't," he said. "They're confused, and the vacuum of official information is being filled with speculation and rumor."

She put their mugs down on the table and took a seat opposite him.

For a moment, they took each other in.

"I'm sorry I couldn't get here earlier," he said.

"You didn't need to rush back," she said, relieved that he had.

From the moment things had erupted online, she'd needed his presence beside her. They were a team in this; everyone else involved had other priorities. H was Fiona's only concern. For the publishing team, the book was at the top of the list. Only Charlie was thinking about how all of this impacted Kate.

"I got a train as soon as I heard," he said.

"Did Fiona tell you about this afternoon?"

His expression shifted. "I had to turn the volume down on my mobile, she was . . . expressive," he said. "She mentioned something about a dinosaur?"

Kate sighed and closed her eyes. "An angry seven-foot T-Rex."

Charlie laughed into his coffee mug. "At least that bit hasn't made it online," he said. He squared his shoulders. "Look, it's going to be a rocky few days. I've just come from a meeting with Prue and the team. They're going to issue a statement tomorrow."

She nodded, her hands clasped around her mug. "Do you know what they're planning to say?"

"Not precisely, but it'll go some way toward explaining the behind-the-scenes business decisions and give people something else to focus on. They won't name the author, of course, and they'll thank you for your help in bringing the book to market."

"Do you think that's going to be enough?" she said, finding it hard to imagine.

He took a few moments to gather his thoughts. "As far as the book's concerned, I think this whole scenario is nothing but good publicity," he said. "Sales will increase. Reader speculation will turn to who the real author is, and it's on Fi and the team to handle that."

"H deserves the privacy he was promised," Kate said, worrying for the angry Welshman she'd almost met that afternoon.

"Prue and the team think it's best if you lie low going forward," he said.

She wasn't surprised, after Fiona's sharply delivered message earlier. "And you? Do you agree with them?"

He turned her question over before speaking. "Having sat through the meeting this afternoon, I can honestly say everyone genuinely feels bad for you over there," he said. "But they have to make the book their number-one priority." He looked her straight in the eyes, leaning toward her. "Kate, I'm thinking only about you when I say this. The best thing you can do right now is absolutely nothing—trust me, I learned that the hard way. Don't engage, don't try to defend yourself while you're emotional, you'll leave yourself open to attack. In fact, don't go online at all if you can help it."

"Everyone is telling me the same thing," she said, rubbing her hand over her forehead. "You, Fiona, Prue, even Liv. Say nothing, do nothing. But I hate it, Charlie, all those things being said and thought about me that aren't true. Surely I could put my own statement out tomorrow too, just to apologize at least?"

He reached across the table and covered her balled-up hands with his own.

"Let the publishing team do their job and see how that changes things. You don't need to make all the decisions at once, okay?"

Kate's phone pinged a message from Liv she couldn't make any sense of.

Shit! I'm so sorry, sis, it all happened
in the heat of the moment! You know
how much Nish loves their trifles, it was
in my hand and she was being such a cow.
Call me if you're awake Xx

She pulled her hand reluctantly from Charlie's, shaking her head.

"I don't know what she's talking about, but whatever it is doesn't sound good." Wondering how many times you can get that sinking feeling without touching the bottom, she clicked her phone open.

It didn't take long to unravel the meaning behind Liv's cryptic text. Charlie scraped his chair around the table to look at Kate's phone screen as the latest installment in the seemingly never-ending saga played out in front of their eyes.

Claire, the supermarket worker who they'd met in-store on publication day, looked down the camera. "Can't keep this one on the shelf today," she said, piling copies of *The Power of Love* into the empty space before rolling her eyes at the camera. "Bet the 'author' doesn't show her face in here again, though!" She made sarcastic air quotes as she spoke, sparking a flurry of hearts and thumbs-ups near the little livestream symbol winking in the corner. Kate had checked out Claire's book-blogging page after they'd met; it was full of shelving videos as the latest books arrived in the shop, accompanied by book recommendations and reviews. She'd grown quite a following.

"Say that again and you'll be wearing this trifle," someone off-camera yelled.

"Holy shit," Kate whispered. "Liv, what have you done?"

Charlie leaned in as Kate turned the volume up.

"You again," Claire said, filming Liv now. "Fake author's side-kick," she said into the phone, for the benefit of anyone watching.

"Sidekick?" Liv said. "Sister, actually, and I'm going to give you one chance to stop being rude about someone you know nothing about and do the job this place pays you to do rather than creating content when you clearly should be working."

"I'm on my break, actually," Claire spat. "So I'm going to give *you* one chance to get out of my aisle and go and pay for that trifle instead of waving it around."

Liv glowered into the lens, then turned on her heel and stalked away slowly.

"At least she didn't throw the trifle," Charlie said.

"Let's hope the phony author has more dignity than her sister, eh?" Claire said to her followers. She'd probably imagined Liv was out of earshot, but she'd underestimated the power of a woman scorned. Liv, still on camera, swung back around and marched straight up to Claire, tearing the plastic lid off the family-size trifle.

"Dignity?" she said, furious. "Dignity? I warned you."

The last thing visible on the video was the trifle flying through the air toward the screen. Cream obscured the lens with a splat, but Claire could be heard screeching with shock as Liv yelled she'd happily pay for the fucking trifle now.

Kate clicked her mobile off. First Alice and now Liv. She loved her family to their bones, but it felt as if today was the day they'd decided to ruin her life.

"Well, that's not going to help, is it?" she said, flat, not even looking at Charlie.

"Fiona mentioned she'd met your sister."

Kate heard the subtext; Fiona had no doubt done a complete hatchet job on Liv, having been stuck in a storeroom with her for a chunk of the afternoon.

"We lost our mother when we were really young," Kate said, feeling the need to defend her sister. "It's been us against the world ever since." She shook her head, remembering all the times Liv had waded in, both feet first. "She has this"—she splayed her hand flat on her chest—"this fire in here, a protective instinct that kicks in hard at the first sign of trouble." She sighed and turned to look at Charlie. "You must wish you'd never opened my letter. What do we do now?"

BOTH OF THEIR PHONES BLEW up over dinner, Chinese grabbed from the place a few doors down. Kate's social media was on fire, and Charlie's missives from Fiona and the publishing team were incessant. In the end, he turned both phones onto silent and placed them face down.

"Just eat," he said. "Everyone can wait."

"Today has felt at least four days long," she said, pushing noodles around her plate. "If I'd known what was coming, I'd have stayed in bed."

"It would still have come just the same," he said. "The world keeps turning, even if you hide yourself away from it."

"I know," she said. "I just wish I could click my fingers and be somewhere else."

"I was thinking exactly that on the train," he said. "Now would be a really good time for you to be somewhere else for a few days."

Kate pushed her plate away, done. "It feels like running away from my problems."

Charlie's phone rang, and he declined the call after checking. "Press again. Taking yourself out of a crazy situation so you can think straight isn't running away. As your agent, I strongly advise it." He held her gaze, and then her hand. "I just want to get you out of here to someplace safe."

Her phone rang again, yet another number she didn't recognize. She let it go to voicemail and listened back to a sharp-voiced journalist from one of the nationals sniffing around for an exclusive.

"My father kept a place in Henley-on-Thames. Let me drive you over there early in the morning," he said. "He also had a ridiculous old sports car, you'll like it."

Of course Jojo had a sports car and a bolthole in Henley-on-Thames.

Charlie's tired eyes reminded her that he'd shifted his entire day around to be here. She'd waited all day to hear his advice; now she needed to take it.

Their phones beeped constantly.

"Am I asking too much of you?" she said, realizing she wanted to say yes.

"I asked you, remember?" he said. "Besides, I've been looking for an excuse to drive the car."

She appreciated the lie, knowing he was downplaying things for her benefit. She had no idea how this whole fiasco was going to play out, but at least she didn't feel alone in it anymore.

32

CHARLIE ROLLED UP OUTSIDE THE SHOP AT A LITTLE BEFORE SIX THE following morning in Jojo's deep burgundy two-seater sports car, soft-top down. Kate had spoken only to Liv about her escape plan, assuring her sister that the whole trifle incident wasn't a big deal in the grand scheme of things. It wasn't necessarily true—Fiona was hopping mad, but the publishers seemed to be running with the "no publicity is bad publicity" chestnut. Things had certainly gained traction overnight. It was turning into just the kind of story social media loved, micro-scandal on top of micro-scandal, with the ongoing mystery of who actually wrote the book constantly fueling the fire. The book community was ablaze with it, names being tossed back and forth, timelines being spliced together, amateur sleuth senses on high alert trying to be the one to get to the bottom of it. Kate had exhausted herself reading threads into the small hours, a dead weight of anxiety lodged firmly in her chest. Her name was being well and truly trashed, her online absence since the reveal the subject of hot debate. People assumed she'd run shamefaced for the hills when she'd been exposed, like a scammer trying to steal someone's life savings.

She raised her hand to let Charlie know she was on her way

down, wheeling her overnight case to the door and standing for a second before closing it behind her. She was exhausted, her angel wings tattered from being so tightly folded around the book.

The small flat had become her haven from the world since the divorce, but it was time to swap one temporary sanctuary for another.

"I can imagine Jojo channeling his inner James Bond driving this," she said, wheeling her case out onto the street.

He loaded her bag into the back seat beside his own.

"Or his inner Bond villain, depending on who he was trying to make an impression on," Charlie said. "It was one of his many props."

Kate settled into the cocoon of the ivory-leather passenger seat, already warmed by the morning sun.

"You look knackered," he said, glancing at her as he pulled away on the quiet street.

"I didn't sleep so well," she said, not needing to add what had kept her awake.

Charlie reached an arm behind her seat and handed her a rolled plaid blanket. "Why don't you close your eyes?"

She unraveled the blanket over herself and sank into the seat, resting her head back. The theme from *A Summer Place* played on the radio, big band music that felt somehow more in keeping with Jojo than Charlie.

"Couldn't bring myself to change stations," he said, catching her looking at the radio set into the center console.

She studied his profile as he lowered his aviators against the glare of the sun, his tanned hands assured on the leather-wrapped steering wheel, then closed her eyes and fell into a deep, dreamless sleep.

——— • ———

SHE WOKE AS CHARLIE EASED the car into a space beside the River Thames.

"God, I'm sorry," she said, blinking her eyes open. "I can't believe I fell asleep so fast. I was planning to stay awake and keep you company." She twisted her head from side to side to ease the crick in her neck. "I blame the blanket."

"You went out like a light," he said. "You must have needed it."

"It's hard to believe we're only an hour out of London," she said, looking around at the bucolic riverside scene. "It feels as if I've woken up in a completely different world. Did you come here much as a kid?"

He shook his head. "I've never actually been to the apartment before. In fact, I didn't even know he owned it until after he died."

She turned to him, shocked. "You didn't? When did he buy it?"

Charlie surveyed the pretty riverside scene, cascades of flowers along the railings, relatively few people around at the still-early hour except dog walkers and runners.

"Ten years ago, according to the paperwork."

She couldn't work out if he sounded pissed off. She'd built up an impression of their father-son relationship based on everything he'd said over the last few months, and this seemed completely at odds.

"Must have come as a bit of a shock?"

"Just a bit," he said.

"And you've never wanted to come and see it?"

He sighed, thinking before he spoke. "I've wanted to, yeah. But . . . I don't know. I've put it off, I guess."

He seemed perplexed by his father's secrecy and relieved to not be there alone. The lot of an only child, no one to share the burden.

"Right," she said, taking charge. "Which one is it?"

He nodded toward an old converted warehouse, once a place of industry, now a screamingly cool apartment block with glass-fronted river-view balconies.

"Somehow it doesn't look very Jojo," she said, squinting up at the building through the windshield. Not that Jojo wasn't a man fond of his luxuries, but he'd been more old school in his tastes, if his car, his captain's chair, and his penchant for bow ties were anything to judge him by.

"I guess you never know everything about someone," Charlie said, getting out of the car. "I'm sure he had his reasons."

He'd brought her here to get away from her problems, and in doing so he seemed to be walking toward one of his own.

"So no one has been here since your father died?" she said, stepping out onto the pavement.

"Just the cleaners," he said.

She was relieved to hear it was serviced, no fridge full of rotten food or unchanged beds to deal with. This was an important window into his father's world, one Charlie had never looked through before; he didn't need to contend with unmade beds and moldy food.

"Thank you for bringing me here," she said. It wasn't a platitude. It was an expression of deep relief, especially now she knew the emotional cost for him. It wasn't as if she could leave her troubles behind her, yet it felt as if she'd gained some distance from them for a short while. Perspective, perhaps. She was at least guaranteed not to see Fiona or any marauding T-Rex.

He patted the roof as he folded it up. "It's a good chance to blow the cobwebs off this old girl."

"You're not talking about me, are you?" Kate laughed for what felt like the first time in days. Reaching for the handle of her case, she wheeled it toward the entrance.

33

Jojo's apartment could have been anyone's. It felt almost as if he'd bought the show home complete with furniture—it lacked any sense of his personality or taste.

Kate stepped out onto the balcony as Charlie walked around the space, inspecting the expensive fixtures and fittings. Obvious nods to the heritage of the building, exposed brickwork and stripped wooden floors, had been paired with modern comforts: deep sofas, discreet high-end tech, a large piece of abstract art taking up most of one wall. The whole place was oriented toward the phenomenal river views, the balcony set with a table for two, and an outside sofa to make the most of the space. It was entirely fabulous, but Kate couldn't picture Jojo there at all.

"Maybe he bought it as an investment?" she said as she came back inside, thinking aloud.

Charlie shrugged. "It would have been a sound one." He continued on through to the bathroom and the bedroom beyond. It was a perfect bachelor pad, or maybe even a love nest, but neither of those options sounded very Jojo.

"I'll take the sofa tonight," she said when he reappeared.

He looked at her levelly. "No, you won't."

"It's fair. You had the sofa in Cornwall."

"If I remember rightly, we shared it," he said after a beat, holding her gaze long enough for heat to climb her neck.

"All the same," she said. "I'll take it tonight."

He didn't push the conversation, probably leaving it to pick up later.

"There's some supplies in the car, I'll go grab them," he said, heading out and leaving her alone in the second-floor apartment. It felt somehow as if they were in the eye of a storm and had taken refuge in a stranger's home, both of them edging around the place as if they had no right to be there. She wandered out to the glass balcony again and drank in the view, the crown of her head warmed by the morning sun. Raising a hand to her eyes, she watched Charlie down below, a confident, broad-shouldered guy and his expensive sports car, fitting seamlessly into the exclusive scene as if he belonged there. She'd rarely seen him out of business dress; there was an off-the-clock intimacy to his jeans and T-shirt. He looked up and waved when he caught her watching him, sliding his aviators on as he slammed the boot.

"Right," he said, nudging the front door open a couple of minutes later with brown bags balanced in his arms. "Here we go."

She followed him to the kitchen and watched him unpack the shopping onto the kitchen surface. Steaks, a preprepared salad, a bottle of red wine.

"Tiramisu." He pulled a clear tub from the bag. "My neighbor is Italian, she feeds me when she's made too much for her family. I think she worries I don't eat enough since my father died."

Kate couldn't imagine anyone feeling sorry for Charlie. He exuded an air of resilience and quiet authority, but perhaps that was just the side of his personality he chose to share with her. His professional side, maybe? The idea lodged itself in the back of her head for further examination later, that he might hold something of his real self back for the people in his life who weren't business acquaintances. Was that what they were? On the face of it, of course they were, but it felt like something more too, something intangible and nebulous and complicated.

One thing was for sure—she'd never needed his advice more than she did right now, with her reputation in tatters online, and Liv inadvertently throwing fuel on the social media fire too. She needed to take these couple of days for what they were, a chance to regroup and work out how to put the fire out.

Charlie unloaded other things from the bags. Bacon and eggs, milk, butter, cheese wrapped in waxy paper with string. She filled the empty fridge, working in easy tandem with him.

"Steaks for dinner, then," she said, sliding them onto the shelf. "How do you like it? You should know I'm one hundred percent going to judge you based on your answer."

"Rare," he said. "Medium rare at a push. Any more than that and I'm wishing I ordered the fish."

"You passed the test," she said, closing the fridge. "Never trust a well-done guy, it's a basic life hack."

He fiddled with the radio system built into the kitchen wall and big band jazz filled the air, the first real sign of his father having spent any time in the place. He sighed before turning it down to background noise.

Kate made coffee, and they sat out on the balcony sofa with their faces turned up to the sun, feet propped on the low table.

"I know we have a lot to work out, but can we just sit for a while?" she said.

He lounged beside her, the press of his arm warm beside hers.

"No arguments here." He rested his head back on the cushion and closed his eyes. Low music filtered from a hidden outdoor speaker, obviously connected to the in-house system.

She opened a door in her head and mentally pushed all thoughts of home and work inside it. The book, Alice, triflegate . . . all on the other side of the door and locked away until she was ready to face them.

She sipped her coffee and studied Charlie's profile instead, watched his brow smooth as the music washed over him, the sooty sweep of his lashes resting on his cheek. He was a charismatic man, always thinking two steps ahead; now it was as if someone had momentarily pressed his "pause" button, and as the minutes ticked by, Kate realized he'd fallen from resting to sleeping.

Keeping the door inside her mind well and truly locked, she put her empty cup down and leaned her head on his shoulder, tucking her legs up and closing her eyes too, letting his serenity become her own. In all of the chaos that had surrounded her life since publication day, it was an unexpected oasis of sun-warmed bliss, and she gave herself over to it and snoozed.

34

THEY WERE AWOKEN BY BOTH OF THEIR PHONES GOING OFF AT ONCE, notifications from Prue that the publisher's official statement had just been released.

> We realize there has been some speculation around the publication of *The Power of Love* by Kate Darrowby, and we hope to clarify things by sharing some of the thought processes behind the publishing decisions.
>
> As always, everything begins with the arrival of the manuscript, in this case a beautiful, impactful love story by a world-renowned author who wishes to remain anonymous. Readers will be aware that ghostwriters and pseudonyms are a regular and transparent part of the day-to-day business of bringing books to market, and although those mechanisms were applied slightly differently in the case of *The Power of Love*, we believe it still sits within the spirit of the usual parameters.
>
> Our priority as a publishing house is to deliver stories we believe in into the hands of readers who will love them, and reviews have certainly proved this to be the case with *The Power of Love*.

They say it takes a village to produce a book, and that's never been truer than the case in point. We're grateful for the incredible support readers have shown the book, and we ask that the author be allowed to retain the privacy and anonymity they've requested.

#itsallaboutthebook #LoveStoriesMatter

Kate read and reread the publisher's statement, unsure how it helped. "I'd hoped they might mention me directly," she said, looking from her phone screen to Charlie. They'd made fresh coffee and settled in the living room to analyze what had been said.

Charlie nodded slowly, thinking. "I guess we wait now and gauge reader reaction. It may be enough to redirect the focus of the attention away from you."

"Onto what? Digging until the actual author is unmasked? I know they've asked people to respect his privacy, but I worry this is going to have the opposite effect and feed the hunger to identify him."

"Which could take the heat off you," Charlie reasoned.

"But I don't want that to come at his cost," she said, exasperated, thinking of H thrashing around Liv's shop with his dino head in his hands.

"There isn't an easy fix to all of this, it's going to have to burn itself out," Charlie said. "The author is well protected. He won't be identified unless he decides to out himself, which is unlikely."

"Do you think it *will* burn itself out?" she said.

He considered his answer. "It isn't going to harm the book, it's outselling all expectations. And it won't harm the author either, he stands to do very well from this in the background. The only person it could potentially have lasting repercussions for is you, and it's my job to make sure that doesn't happen."

"There's only so much you can do," she said. "This whole thing is starting to feel like a monster that keeps growing a new head."

He studied her for a few quiet moments.

"Come on," he said, getting to his feet.

"Where?"

"The whole point of coming here was to get away from all of this for a while," he said. "Let's go take a look down by the river."

She glanced at the constant notifications scrolling on her mobile, then out of the window at the sun-drenched riverside scene, and made a snap decision. Turning her phone off, she placed it on the coffee table and accepted his outstretched hand to heave her up out of the low, insanely comfortable sofa.

It was beginning to feel as if Charlie was the only barrier between herself and complete disaster, but if he was prepared to live in the now just for this weekend, then she was willing to do the same.

"THIS SUMMER HAS BEEN OFF the charts, hasn't it?" she said, glad of the shade of a broad umbrella as they snagged a table outside a riverside bar an hour or so later. They'd meandered inside designer gift shops and artist galleries, browsing at a pace that belied their current lives back home. Kate had picked up a wonky coffee cup for Liv, and Charlie had bought a wide shallow porcelain bowl, midnight blue marbled with bright lava orange, from a local designer's workshop. "There's a vase in the same pattern in the apartment," he'd shrugged by way of explanation.

"It's not hard to see why stressed-out Londoners flock here," he said.

"It gives me that same feeling as Cornwall," she said. "Holiday escape."

"I'd never actually been down there until the signing event," he said.

"Not even as a child?"

He laughed softly. "Unsurprisingly, my father didn't go in for holidays," he said. "He had a brother in Scotland and he'd send me up there on the train for a few weeks in the summer. I guess that counted as a holiday for me in his head."

"How old were you?"

He shrugged. "Nine? Ten?"

She couldn't imagine letting Alice out of her sight at that age. "I don't like to think of you catching the train alone so young," she said.

"Different times, I guess. He always put me in first class and convinced one of the stewardesses to keep an eye on me." Charlie took a long drink. "He was an unconventional father, but a good one."

Kate fell silent. She was seventeen when she'd first met Jojo, and had no recollection of ever knowing he had a son just a couple of years older than she was.

"It would have been his birthday today," Charlie said, not meeting her gaze. "The first one since he died."

She swallowed, taken aback. "Really? Charlie, you should have said. I feel awful—did you have plans this weekend?"

He finished his beer, dropping his aviators from the top of his head down over his eyes. "I was glad of the distraction to be honest. What do you do to mark the birthday of someone when they're not here anymore?"

Kate's father had always kept his daughters at a distance; his passing when she'd just turned thirty had been joltingly sad, but not out of the blue, and in truth they'd seen very little of each other since her marriage. He probably wouldn't have been able to pick Alice out in her class photo.

"Well, we could do something to celebrate Jojo?" she said.

She could see him frowning behind his sunglasses. "What kind of thing?"

"What would you have done if he was here?"

Charlie huffed. "He'd have booked a table at the most expensive place he could think of and ordered the best champagne on the list, and then made a scene when I insisted on paying for it, even though we both knew I was always going to."

She nodded, finding the scene easy to envisage.

"Right, so let's do that. I just happen to have booked us the balcony table at this super-cool secret restaurant overlooking the river. I hear the chef does a mean rare steak."

He laughed softly, looking out across the street, and she picked up the wine list from the table and caught the waiter's eye.

"Could we have a bottle of this to go, please?" She skimmed her finger down the menu to the more expensive of the two champagne choices at the bottom.

The waiter nodded his approval. "Celebrating something special?"

"Someone special," she said.

"Thank you, Kate," Charlie said, scrubbing his hand over his jaw.

"Let me get this," she said, reaching for her bag.

"No chance," he said, opening his wallet.

"Oh, I absolutely insist," she said, louder than intended as she summoned her inner Jojo.

He caught her eye and laughed softly, onto her.

"My treat," he said, handing his card to the waiter when he reappeared with the champagne and the bill.

Kate gathered her things together, ready to get back to the cool interior of the apartment and prepare a dinner fit for the inimitable Jojo Francisco.

35

KATE CAST AN EYE OVER THE TABLE FOR TWO SHE'D LAID ON THE BAL-
cony. A simple white cloth and a creamy pillar candle, silverware and
stem glasses, plus some napkins and fine white crockery she'd found
in the sideboard. She was quite pleased with the overall effect. The
spectacular view helped, of course, a living work of art with the slow
appearance of pink and orange streaks across the golden evening sky.

Charlie emerged fresh from the shower, his hair still damp,
casual in jeans and a faded band T-shirt that highlighted his tan.

"I feel as if I should have checked the dress code, this place
looks fancier than I remember," he said, casting his eye over the
table, and then over Kate. She'd changed into a strapless black
sundress with a simple gold locket Alice had given her a couple of
birthdays ago, although she was barefoot with her hair tied back
in a ponytail.

"Have you made a reservation, sir? It's terribly exclusive
here," she said. She was relieved to have been able to flip into
cooking mode. Taking care of Charlie had pulled her out of wal-
lowing and given her something different to focus on, for a few
hours at least.

"I think my friend made the booking," he said.

She nodded. "Can I take her name?"

"It's Kate," he said. "No surname."

She smiled. "Ah yes, I think she's here already. She ordered a glass of champagne a little while ago, but I don't think anyone remembered to deliver it."

"Can't get the staff." He shook his head as he headed for the fridge.

He twisted the cork out with a practiced hand and poured the first glass. "For you."

"To Jojo," she said, touching her flute to Charlie's.

He nodded, looking as if he'd like to say something but didn't trust himself to speak.

"Right," she said. "You grab a seat so no one else snags the best table and I'll go chase up the chef."

Champagne in hand, she plated the steaks with the salad and green beans. During the course of her marriage she'd hosted countless parties and business dinners, and in that moment she was grateful to all of those nights in the kitchen for making her secure in the knowledge that the steak she was serving Charlie was exactly as he'd asked for. She wanted to impress him tonight, for the food to take his mind someplace other than down melancholy avenues.

Sudden, unexpected nerves shivered through her veins as she straightened her dress and smoothed her hands over her hair. Along with the rest of the nation, she'd caught the sun in recent weeks, a fresh smattering of freckles across her nose, a hint of gold on her shoulders. She looked date-ready. It wasn't a date, but the fact was she'd just cooked dinner for a crazy-handsome guy, and now she was planning to sit down and enjoy an evening by the river with him. For one night only, they were just going to be Kate and Charlie, eat steak and drink champagne, and try to give each other something to smile about.

"This looks amazing," he said as she placed the food down and took her seat.

"I know it does," she said, then laughed and accepted a refill of champagne.

"Even my father would have been hard pushed to find fault," he said.

"Definitely not with the view," she said.

"Definitely not." His gaze lingered on Kate.

The steak was perfectly rare, the champagne chilled and delicious, and they spoke mostly of Jojo. Charlie shared memories of him as an over-competitive father; Kate told him how Jojo had changed her life overnight as a teenager.

"I'd only gone to the audition to keep my friend Sophie company, she was mad into acting," Kate said. "She wasn't suitable for the part, too short, and we were both too scared to say I hadn't come to audition when he put me on the spot. Things went from there really, and everything just clicked into place."

"I can easily imagine it," Charlie said. "He always found a way to get what he wanted."

"I wasn't even eighteen at the time, I'd never met anyone like him before. He was a real dynamo, wasn't he? I had to work myself up to every meeting with him."

"My friends used to say the same thing," he said. "Mine was never the house we hung out at, let's put it that way."

"You sound as if you were close, though?"

He nodded. "He was around the age I am now when he found himself widowed with an eight-year-old son and the agency to run. I don't know how he kept everything together-looking back, but he did his best."

"A case of having to, for you, I suppose," she said. "Kids make you strong, even when you feel anything but."

"Credit where it's due, Fiona helped us a great deal over the years," he said. "I know she seems tough, but her heart is in the right place. It was hard for her when she lost Bob, and I know she's struggled without my father."

The snippet of behind-the-scenes insight into Fiona added yet another facet she hadn't seen before. No less scary, but multi-faceted. Like everyone, really.

"She seems career-driven, similar to your father?"

"I honestly don't think she knows who she'd be without it," he said.

"Does that make you feel as if you have to stay around to fill Jojo's shoes?"

"As if I could," Charlie said, refilling their glasses as they de-camped inside to the sofa. "It was just so sudden, losing him like that. My big, busy life had already shrunk down to just the two of us, and now it's just me."

His voice thickened with loss, and Kate placed an instinctive hand on his shoulder.

"It's okay to be emotional," she said. "You lost someone you love. And today is his birthday."

Charlie didn't reply, his gaze fixed on the river beyond. She studied the way his dark hair fell forward over his brow, the setting sun scattering rose-gold glitter in his whiskey-cola eyes. He was the kind of guy who stood out in a crowd, and the effect he was having on her champagne-honest mood was intoxicating.

"How old would he have been today?"

"Seventy."

"Wow, a big birthday."

"I miss him so much, Kate. I don't know what to do with the life he left behind. It's his house, his business . . . his captain's chair."

Charlie was fortunate in many ways to have been left such a legacy, but it was a lot to ask of one man, of an only child, to carry the weight of Jojo's world along with his own.

"It's blown a hole straight through the middle of my life again. Isn't it just so damn typical of him to die in the Ivy?"

She'd read a couple of articles online, enough to know Jojo had died at his favorite table while eating his favorite shepherd's pie.

"A legendary place for a legendary man," she said.

"I'm glad you knew him," he said.

"I'm glad I know you," she said, unable to keep the words in.

Charlie turned toward her, their knees almost touching. He looked into the depths of his champagne, his arm along the back of the sofa, his fingers resting lightly on her hair.

"He never once asked me if the rumors about my marriage were true." Charlie glanced up at her. "I know you'll have heard them. People love to talk, as Fiona was quick to point out recently."

Kate nodded.

"I didn't cheat or lie. I just fell out of love and I couldn't pretend otherwise, but that's not sensational enough for a place like that. Hollywood thrives on stories and scandal. Tara's family has been established there almost as long as the hills themselves, and they know how to spin the narrative to make sure they stay there." He sighed. "You're in or you're out."

"You don't have to explain yourself to me," she said.

He twisted the end of her ponytail around his fingers. "I don't want you to wonder if I'm a decent man."

The vulnerable truth of his words struck a nerve. "You've shown me who you are countless times over the last few months."

"I meant what I said that night outside the hotel," he said, leaning forward to put his glass down. "I've never met anyone quite like you before. You have this . . . this translucency, you wear your soul close to your skin and it scares me stupid. It's probably what makes you such a good actor. You look into the lens and show the world exactly who you are, unfiltered."

It was such an unexpected thing to say, she just stared at him. "Why does it scare you?"

"Because I put you in this precarious position in the first place. You walked into the office and I could see all of those things. I knew right away that you were perfect for the job because no one would doubt anything you told them."

"You're not responsible for everything, Charlie," she said. "I wrote the letter, if you want to play the 'who started it' game."

"Do you regret it?"

She swallowed. "I hate that Liv and Alice have been pulled in, and it breaks my heart that readers feel deceived. But do I regret being here, right now, with you?" She shook her head and slid her champagne glass onto the table, then moved closer to Charlie. "No one knows we're here. It feels like a pause, a place for an intentionally blank page."

She'd known coming here that there was potential for something to happen between them, and she appreciated that even though he must have thought the same thing, still he didn't make the first move.

"If you could write something on it, what would it be?" he said.

"I'd write that she wondered what it would feel like to be kissed by him," she said, watching the subtle shift in his eyes in response to her directness.

He nodded, his hand on the back of her neck now, stroking. "And then what does it say?"

She bit her lip. "I think you should write the next line."

He thought about it before he spoke again. "I'd write that in the ordinary run of things he'd like to take her dancing and see a movie and buy her flowers, but that isn't how their story goes. They only have this one deleted scene, so they pretend they've already done all of those things and skip to the part where he kisses her breathless and asks her to spend the night in his bed."

"You're too good at this," she said. Quiet music still played through the sound system, stripped-back, late-night stuff designed for lovers, and Charlie slid the silk band from her hair and let it fall around her shoulders. He frowned at the pale-blue band momentarily, then dropped it behind the sofa.

She placed her hand flat on his chest, his heart banging beneath her palm. "I'd write that he took her hair down, and it was the single most sexy thing that anyone had ever done to her in her entire life," she said. "Ask me and I'll say yes."

Charlie held her face between his hands. "Come to bed with me?"

"Yes," she said, his breath warm on her lips. "I think this is the bit where you kiss me breathless."

He slid his hands into her hair and lowered his mouth onto hers, achingly slow and sexy. He said her name, and he let his tongue slide over hers, and he tipped her head back and pressed her body into the sofa with the weight of his own. She closed her eyes when his mouth moved over her neck, her hair bunched in his hands. And then he straightened and stroked his thumb over her lower lip, watching her eyes.

"Or we could just stay here," he said.

She reached for the hem of his T-shirt and pulled it up, and he finished the job and dragged it over his head. "Let's do that," she said, swallowing hard because he was a lot without his top on.

He sucked in a breath when she stroked a hand down his chest, the smoothness of his stomach, and she gasped when he reached for her and pulled her on top of him as he lay down.

He dragged her dress down to her waist, exposing her breasts, making her gasp again and cover her face with her hands. He reached up and moved her hands away, holding on to them as he looked at her body and then slowly back up to her eyes.

"Don't hide from me," he said.

She shifted against him and enjoyed the way his body responded, the lift of his hips, the groan in his throat. It was heady to be wanted with such blatant need.

He let go of her hands to hold her breasts, the intimacy of his thumbs on her nipples making her squeeze her eyes shut. She opened them wide again when he reached down and rucked her dress up her thighs.

She bent close to him, searching for the press of his skin against hers, sucking in a breath of almost panic-desire when his hand slid between her legs, because she'd never felt such out-of-control intensity before. His mouth found hers, urgent now as he rolled her underneath him and looked down at her with undisguised lust, dragging his mouth over her skin in a way that melted her bones.

He moaned ragged in his throat when she reached between them to unbutton his jeans, her eyes staring into his soulful ones, his hands pulling her underwear down her hips until they were both naked and breathless. He pushed her knee outward with his own, and she made space for him between her thighs and wrapped her arms around his back. He stopped to give them both time to be in the moment, then held her jaw and kissed her with sudden gentleness as he pushed his hips down.

"Oh my God, Charlie," she whispered, overwhelmed by the shock and pleasure and relief of him inside her. "I'm so glad I didn't die without having sex with you."

He half laughed, half moaned, thrusting deeper, harder. "Don't tell me you're going to start one of your speeches," he said, and she wrapped her legs around his thighs and sank her teeth into his shoulder.

"I can't remember any words," she whispered as he smoothed her damp hair from her face, his other hand between her legs. He watched her eyes, knowing when it was too much, sliding his fingers into her mouth when she stroked her hand down over his ass and pulled him over the edge with her.

They stilled afterward, hearts banging, his head on her chest. She held him to her, her fingers smoothing his hair.

"She wrote that it felt as if they'd danced, and been to the movies, and he'd given her all of the flowers," she whispered.

He moved so she was in the crook of his shoulder and wrapped his arms around her, and she closed her eyes and slept.

36

THEY PACKED THEIR BAGS ON SUNDAY AFTERNOON AND LEFT THE APART-ment exactly as they'd found it, except for one new addition. The midnight-blue bowl with lava-orange marbling, now sitting in pride of place on the coffee table beside the matching vase in the lounge. It was the closest Charlie could get to giving a birthday gift to his father.

They sat side by side on a bench beside the river, car loaded ready to go, neither of them sure what to say. As they'd turned the key in the lock of the apartment, the door inside Kate's head had cracked open under the weight of reality piled against the other side of it.

He turned to her with a quiet sigh. "Kate . . ."

She put just enough space between them to allow for the conversation they needed to have. "Can I go first?" she said. "The thing about a deleted scene is that it isn't supposed to knock on to the main story, is it? It sits between the pages unseen, informing the story in ways no one else can know."

He watched her and waited for her to go on.

"We're grown-ups with crazy lives. Responsibilities, people who are relying on us. Can you imagine what would happen if we rolled back into London now and decided to make this, us, part of the plot?"

"I had the KISS acronym framed on my office wall in L.A.," he said. "Keep it simple, stupid. It's an old military saying, but it works for script writing too. Don't overcomplicate things. Don't make your characters TSTL." A resigned half smile ghosted his lips. "Too stupid to live," he explained. "Don't have them run upstairs to escape danger instead of out the door."

"I hate it when that happens," she said. "It makes me want to throw things at the screen."

They fell silent, watching a family of ducks emerge from the riverbank.

"It wasn't stupid to come here," he said.

"But it would be stupid to let it define the story when we leave," she said.

"There's something else." He turned his mobile over in his hands, looking at it. "I had a text last night, while you were sleeping."

He'd been quiet over breakfast. She'd assumed he was recalibrating, as she was, because they needed to press "reset," but perhaps there was more to it. She waited, knowing he had something else to say.

"There's interest from a major studio in a script I worked on a couple of years ago. The project faltered at the final hurdle last time. It was pretty crushing for everyone involved."

Kate didn't know what to say. He'd told her the L.A. part of his life was over. That he never wanted to see those hills again.

"What will you do?"

"I don't know." He looked away, sighing into the morning air. "I figured that part of my life was done with, but if I'm brutally honest my gut reaction to the news was elation. An emotional muscle memory, maybe, because writing is a tough gig and chances of success are vanishingly small even with connections.

Good stuff doesn't happen often. I sat outside on the balcony for a while after reading the message, trying to work out whether to take the stairs toward potential danger or head out of the front door to safety."

The conversation had gone so far away from where Kate had expected that she wasn't sure how to respond. "Was the text from your ex-wife?"

He nodded. "We wrote the script together."

"What about Fiona and the agency?" she said, when what she really wanted to ask was *What about me, what about the book, what about the landslide I'm caught in the middle of?*

He closed his eyes, and she could see the strain he was under. "I need to go home and think."

It felt, in the moment, as if his news had wiped their deleted scene from the script altogether. She drew in a breath and gathered herself, feeling as if she needed to rebalance the scales.

"I've been thinking about what to do next too," she said. "I obviously don't plan on living above the shop forever—I'm basically borrowing Liv's life. More than that, I've taken it over. She'd never say it, but she and Nish have spent years building their family together. They don't need me setting fires underneath them all the time."

"What are you saying?"

She shrugged. "I've scuppered my chances of acting with everything that's happened with the book, but in all honesty I've changed my mind about the idea anyway. I've had enough of London. It's too big, too all-consuming. Once all of this is over with the book I might rent a place down south. Cornwall maybe, I love it there."

She wasn't lying, exactly. She'd thought all of those things in recent weeks, but not in any solid form.

They looked at each other steadily, moments of silent connection and then disconnection.

"We should hit the road," he said, sliding his aviators over his eyes.

"Liv's expecting me," she said, getting to her feet and dusting herself down.

37

CHARLIE'S MOBILE RANG AS HE TURNED THE ENGINE OFF OUTSIDE THE fancy-dress shop. "It's Fiona," he said, frowning. "She's taking meetings in New York before she boards a cruise around the Caribbean, I better answer it."

Kate turned her face toward the window as he stepped away from the car, watching the quiet street. The drive home had been subdued, returning to reality with a jolt rather than a soft landing. She'd felt bolstered by the thought that, however bad things got, they were in it together. She didn't feel that way anymore, because the reality was that however much the book had taken over her life, it hadn't taken over Charlie's. He had other clients, and other pulls on his time and emotions. His conversation with Fiona sounded heated, his tone reaching her even though she wasn't attempting to listen. If it concerned her, he'd share it with her. Perhaps Fiona had heard the Hollywood scoop already; she seemed to have eyes and ears everywhere. Kate waited in the car until he'd ended the call, affording him some privacy.

"Sorry about that." He opened her door, weary concern all over his face.

"Everything okay?"

He rolled his shoulders. "Depends how you look at things." He paused. "Fiona has sold the rights to the book in the U.S."

"What will that mean for me?" She frowned, getting out of the car.

"It means the book will be published in the U.S. soon, very soon actually, in order to ride the current wave of interest here."

"Will it be published with my name on it and my photo and everything?"

"The success here has caused a ripple effect," he said, not directly answering the question.

"Can I opt out of all this?"

She stared at him, and he didn't look away. "I don't think you can, Kate. It's in the contract."

They stood face-to-face in the street, feeling a million miles away from the closeness they'd shared together. It felt more like a page torn out and screwed up than a deleted scene.

"But people know now, it's not the same anymore," she said. "How can they publish it as it is when everyone knows that Kate Darrowby doesn't exist?"

Charlie looked uncomfortable. "Because that's the hook that's driven the offers up sky-high. The book community is international and all of the publicity generated around *The Power of Love* here has fueled massive global interest. Everyone wants a slice of the pie while it's hot."

"At my expense," she muttered, squaring her shoulders. "What if I say no?"

He shook his head, his expression telling her what his words didn't. There was no get-out clause. "I should have seen this coming. My father would have."

"And no doubt Fiona did."

Charlie's silence spoke volumes.

"Just so I'm clear . . . All of the humiliation that's happening here is going to escalate, but a million times worse because this time it will be readers from all over the USA chipping in," she said, flat with distress. "And I can't do a damn thing about it except sit here and wait for the onslaught, let everyone call me a fraud, and a liar, and an opportunist."

"You're none of those things."

"It doesn't matter what I am, though, does it? It matters what everyone says I am. People believe what they read, Charlie." She grabbed her overnight bag and swung on her heel. "I'm going inside."

"Shall I come in and talk this through?"

She shook her head. "I want to be on my own. You're not the only one with things to think about."

SHE MADE COFFEE ON AUTOPILOT, fear and anxiety deadweights in her chest. It was all so messed up and about to get worse. There had already been too much collateral damage to the people she loved. Liv was putting a brave face on it but she'd definitely taken heat online for her trifle-hurling stunt, and Nish and the kids were all feeling the aftermath from school friends and colleagues. Alice had had such a torrid time with Flynn the Aussie heartbreaker, although in a way Kate was relieved he'd at least shown his true colors early. Richard had left her a curt message the night before to let her know he'd collected Alice from Leeds and taken her with him and Belinda on a planned trip to the south of France. Conflicted feelings had battled for supremacy at the news—relief, of course, that Alice would be spending the first weeks of her summer break recovering in France, but a selfish envy too, that Belinda would be the one giving out motherly hugs and pep talks. She wasn't in a place to offer Alice the same escape, but still it stung that someone else was. At least for them it was only a part of their bigger picture. For Kate, it was her entire canvas, mud-brown and battleship-gray paint slung in every direction, obscuring any of the brighter stuff she'd managed to build since the separation. The past weekend in Henley had felt like momentarily stepping into someone else's shoes, and then this afternoon it was as if life had spotted her smiling and kicked her hard in the teeth.

Did she wish, on balance, that she'd never written that impulsive letter to Jojo? She'd said no when Charlie asked her that same question just yesterday, but now on this drizzly Sunday afternoon, she finally concluded that the answer was yes. She was exhausted. She didn't want her personal story dragged out for public consumption all across the United States, or to be the topic of watercooler conversation in Germany, or the hot gossip anywhere else the book found its way to over the course of this long, hot summer. She remembered one of the early meetings at the publishing house, when they'd likened the spread of the book to a tidal wave. No one had thought to mention that she might actually drown.

Rain splattered the window as she dumped her bags and lay down on the small sofa, cold and curled into herself. Gardeners around the country would be waving flags in relief, but for Kate the rain seemed more like a reflection of her mood. Cloudy with a fair chance of disaster. More chaos. More online debate, more hounding to find H, more anxiety for her family. Global interest, Charlie had said. Just the phrase had her screwing her eyes tighter, burying her face in the cushion until sleep came and rescued her for a while.

38

"YOU LOOK TIRED," KATE SAID, WATCHING HER SISTER STRAIGHTEN UP and roll her shoulders after an afternoon bent over the sewing machine.

Liv had been working solidly for the last few weeks on a set of six *Bridgerton*-inspired bridesmaid gowns for a bridal party, dresses that would come back into the shop afterward to be used as hire-outs.

"This is the most intricate one of them all," she said, lifting the finished sea-foam-green silk dress carefully from the machine. "Will you try it on for me? I need to check the seams."

The other five gowns hung together on a rail behind Liv, each a different shade of muted silk, all empire-line bodices with chiffon cap sleeves, delicate embroidery, and jeweled adornments to individualize them.

Kate peered down the neck of her T-shirt to check which bra she'd put on that morning. "You're in luck," she said. "Push-up."

"The dress should do everything for you anyway," Liv said. "I tried the peach one on at home the other day—Nish thought all his birthdays had come at once."

Kate laughed, stepping into the changing booth to get undressed in case any customers came in. "How did women ever get anything done when they had to dress like this all the time?" she said, stepping into the intricate dress and pulling the delicate-sleeved bodice carefully up her arms. Liv fastened the back, hoisting her up in all the right places, which pushed her cleavage up considerably higher than its usual place.

"Oh my God, look at my boobs," Kate gasped, staring at herself in the mirror.

"I can't look anywhere else," Liv said, sweeping Kate's hair up with a jeweled comb she'd ordered to accessorize the dress. "Come and stand on the stool so I can see it in the light."

Liv propped the door open to let some cool air in as Kate stepped up onto the alterations stool in the middle of the shop.

"Let me just take some reference photos." Liv circled slowly around, coming in close for detail. "Could you hold this for the pics?" She handed Kate a fan. "I'm going to send them over to the bride."

Kate flicked the fan out and gave it a go in the stuffy shop. "I feel like someone should ask me if I'd like a cooling glass of lemonade," she said, wafting herself.

"You could do with a randy lord," Liv said.

Kate hadn't told Liv anything about her deleted scene weekend with Charlie. They hadn't seen each other since, communicating through messages and emails rather than calls. It wasn't just Charlie's choice; Kate had found herself fragile and jaded, badly in need of some space from the publishing industry in general and from Charlie specifically. The online piranha frenzy hadn't abated; every time she clicked on her Kate Darrowby social media profiles she was swamped with a deluge of comments, questions, and demands to know who the actual author was. It had become so demoralizing, and so out of her control, that she'd started to avoid looking at all.

Kate fanned herself, preferring to stay in the here-and-now

safety of her sister's company. "I'm quite overcome by the heat, sister dearest," she laughed. "I rather like all this, I think I was born in the wrong era."

Liv stuck a stray pin into the cushion attached to her wrist. "You'd miss your jeans within a week."

"Probably. Shall we have a little waltz?" She braced her arms in hold position.

Liv flopped onto the nearest chair. "Find someone else to mark your dance card, I'm boiling."

"I'm no lord, but I'll give it a go if you're stuck?"

They both turned at the sound of a male voice from the doorway.

"Charlie!" Kate fanned herself harder without thinking, then snapped the fan shut because she felt ridiculous. "How long have you been here?"

"Charlie?" Liv said, because despite his heavy involvement in Kate's life over the last few months, this was the first time they'd actually met face-to-face. She raised her eyebrows toward Kate, then offered her a hand down off the alterations stool.

"This is my sister," Kate said, flustered.

Liv glanced between them and seemed to pick up on the fact you could cut the atmosphere with a knife. Kate speed-read the unspoken questions in her sister's blue eyes—*Do you need me to stay, can I trust this guy with you?* She nodded imperceptibly, adding the ghost of an I've-got-this smile. She squeezed Liv's fingers briefly, feeling bolstered by the answering squeeze of solidarity.

"I'll be out the back if you need me, madam." Liv dropped a cute curtsy before turning on her heel and disappearing smartly into the storeroom.

Kate's pulse raced, both because of the tightness of her bodice and Charlie's sudden proximity.

"I was in the area," he said, looking at the ceiling rather than her heaving cleavage. "I should probably have called first . . ."

"I don't usually dress like this at home," she said, remembering his mouth on her skin, the weight of his body over hers.

"I guessed as much," he said.

The heartbreaker half smile, the whiskey-cola eyes; she took a couple of steps back so she couldn't smell the familiarity of his skin.

"Have you come to tell me something has happened?" she said, opening and closing the fan for something to do with her hands.

He swallowed hard. "I fly to L.A. tomorrow. I'll be gone for a week or so."

"Oh," she said, floored. Things must have progressed with his manuscript. "I see. Congratulations." Her hand fluttered to the neckline of the dress. If she'd been wearing pearls, she'd have clutched them. *What about me,* she wanted to shout, *and the shitstorm about to hit the fan when the book comes out in the U.S.? I'm relying on you,* she wanted to say, *don't go, I need you here.* She kept all of the unreasonable thoughts in her head, choosing silence as her method of communication.

"It isn't finalized yet. I'll be back before the book releases in the U.S.," he said, his voice gentle, his eyes searching hers for something more than surface conversation. "How have you been?"

She wasn't sure what he expected from her. Permission to not feel awkward? Had he come to ease his conscience?

"I'm fine." She straightened her shoulders. "Keeping busy, helping Liv, seeing . . . people." She almost threw her husky-eyed first love from the train into the mix and then realized she didn't have the energy to maintain the lie anymore. "Don't worry about me. I know I can rely on Prue if I need anything."

For a heart-stopping, statue-still second she thought he was going to dip his head and kiss her, and then he nodded curtly and stepped back. At this rate they were going to be on opposite sides of the shop.

She clenched her jaw, blindsided by the fact that he was actually leaving, and that she was in full Regency dress, and by the unreadable messages in his dark eyes. He looked as if he was going to say something urgent but then just spun on his heel and left the shop, as swiftly and unexpectedly as he'd appeared. Kate stared at the empty space he'd inhabited moments ago, the familiar warm-amber trace of his cologne left behind in the air.

"So that was Charlie," Liv said, emerging from the storeroom.

"I can't believe I was wearing this bloody dress," Kate breathed, her eyes lingering on the empty doorway.

"Proper Mr. Darcy moment."

"Proper mortifying," Kate said. She dropped into the chair, fanning herself dejectedly. "My life feels like a TV drama, and someone else is writing the script."

"Can it be me?" Liv said. "I'd make sure Fiona's cruise ship hit an iceberg." She was still simmering about being shut in the store cupboard with Fiona.

"They don't have icebergs in the Caribbean," Kate said.

"I'm the scriptwriter. It's a freak iceberg and it's happening."

Kate shook her head, letting Liv entertain herself. "I think that one's already been done," she said.

"Meanwhile, in the south of France, a tiger escapes from the local zoo," Liv said, looking pleased with herself. "It mauls Richard to death. Slowly. Belinda tries to save him and loses an eye. And an ear. She becomes a one-eyed, one-eared widow recluse, penniless because he's secretly gambled away all the money."

Kate held her fan up to stop her sister's flow. "You're wasted on costumes—*EastEnders* would snap you up in a heartbeat."

"And, of course, every good drama needs a central love story," Liv said, taking her fan back. "A tall, dark, and handsome stranger who walks into the scene when we least expect him to and saves the day."

Kate stood and turned her back to Liv. "Unzip this dress, will you, I can't breathe." She held the front of the dress against her body as the zip slid down. "And if you're clumsily trying to shoehorn Charlie in there, you should know that he only came by to tell me he's leaving for L.A. to work on a rom-com script with his ex-wife."

"Shit." Liv made clapboard signals with her hands. "Cut. That wasn't in the story."

Kate stepped behind the changing curtain and out of the dress, handing it to Liv. "I've changed my mind, I don't wish I lived in the Regency era anymore. I don't want to hang around on the edge of my own life waiting for some guy to dance with me or take me to the movies or buy me flowers."

"Not sure they had movies in those days," Liv said, hanging the dress up as Kate emerged from behind the curtain in everyday jeans and T-shirt.

"Lucky them," Kate said. "Rom-coms are a crock of shite anyway."

39

Dear Kate,

I'm sorry to have gone AWOL—I've escaped to my safe place, Formentera, for a while. The T-Rex incident was the final straw.

I'm not sure what to say, I'm genuinely heartsore over how this has rebounded on you and your family. My offer stands—say the word and I'll reveal my identity. I don't give a damn what Fiona or anyone else says.

I hope the costume found its way back to the shop safely. What a ludicrous turn of events—my darling girl would have found the whole thing hilarious. Laugh in the face of adversity, she always said.

I hope you can find some humor in the situation, Kate, you seem to be someone who likes to laugh. You share that in common with my late wife. I think you would have liked her very much. Everyone did.

Yours,
H x

Dear H,

I'm relieved you've been able to get away, that feels like the right thing to do. I've been worried about you after the aforementioned T-Rex incident.

Getting away helps with perspective, doesn't it? I found that on a recent trip, like stepping into someone else's shoes for a while. Or into your own most comfortable ones, maybe.

I genuinely appreciate your offer—I can't imagine I'll ever need to take you up on it, but I promise to keep it in mind just in case.

Your wife sounds like sunshine in a bottle. I hope in time you find your smile again. From everything you've said, I'm sure your happiness would be her greatest wish. Until then, soak up the sun and try to relax at least.

Speak soon,

Kate x

———————

From: PrudenceAtwell@JJPPublishing.com

Dear Kate,

Hope you're well and making the most of the summer!

I wanted to let you know in advance that the *Sunday Times* bestseller listing for *The Power of Love* is going to be retracted tomorrow because of the controversy around its authorship.

It isn't a problem in terms of the book, sales continue to be robust. I realize, however, that you may encounter fresh negativity online, so I wanted to make you aware of the situation prior to it being made public.

Please do let us know if we can help at all.

Best wishes,

Prue

**SUNDAY TIMES column by
Muriel Blackstock to accompany
the removal of *The Power of Love*
from the *Sunday Times* bestseller list.**

Passing through the airport this morning, I stopped by the bookstore to check out what's being touted as this year's hot read for my Greek sun lounger. Three celeb-turned-fiction authors, a couple of TV tie-ins, and an ex-politician's wife's scandalous memoir. So far, so normal. And then an entire stand dedicated to the summer's runaway success story, *The Power of Love* by debut author Kate Darrowby. Published in hardback, Darrowby took part in an ambitious TV and radio launch campaign, regaling the nation with humorous anecdotes about her misadventures in pubic topiary and a viral search for her husky-eyed first lover. It's since been revealed, however, in rather tawdry circumstances involving an Aussie surfer and a family-size trifle, that Darrowby isn't actually the author after all—just a jobbing actor hired to pose as such. All rise the publishing industry's newest invention, the ghost author.

Readers will be familiar by now with the use of ghost-writers behind celebrity authors, but is this a step too far for them to stomach? Given that the messy scandal has now resulted in the loss of its *Sunday Times* bestseller status, perhaps an AI ghost would have been a more appropriate choice. Certainly a more discreet one.

Oh, and for those wondering, Marian Keyes came to Greece with me in my suitcase. I sobbed into my souvlaki.

40

"BLOODY SMUG-ARSED MURIEL-SHIT-FOR-BRAINS-SCUMBAG-Blackstock!" Liv hurled the paper down in disgust after reading the article out loud to Nish and Kate. "Get Charlie on the phone, wake him up in L.A., and ask him where exactly in your contract you agreed to being stabbed repeatedly in the back by every journalist and keyboard warrior in the entire fucking country?"

Nish placed a mug of coffee on the table in front of Kate. "She'll calm down in a few minutes," he murmured under his breath, as they watched Liv stomp. "This whole book thing has got her really worked up."

Kate nodded, miserable, aware that *this whole book thing* was her fault.

"You know where this belongs?" Liv strode back to the table and grabbed the paper with both hands. "I'll show you."

She ripped the page out and marched into the garden, Kate and Nish close behind her, until she reached Nish's carefully managed compost heap. They stood in the Sunday-morning rain and watched as she flung the page on top of the pile, then reached for the garden fork and speared it viciously through Muriel's face. She stuck her foot on the fork and turned the compost pile over until the page disappeared altogether.

"That's better," she said, straightening up, red-faced with effort, leaving the fork sticking into the compost heap.

"Come back inside," Kate said. "You're getting drenched."

"It was worth it," Liv said.

Kate caught Nish's eye and saw concern crease his forehead. He was a glass-half-full kind of guy; it took a lot to push his buttons.

"I've been thinking about booking a holiday," he said, once they were all back inside. "What do you think, love? I have enough time off accrued at work, we could get the kids away for a couple of weeks. Stevie could do with it now her GCSEs are over, and you've been working flat out on those bridesmaid dresses."

Liv frowned, as if her husband was speaking a language she didn't understand. "Shut the shop?"

"I can watch it for you," Kate said. "In fact, I'd like to, it'd keep me busy. God knows I could do with something to occupy myself at the moment."

"I can't leave you alone in the middle of all of this going—" Liv stopped mid-sentence and reached out to grip the mantelpiece. "Nish, I don't feel right."

The color drained from her face like bathwater down the plughole, and Nish and Kate both lunged forward as she lurched sideways, catching her before she fell and hit her head on the fire surround.

"Oh my God, oh my God, oh my God," Kate said, fast and panicked. "What's happening to her?"

"I don't know," Nish said, stricken, cradling his out-cold wife in his arms.

"I'll call an ambulance," Kate said, her mobile already in her hand. "Oh Jesus, Nish, is she breathing? Please tell me she's breathing, I'll never forgive myself if anything happens to her because I—"

"Just make the damn call, Kate, she's breathing," Nish snapped, cutting her off mid-sentence.

She nodded, her hands shaking violently, her voice shaking almost as badly when she spoke to the first responder, who assured her they'd get an ambulance routed to them straightaway.

"I can't believe this is happening," Kate said, kneeling beside her sister, picking her limp hand up and rubbing it hard. "Come on, Liv, wake up, you need to wake up now. Please, Liv, please wake up."

She'd only seen Nish cry once before, on his wedding day. To see his fearful tears now was unbearable. Thank God the kids were at his sister's for a few school's-out-for-summer celebratory days with their cousins.

"Did her eyelids just flicker?" Nish said, after what felt like hours staring at Liv as the sound of a distant siren grew closer.

Kate felt her sister's fingers move in her hand, and gasped. "She moved, Nish, she moved! I think she's coming around."

The ambulance turned onto the drive, and Kate jumped up. "I'll let them in."

The crew bustled in with some urgency, asking direct questions as they took stock of the situation. One knelt beside Liv, who in that same moment opened her eyes and squinted up into the paramedic's face.

"Who are you?" she said, struggling to sit up.

The woman placed a hand on Liv's shoulder. "Stay there a second for me, Liv, get your breath while I do a few checks."

"You passed out," Nish said, smoothing Liv's hair back from her face.

"Have you any history of fainting?" the paramedic said, wrapping a blood-pressure cuff around Liv's upper arm.

Liv shook her head. "Never."

"And have you been generally well the last few days?" the other one asked, pegging an oxygen clip on Liv's finger.

Liv nodded. "Normal, I think? A bit tired maybe. I haven't really felt like eating."

"She's been busy with work," Nish said. "And under a lot of other stress too."

He didn't look up at Kate, but he didn't need to. She'd already absorbed the guilt, slow horror creeping through her bones. She'd leaned too hard on Liv for support without realizing that her ballsy big sister had a breaking point too.

The paramedics busied themselves with checks and quiet conflabs, and eventually said they needed to take Liv to the hospital for a once-over by a doctor to be on the safe side.

"I don't need to do that," Liv said, once they'd detached her from their monitors. "I feel fine now." She got to her feet and then reached a hand out to steady herself on Nish, who shook his head.

"You're going, and I'm coming with you," he said. "No arguments."

Liv looked at her uncharacteristically direct husband, and then nodded, probably because she saw the fear and love written all over his face.

Kate stepped forward and hugged her sister tightly. "God, you scared me," she whispered. "Don't ever do that again." Letting go, she slipped her silver bangle from her wrist onto Liv's, then looked at Nish. "Call me as soon as you know anything."

She watched them board the ambulance and drive away, then closed the front door and pressed her back against it, tears streaming down her face.

41

"YOU'RE *PREGNANT?*"

Liv and Nish sat side by side on the sofa, clutching hands like a pair of naughty teenagers.

Kate sat in the armchair by the fireplace, almost as shell-shocked by their big news as they were.

"I'm forty-two," Liv said. "How can I be having another baby?"

"I think we both know the answer to that," Nish said.

"I blame that *Bridgerton* dress," Liv said, shooting him a pointed look. Confusion filled his eyes, followed swiftly by a knowing groan of recollection.

Liv scrubbed her hands over her pink cheeks. "What are the kids going to say? And your mother will be horrified."

"Will you stop worrying about what everyone else is going to think and worry about yourself for once?" Nish said. "We're having another baby, Liv."

She fell silent and looked at Kate, who was doing her best to read the situation and keep up with the fast-flowing emotions in the room before she said anything. The moment to speak was now, judging by the way they were both staring at her.

"What a lucky, lucky little baby," Kate said, a slow smile

spreading over her face as she held Liv's gaze. Liv swallowed, then nodded, her eyes filling with tears. Kate jumped from her chair and knelt by the sofa, somehow managing to pull both Liv and Nish into one big embrace. They sat huddled for a while, Liv crying, Kate and Nish both liable to join her at any moment. Liv's sudden collapse that morning had filled them both with abject terror; to now be celebrating such life-affirming news was a whole heap of emotion to process in the space of a few hours.

"That bloody holiday is happening," Nish said. "You're not going to work tomorrow." He looked at Kate for backup.

"Nish is right," she said. "You need some proper rest, a break to get your heads around all of this together. Take the kids somewhere nice for a couple of weeks, I'll watch the shop."

"You think?" Liv said. "Are you sure?"

The fact that Liv wasn't arguing was answer enough for Kate. Liv might be the big sister, but it was Kate's turn to step up.

42

KATE HEADED DOWNSTAIRS TO OPEN UP, FILLED WITH NEWFOUND PUR-
pose. She'd run the shop for the last two days without incident, glad
of the distraction to keep herself from constantly checking her phone.

The *Sunday Times* delisting notice had had the predicted
effect—reignition of the speculation over who the real author was
and a deepening of the scandal and disparagement toward Kate.
Liv's trifle-throwing incident had taken on a viral meme life of its
own, and the fact that Kate had made no attempt to defend either
herself or her sister was seen as admission of both her guilt and
her shallowness.

Her fingers itched to reply, and her heart burned with shame
at the suggestion that she couldn't be bothered to defend her sister.

Prue had been in touch most days to reassure her that no
reply was the best reply, that you don't stick your finger in a piranha tank and expect it not to get bitten. It was starting to feel like
losing a finger might actually be worth it. Her wedding finger,
maybe. She didn't need it anymore.

She sent Liv a quick "good morning" text to check all was
well in Portugal as she put the kettle on in the tiny kitchen behind
the shop, then headed across to unlock the door. It took her a

couple of confused seconds to register that something wasn't quite right, her hand resting on the door to flip the CLOSED sign over to OPEN. She couldn't see clearly through the glass. Frowning, she peered closer, then opened the door carefully to find something smeared all over it and pooling in a congealing heap on the step. The plastic bowl was the give-away clue: trifle.

She looked left and right along the street, but all was quiet.

"Bloody hell." She twisted her bangle, pressing the solid silver between her fingers for comfort, relieved Liv wasn't here to see this because her blood pressure would have shot through the roof. It was only trifle, but the subtext of the attack said *I know where you live, where you work, what you did.* She went back inside and slammed the door behind her, heart thumping, trying to decide what she should do. Clean it up, obviously, but should she tell the police? What would she say, someone's thrown a trifle at my window? Surely they had more important things to worry about, she'd feel ridiculous. Filling a bowl with soapy water, she headed back outside and washed the door down, watching the pink-and-yellow mess slime away toward the drain on the road.

It's only trifle, she kept telling herself. *Probably just kids.*

She could rationalize it, but nonetheless it had struck a vulnerable note within her. When she was much younger, her first car had been stolen. She'd got it back, luckily, but her first few times behind the wheel afterward had left her unsettled by feelings of invasion. Those same emotions ran through her now. Anger, because how bloody dare they come for Liv? Fear, because what if they did it again, or worse? And on top of that, a creeping sense of shame, as if she somehow deserved to be punished.

Her phone bipped as she went back inside. A message from Liv, a photo of the kids jumping into the pool with their clothes on the moment they arrived at the villa.

She sent back smiley faces and thumbs-up emojis, then sat

down on the stool in the quiet of the morning and stared at the closed door, unnerved.

IT HAPPENED AGAIN THE FOLLOWING morning. Kate had slept badly, her senses on high alert, and she saw it as soon as she came down to the shop floor. She hadn't heard a thing—the obscured bathroom window in her flat upstairs overlooked the street, a setup which was better in every way apart from not being able to watch out for trouble. She took photographs of the mess, and then, just like the morning before, used several bowls of hot soapy water to wash away the evidence. And just like the day before, she didn't tell a soul.

43

SHE WASN'T PREPARED TO LET THE SAME THING HAPPEN ON FRIDAY morning. Unlocking the shop at half past five, she stepped into the deserted street and stood sentry outside her door. The occasional car idled past, a woman jogging with her dog in the pale early-morning sun on the opposite side of the road. Maybe they wouldn't come today, she thought, crossing her fingers, jiggling her foot against the wooden frame of the door. Turning her options over in bed last night, she'd concluded that she needed to be more Liv in this situation. Her sister wouldn't passively wait for it to happen again. God, what she wouldn't give to have Liv standing beside her now, although in reality she was grateful, of course, that she'd be snoozing in bed in Portugal, oblivious.

In the distance she could see a pushbike approaching, some-one dressed in dark clothing, and as they came nearer, her stom-ach clenched with fear when she saw the balaclava too. Was this it? The bike slowed and, sure enough, the rider paused a few feet away and reached down inside their jacket, too preoccupied to notice her standing in the shadows to the side of the door. He—definitely a he, by the build of him—ripped the lid from the large trifle and raised his arm, and in that same moment Kate stepped forward to challenge him. He wavered, already committed to the act, and she raised her phone to record him, hoping her unexpected presence would be enough to throw him off guard. Adrenaline surged through Kate's body as she moved toward him, but then the trifle smacked her full in the face, making her splutter and gasp as it went inside her mouth and her eyes, splattering the window behind her with the force he'd thrown it. She heard rather than saw the click of photos being taken, wiping cream from her eyes just in time to see the rider give her the middle finger before disappearing down the street.

She stood alone on the pavement, trifle dripping down her face and T-shirt. It hadn't hurt her, physically, but the force of it slapping her in the face, the shock of it going into her mouth . . . she sat down on the shallow windowsill outside the shop and lowered her head between her knees, winded, full of fury and fear. Had she escalated things rather than put a stop to them? She'd expected kids, not a fully grown man in a balaclava. It felt sinister and unsettling. Was it time to call the police now? Even after this, the idea sat badly with her. She should be able to handle this herself. Involving the police would mean involving Liv, and that was the last thing she was going to let happen. Right. Okay. She straightened her shoulders and checked her watch. Not much after seven A.M. She'd wash the window, go upstairs and shower, and be back down in time to open the shop bang on nine o'clock. No way was some pathetic guy with a BMX and a grudge going to get the better of her.

IT WASN'T EASY TO STAY resolute as she cleaned the scene with trifle crusting on her skin, and she might have cried a little in the shower as she shampooed clumps of cream from her matted hair, but nonetheless, nine A.M. found her flipping the CLOSED sign to OPEN and stepping out onto the street to check the coast was clear. Just

the usual morning hubbub. People headed to work, parents grabbing coffee after dropping their kids at school, a couple of college
girls carrying huge cups of Barbie-pink bubble tea from the new
place farther down the street. They made her think of Alice, a
sharp twist of longing in her gut to hold her daughter close. Everyone she'd normally turn to was somewhere else: Alice, Liv . . .
Charlie. He'd have made that list in the past too. He messaged
most days to ask if she needed anything from him. It was difficult
to discern if the texts were personal to her or bcc'd to all of his
client list. Some days she replied with a polite no, other times she
left them unanswered. She hadn't breathed a word to him or anyone else about what had been happening every morning. Perhaps
she'd tell him when he was home again, if she hadn't miracu-
lously found a way to resolve it before then. Pulling out a notepad,
she made coffee and tried to brainstorm solutions.

Report it to the police. She wrote it down then put a line straight
through it because she didn't want to do anything that risked involving Liv.

Talk to Prue and the team. But what could they do, really? She
drew a line through that one too, because how could they practically help her at six in the morning?

Talk to Fiona. She didn't even know why she'd written the option down in truth, because the only thing she'd get was an earful.
Kate had concluded that Fiona had no recollection of her from
twenty years ago and little respect for the woman she was now.
She seemed to expect trouble to follow Kate around, and to take
pleasure in her downfalls.

Buy every trifle within a five-mile radius. So that would be time-
consuming and costly, and what the hell would she do with them
all, and anyway, the shops would just keep restocking. It'd be a
never-ending cycle. Line through.

Throw something back at balaclava man. But what? Should she stick to the pudding theme and pelt him with a lemon drizzle cake? Knowing her luck, she'd probably injure him and he'd sue her for every penny she didn't have. Liv would probably go big on this strategy, Death by Chocolate, but it just wasn't in Kate's nature to start hurling things at strangers in the street. Which left her with a cold cup of coffee and a big old list of crossed-out nothings.

44

AT SIX O'CLOCK ON SATURDAY MORNING, KATE SAT BEHIND THE COUNTER in the shop and stared at the door, utterly miserable. She hadn't slept, she hadn't showered, and she wasn't brave enough to go out there and face balaclava man again. In truth, he had her running scared.

He appeared at half past six, exactly as before. Stopped in the street and surveyed the scene for a minute, scanning to see if she was out there hiding again, most likely. She pressed her back to the wall as she watched him climb off his bike this time, her heart hammering, her hands shaking, her fingers clasped around her bangle. He peered through the glass door and for a horrible moment she feared he was going to open it, even though she'd triple-checked it was locked. He didn't. He ripped the lid from the trifle and scooped it out with his fingers, smearing it down the door again and again until he'd made as much mess as possible, then chucked the bowl on the ground and stamped on it before getting back on his bike, taking photos of his handiwork and disappearing.

Kate slid down the wall behind the counter and sat on the floor, her arms wrapped tight around her knees. How the hell had sending that speculative letter to Jojo come to this? How had agreeing to represent H's beautiful book led to her sitting alone on the cold shop floor, scared of her own shadow? She'd spent the last year and a bit scraping herself up after the divorce, and just when she'd thought she was finally getting somewhere, life had gone completely off the rails again.

HER PHONE BUZZED IN HER pocket, startling her. A video call from Charlie. She stared at his name on the screen, her finger hovering over "Accept," before she declined the call. She longed to talk to someone about all the things that had been happening and, in truth, Charlie was the person she wanted to speak to. He'd know what to say, what to do, but she was having a hard time shaking her lingering anger with him. Her feelings about what had happened between them had tangled themselves around the complicated trust issues she'd been left with in the aftermath of her marriage. Charlie had categorically told her that the L.A. chapter of his life was over, yet it had only taken his ex-wife to open the door and he'd run through it. She knew it wasn't as straightforward as that, and she wasn't proud of the messy, mixed-up thought processes his decisions had raised in her head, but it was what she was. She'd backed away to protect herself and she wasn't ready to lower her guard, but now she was out on a limb with none of her usual support system, just when she most needed someone.

She was just trying to summon the wherewithal to haul herself off the floor, when she heard a noise she didn't recognize outside the door. She braced instinctively, holding her breath. Had he come back? Raising her head slowly over the counter, she squinted toward the door, then jumped to her feet. Someone was hosing the door down, making light work of the cleanup job. She waited until they'd finished, then flung the door wide to say thank you.

"I saw what happened," the woman standing there said.

Kate recognized her as the owner of the Chinese restaurant

a couple of doors down; she'd seen her taking her kids to school most mornings. She'd trailed a green hosepipe along the shopfronts in order to clean Kate's door, and was now directing the spray toward the gutter, job done.

Kate nodded, overwhelmed by the kindness of a stranger.

"Thank you," she said, more of a tearful whisper than she'd have liked. "I appreciate it more than you know."

The woman smiled, shy, and shrugged. "You're welcome."

Kate really wanted to lunge in for a hug, because, in truth, she badly needed one herself. "I'm Kate," she said instead. "I live upstairs."

The woman laid her hand on her chest. "Yushu." She looked away, distracted as one of her children appeared in her doorway and called out to her in Chinese. "Kids. I better go," she said, smiling again.

Kate wrapped her arms around herself and nodded, watching her neighbor walk away. "Thank you again."

Yushu probably didn't realize it, but that single act of neighborly solidarity was exactly what Kate needed to stiffen her backbone. Walking back inside the shop, she flipped the sign over to OPEN, bolstered by the kindness of a stranger.

45

"ANYTIME ON THURSDAY IS FINE TO RETURN THEM," KATE SAID, WAVING off a group who'd turned up in need of emergency TV-themed fancy-dress outfits and left the shop in head-to-toe *Peaky Blinders* chic. It had been her busiest day by far; she was glad to finally close the door and flick the bolt across. Her eyes skimmed the street scene, pretty certain balaclava man wouldn't put in an appearance while other people were around.

Her social media alert pinged on her mobile in the back pocket of her jeans as she headed upstairs, and then again, and again. She slowed on the steps, not reaching for her vibrating mobile, because these days her phone going frantic was a sure sign of incoming trouble. Dropping onto her sofa, she screwed up her face ready for impact and pulled her phone out. As long as it wasn't about Liv, it was okay.

So, it wasn't about Liv, but it wasn't okay either. Far from it. One of the big gossip sites had run a huge piece speculating on H's identity, listing their top-ten authors in the frame against their odds, none of whom were even male. And, of course, the article covered every last salacious detail of her own involvement, including snippets of her TV and radio interviews and snapshots of distressed readers who felt duped and lied to. All of it was damning, but none of it was new, until she reached the last paragraph, where her mouth fell open and stayed that way.

> Elliott's ex-husband Richard remained tight-lipped on the situation when we reached out to him for comment:
>
> "Out of respect for our daughter, I do not wish to comment on my ex-wife's erratic behavior in recent months, despite her having recently broken into and entered my home whilst I was out of the country. I hope she's receiving adequate support and the help she clearly needs at this time."

Kate read and reread it, then huffed and read it a third time. "You absolute bastard," she spat, incensed. It was hardly refraining from comment, was it? In one short paragraph Richard had called her erratic, accused her of burglary, and suggested she was in need of medical intervention. "No comment is two bloody words," she muttered, furious at the nerve of the man.

Clicking on social media confirmed what she'd expected: his non-comment was all over her author pages and many others besides, keeping the fire well and truly burning under the speculation and scandal.

**This really is the story that
keeps on giving**

someone posted, with a row of laughing faces.

It really is like being chopped into small pieces and fed to the lions every day, she thought, but stopped herself from typing. She cringed when she realized some big-name writers mentioned in the article had already taken steps to publicly rule themselves out as the secret author, people whose books she'd read and admired over the years. A chunk of her self-respect quietly broke off and dissolved into her bloodstream at the idea of them being hassled for comment, solidifying her determination that H should never reveal his identity. One person sitting on the bench of shame was more than enough.

At least the book itself hadn't been targeted, she thought, checking the online reviews as she did every day. No one could deny the quality and beauty of the story. Or they hadn't, up to now.

"Oh, fuck right off," she whispered, reading the most recent review from Disgruntled of Devon.

> Shame on Darrowby. If I hadn't bought this
> as an ebook I'd have set fire to it.

Twenty-nine people had already liked Disgruntled's comment, and it had only been posted that day.

MargoInManchester had also hopped online to vent her annoyance.

> I queued for a signed copy of this
> book by the fake author. I've re-gifted
> it to my boss for her birthday, because
> I hate her.

Kate gasped out loud at the whip-smart venom, and the fact that more than sixty-five people had clicked "like." There were more, but she turned her phone off and dropped it face down on the sofa.

She'd been hired to quietly represent H's book, and the way things were going the publisher would be asking her for their money back, citing breach of contract. They'd asked for a ghost author and ended up with a circus, and whether she liked it or not, Kate was the clown. People were laughing at her, adding the by-now familiar #calamitykate hashtag to their posts. And still she said nothing in public, keeping her fingers out of the piranha tank.

She panicked at the thought of Liv seeing all this, and messaged Nish to tell him to throw her mobile in the pool if necessary. He came back with the welcome news that Liv had put herself on a social media ban at his suggestion, and she was currently in the pool with the kids. He was too kind to be intentionally short or want to make her feel unnecessary, but something in his words left her feeling unbearably lonely.

BALACLAVA MAN DIDN'T TURN UP on Sunday. Whether it was because the shop was closed or he'd had a skinful the night before, she didn't know, but whatever the reason for his absence, Kate's relief was immense. She'd crouched behind the counter from six A.M. till eight, her stomach in knots and her eyes nailed to the door, then afterward crawled back upstairs to bed and pulled the covers over her head until midday.

Richard's knife between her ribs had upset her more than she cared to admit. Not because she still harbored feelings for him, but because their shared history obviously meant nothing to him, and he'd certainly not shown her any respect as the mother of his child, even though he was at pains to suggest otherwise. It probably wouldn't have cut so deep if everything else around her was peachy, but as it was, it felt like another kick in the teeth. The rate she was going, she'd need to ask Richard for his Turkish dentist's number.

Knowing Liv was safely out of the way for nine days more was a temporary relief, but also a ticking clock. There was an outside chance balaclava man wouldn't come back again, and an outside chance that the book being published in the United States wouldn't increase the scrutiny around her too much, and an outside chance that Liv would come back from Portugal and not be pulled straight back into the drama.

But Kate wasn't a gambling woman. Outside chances weren't enough to bet the house on. She couldn't leave Liv and the baby's safety in the hands of fate. She needed a plan.

46

"GOOD TO HAVE YOU BACK," CHARLIE SAID, AFTER TAPPING ON FIONA'S office door with his morning coffee in his hand. He'd arrived back in London late the night before; it was the first time they'd both been in the office since her trip away.

"Don't bother with pleasantries unless that coffee is for me."

The Caribbean sun might have warmed her usual pallor, but it had clearly done nothing to soften her approach. That was fine, because Charlie had some straight-talking of his own to do. He considered giving her his coffee, but instead turned to Felicity on reception and asked if she'd mind bringing another cup through when she had a moment.

Fiona made a point of checking her slim gold wristwatch. "We might need to reschedule this catch-up meeting to later," she said.

He didn't wait to hear why. "I'm afraid I can't," he said. "I've got an appointment this afternoon."

"Not in the diary," she said, arching her penciled brows.

He swallowed his annoyance. Fiona rarely bothered to keep him abreast of her schedule yet kept a keen eye on his.

"We need to talk about Kate," he said, stepping into the office and taking the seat opposite hers.

She made a show of slowly screwing the lid on her pen and placing it down in a ceramic pen tray on her desk. His gaze snagged on the tray. Deep blue marbled with lava orange.

"Indeed," she said, looking at him over the top of her glasses.

They paused while Felicity came in and set Fiona's coffee down, waiting until the door clicked to pick the conversation up.

"I have concerns about the way things are being handled," he said.

Fiona's expression flickered, a micro-tell of annoyance, gone as soon as it was there. "I spent time with her U.S. publisher a few weeks ago. They want her out there to do a raft of media interviews. She flies on Friday."

He put his coffee down and stared across the desk. "You're not serious."

She glared straight back. "I'm deadly serious. The backstory around the publication has become *the* story that's selling the book. They've paid big money to get their slice of the action and they want her out there to fulfill her contractual obligations, which in this case means national TV and radio slots to apologize for things in her own inimitable way, without revealing Hugh's identity, of course. God knows the woman is fond of her own voice, never one to use three words when three hundred will do—it's right in her wheelhouse, and for some unfathomable reason, she sells copies."

Fiona picked up her coffee cup, indicating the conversation was over as far as she was concerned.

"There's absolutely no way on this earth Kate is going to the U.S. or anywhere else to do some goddam hideous apology tour." Charlie banged his hand on the desk in temper. "She's taken too much heat because of all this already, not to mention the detrimental effect on her family. It was always an experiment, Fi, and however successful it's been in terms of sales, it's not sustainable on a personal level for Kate."

"Business strategy isn't personal," Fiona said, then sighed and slid her glasses down their golden chain, headmistress to pupil. "Charles, can I respectfully suggest you take a couple of steps back from the situation and let me handle things from here on in? You've allowed yourself to become rather too . . . embroiled."

"Respectfully, Fiona, you're overstepping the mark," he said.

Her eyebrows fired up into her rigid hairline.

"I'm not sure I've made myself properly clear, so for the purpose of clarity, let me speak plainly," he said. "Kate is my client, not yours, which means you don't get to make the decisions about what she does and doesn't have to do."

Fiona sipped her coffee, unaffected. "It's all there in the contract."

Charlie knew Kate's contract inside out and, technically, Fiona was right. He had one more ace to play, though, and now was the moment to show his hand.

"How does Hugh feel about your plan to send Kate to scrape and grovel on American TV?" he said, watching her reaction carefully.

She lifted one shoulder, her shoulder pad skimming her earlobe. "You know perfectly well that Hugh doesn't wish to have any involvement."

"So he doesn't know," Charlie said, flat.

Fiona's eyes narrowed. "He's away and uncontactable."

"As far as I'm aware, they have excellent mobile signal in Spain."

She leaned in, a crack finally appearing in her armor. "Leave Hugh out of this, he needs a break."

"As long as you leave Kate alone, because she needs one too."

Fiona stared at him, shaking her head with disappointment. "Jojo would have handled this very differently."

Charlie had had just about enough of having his father's memory held over him.

"Leave my father out of this," he said, shaking his head. "You know, Fiona, I've worried since he died that I don't have his famous gut instinct, but thanks to you, I know I do. Something about this whole experiment hasn't sat well with me since day one, and now, finally, I see what it is—it didn't take human unpredictability into account. The arrangement protected everyone but Kate, and now the shit has hit the fan, you're happy to hang her out to dry for financial gain, to ask her to publicly humiliate herself over and over again on international TV for the sake of sales. Muriel Blackstock was right—an AI ghost author *would* have been a better option, because real people are messy. Sometimes they screw up, and sometimes they say the wrong thing, and sometimes they put everyone else's needs in front of their own until they practically disappear."

Charlie paused for breath, and Fiona didn't take the chance to jump in.

"And you're right, with the benefit of his experience my father *would* have foreseen all of the things that could possibly go wrong, and he'd never have allowed Kate to sign that damn contract in the first place. But then you knew that all along, didn't you?"

Fiona folded her arms and put her head on one side. Her silence told him everything he needed to know.

"Cancel the U.S. tour, Fiona. Kate has nothing to apologize for and she isn't going anywhere." He pushed his chair back and left her office, and for once Fiona didn't insist on the last word.

47

BALACLAVA MAN RETURNED AGAIN THAT MORNING. KATE HAD DARED hope it was over after his absence the day before, but her heart dropped into her trainers when she came downstairs at a little after seven to find he'd already been and sabotaged the front door.

As she'd cleared away the mess, Kate considered whether it was time to involve the police; she couldn't allow this abuse to go on indefinitely. Balaclava man might eventually get bored and stop, but then again he might get frustrated by her lack of response and escalate his behavior. A brick instead of a trifle, perhaps, or something worse.

She flicked through the latest pictures from Portugal, her heart full at the sight of them all looking so relaxed. Sandy toes and sunburned noses, a shot of all of them pointing at Liv's belly, her hands pressed over her face as she laughed. The thought of her sister walking back into trouble turned her blood cold.

"DID SOMEONE ORDER LUNCH?"

She looked up as Charlie came through the shop door with a brown paper bag in his hand a little after midday. His latest text had let her know he was back in the country, but he hadn't mentioned coming over. She tried not to notice his deepened L.A. tan, and she didn't love the way her body reacted to the unexpectedness of him being there. The quickening of her breath, the warm flush on her neck.

"Depends what it is," she said.

He placed the bag on the counter in front of her.

"How have you been?" he asked.

She lifted one shoulder. "Busy. Liv's on holiday so I'm minding the shop for her."

He nodded. "You look tired."

The truth about what had been happening hovered in her throat, desperate to spill out. "How was L.A.?"

His jaw tightened. "Same as it always is."

"I wouldn't know, I've never been beyond Europe." She knew she was being obtuse, and she didn't like herself for it.

"I came to tell you that you won't be asked to have any further involvement with the book. No one is going to lean on you for interviews or appearances."

Kate all but laughed. "Oh, that's good, then, I'm glad I've served my purpose."

He faltered, frowning. "That isn't what I meant."

She shrugged, tired. "I'm sure it wasn't, Charlie. I'm glad the book has been such a success, I truly am. The author wrote something beautiful and readers love it, so you can all give yourselves a big old pat on the back for a job well done." She paused. "Hey, here's an idea—you could even write a rom-com about it with your ex-wife."

He looked as if she'd slapped him, and she closed her eyes and sighed.

"Sorry," she said. "You're right, I'm tired and cranky."

For a moment she thought he was going to leave, but he pushed the brown bag toward her instead. She looked at it, and then at him, then sighed and unraveled the top. The smell hit her first, taking her straight back to Cornwall.

"Cornish pasties," he said.

"I see that," she said. "Thank you."

"I was kind of hoping we could talk," he said.

She'd been feeling so alone over the last few days, his quietly spoken request was enough to soften her resolve. Crossing the shop, she flipped the sign to CLOSED and dropped the latch.

LIV HAD THE SMALLEST OF courtyards shoehorned in behind the shop, a tiny sun-trap she'd made the most of with a bench and a couple of potted plants. It served them well as a place to escape to with a sandwich, or a Cornish pasty with your agent who you just happen to have slept with. It might have been a blank page in their story, but she was having a hard time deleting it from her head as they sat either end of the bench with the brown paper bag between them.

"Liv's pregnant," she said.

"Wow, that's big news," Charlie said.

She nodded. "That's why she's away, getting over the shock."

"Have you been all right here on your own? No runaway T-Rex's giving you grief?"

"No." She looked down, ripping the paper bag open, suddenly so overwhelmed with the need to off-load that she couldn't meet his eyes.

He put his head on one side, studying her. "Sure?"

"For God's sake, Charlie, I said everything's fine, okay?" she snapped, tipping her head back to stop the tears gathering in her eyes from falling.

"It clearly isn't," he said. "Talk to me."

She looked at him fully then, hating the fact that the tears were sliding down her cheeks. "What do you want me to say? Congrats on your movie deal? I'm pissed off that my daughter is being comforted by my ex-husband's lover? I hate that you left the bed we were sharing to sit on the balcony and text your ex-wife? I'm scared my sister might lose the baby because she's so stressed about all the shit that's been happening with the book? I'm being terrorized by a guy in a fucking balaclava defacing the shop every morning and I don't have a bloody clue how to make it all stop?" She threw her hands up in the air, then stomped back inside the shop and stood with her back rigid against the wall, her hands pressed over her face.

Charlie followed her in, and pulled her hands down to look in her eyes.

"There was a lot there, and we can talk about all of it at some point, but a guy in a balaclava? What guy?" He was still holding on to her hands.

"I don't know who he is," she huffed. "He comes early every morning and throws food at the door, smearing it with his hands sometimes. I confronted him the other day and he threw it in my face."

"Fucking hell, Kate, you should have told me," he said, his tone harsh.

"Why? You were on the other side of the world, and I don't know if you're even my agent anymore. The book's done with, you said so yourself."

"I'm not just your goddam agent," he muttered, letting go of her hands to grip her shoulders instead. "Did he hurt you?"

"No." She was furious with herself for crying. "I need to make it all stop before Liv gets back. She's under doctor's orders to stay calm for the baby's sake. She's always been protective over me, but it's my turn to protect her now. And the baby."

"We go to the police," Charlie said, sure. "Right now."

She shook her head. "I can't. They'd involve Liv, it's her shop."

"Maybe she needs to be involved, it sounds as if someone has a grudge. A pissed-off customer?"

Kate looked at the floor. "It's trifle, so I think we can safely assume it's book-related." She felt ridiculous.

"Jesus." Charlie closed his eyes and scrubbed his hands over his face.

They stood in fraught silence. "Just go," she said, weary. "It's my problem to solve."

He reached out and took her face between his hands. "Is it fuck. I'm not going anywhere."

She stared into his cola-dark eyes, so close she could see the sunburst whiskey shards, and she leaned into him, because she was exhausted and she'd wanted to tell him every day, and she was sick of keeping up the pretense.

The heat of his body warmed hers, and his hands softened from a grip to cradling her jaw.

"You're not on your own anymore. Let me help you."

Kate let her face rest against his palm and finally allowed herself to feel relief. She'd been turning things over in her head all morning, an idea forming that would be much easier with Charlie's help.

"There is one thing you could do," she said. "Get me back on the sofa with Ruby and Niall."

48

HAVING ALREADY BEEN ON THE *Good Morning Show* SOFA ONCE BEFORE, you might imagine Kate would feel less overwhelmed at the prospect of doing it again. You'd be wrong. She was a bag of nerves by the time the car eased to a stop beside the river embankment outside the studios, shivering inside her cap-sleeved, full-skirted black dress. It was an old favorite, one of those pieces you reach for when you need something that makes you feel ready for anything.

Charlie was waiting for her and opened the car door, scanning her face. "Okay?"

She half nodded, half shrugged, not feeling okay at all. She'd stayed over at a hotel nearby last night and left the shop closed up, aware she'd probably return to a sour mess congealing in the summer heat.

"I think so," she said. "I mean, I'm terrified, I just want to get it over with."

She touched the small pendant around her neck, a delicate silver oyster shell and pearl she'd found in one of the harbor shops near Pink Cottage. It was her only jewelry beside her bangle. Just one bangle today, although she felt badly in need of two for good luck.

"Let's go inside," she said, anxious to get the ball rolling.

She appreciated the light you've-got-this touch of Charlie's palm against the base of her back as she walked a step or two ahead of him. He hadn't faltered when she'd asked him to book her onto the show, pulling all the necessary strings to make it happen. It hadn't been all that difficult in actual fact: the promise of an exclusive reveal had had the bookers juggling guests like oranges.

FORTY MINUTES LATER, KATE FOUND herself being quickly hugged by Ruby and Niall during the ad break, neither of them hiding their interest in what she was going to say. They knew she wanted to set the record straight; social-media-fueled drama was the show's bread and butter, they were gagging for the scoop.

"Ready?" Niall said, as the floor manager began to count them down. Kate caught Charlie's eye from his spot behind the camera, drawing strength from his steady presence. Ruby gave Kate's hand a quick squeeze beside her on the sofa, and then they were live to the nation.

"As promised before the break, novelist Kate Darrowby is here with us again, this time to set the record straight about the ongoing saga surrounding her debut book, *The Power of Love*," Niall said.

"Let's take a look back at the story so far." Ruby smiled, breezy, and the feed cut to a whistle-stop VT montage of the book's release, a snippet of Kate's previous sofa interview, the bestseller delisting scandal, snapshots of some of the avalanche of damning social media posts and speculation, all set to dramatic music. It played out like a soap opera, complete with stand-up rows and trifle-slinging. Kate kept her eyes focused on her laced fingers in her lap, not wanting to see the negativity right before she spoke up for herself.

"That all looks like quite the tumultuous ride," Niall said, as Ruby nodded and gazed at Kate.

"That's one way to put it," Kate said.

"Do you feel you've been treated unfairly?" Ruby said.

Kate shook her head. "No, no, I don't. People have reacted to what they've seen, and I haven't responded or defended myself up to now on the advice of the team around me, which I totally understand and agree with. But circumstances have changed recently and I need to at least try to explain myself so people can understand, if not forgive me."

"Go on," Niall said, clearly being told by the producer in his ear to say as little as possible.

Kate forced her shoulders down and her chin up. "My name isn't Kate Darrowby, and I'm not an author," she said. "I'm Kate Elliott, a divorcée who needed a job, and the only job I'd ever done outside of my husband's company was act on a soap when I was nineteen. I'd had a couple of glasses of wine one night and wrote to my old agent, and that was how I came to be in the right place at the right time—or my letter did, anyway. I was invited in to read an as-yet-unpublished novel, and if I loved it, they were looking for an unknown actor to stand in for the actual author who wasn't able to publish it under their own name."

"And do you know who that author is?" Ruby leaned toward her, straight in with the question the nation really wanted the answer to.

Kate paused, feeling pressure on H's behalf. "I genuinely don't," she said. "I wanted to, at the beginning, but given how things have turned out, I'm glad I don't."

"In case one of your family accidentally revealed that too?" Niall softened his smart aside with a rueful smile, but Kate wasn't ready to let the dig slide.

"No," she said. "My family has been dragged into this through no fault of their own."

"The speculation around who the real author is has been feverish, though, hasn't it?" Ruby said, refocusing the conversation back where she wanted it to be.

Kate nodded. "It has, and although I honestly don't know who they are, they've sent me kind, supportive messages and I know that writing this story was a personal catharsis for them, never intended for public eyes. They were brave enough to allow their publisher to share it with the public under certain conditions, and I know they've followed the fallout since with utter dismay. Does it matter who the author is, really? I was in tears on the train the first time I read it, because it's soul-baring, and vulnerable, and ultimately redeeming. I'd come through a horrible divorce and lost any faith in love, and reading that fragile, lionhearted love story made me believe again. I felt the power of the words actually superglue my heart back together."

She straightened her shoulders, and imagined Liv straightening her crown.

"Did I expect it to snowball into such a success that I'd end up on TV and national radio and at events signing readers' books? No, I absolutely didn't."

"And would you have refused the job if you'd known what it was going to lead to?" Niall said.

Kate took a breath. "I don't honestly know. I'll never be sorry that the book is out there. It's been my honor and privilege to help it on its way into readers' hands, but if I'd had the benefit of a crystal ball, there are some things I'd have done differently to protect the people I love."

Ruby nodded. "It's fair to say your family have become quite involved in the whole drama."

Kate swallowed hard, because Ruby had unwittingly cued her up perfectly.

"Yes," she said. "Readers have had their trust broken, something I didn't reckon on, and I'm sorry to my bones for that because I'm a reader too, first and foremost—books are in my blood. I accepted the job because love stories gave me somewhere to turn to when my daughter was tiny and didn't sleep through the night, and when my husband didn't come home at all, some nights. They've made me feel seen and safe, so as of today I'd like to just be Kate Elliott again, part of the reading community. If they'll have me."

Ruby and Niall nodded in unison, and she plowed on before they could ask her any questions.

"I know many people have seen the video online of my sister defending me," she said.

"Trifle-gate," Niall interjected, with an ironic raised brow. He really did play up to the camera.

"She reacted in the heat of the moment," Kate said. "We lost our mum when we were little girls. Liv's the eldest and has always felt responsible for me. She's the kindest, funniest, most loyal person you could ever wish to have in your corner, and I'd really appreciate it if people could leave her alone now, please? She's recently found out she's expecting a baby, and all of this stress is too much on her. She's spent the last ten years building her fancy-dress shop up, she makes all the costumes herself by hand, and every morning for the last week someone has been throwing trifle at the windows."

Kate saw the way Niall and Ruby sat to attention at this turn of events, and she didn't dare even look at Charlie.

"And I know it may sound harmless—my sister's away at the moment, thankfully, so I'm clearing up the mess—but actually it's become quite sinister. I went out the other day to try to see who's doing it, and a guy in a balaclava appeared and threw trifle right in my face. In my hair, in my mouth, in my eyes. I was alone in the street at half past six in the morning, and I'm honestly not telling you all this out of self-pity, but because it needs to stop before my sister comes home."

Ruby looked horrified. "You poor thing, Kate, that's horrible."

Kate swallowed hard, relieved she'd made it through the interview. They'd allowed her to speak for longer than her allotted time slot, and she could see the floor manager urgently gesturing for Niall and Kate to wind it up.

Niall took his cue and delivered his endpiece to the camera, then the familiar jingle sounded to signal the show was off-air for the day. Ruby pulled Kate into a quick hug as they stood.

"I hope they catch him and force-feed him trifle until he fucking chokes," she said into Kate's ear, completely different to the mild-mannered persona she portrayed on TV.

Kate gulped back tears, because it was such a Liv thing to say, and then she found herself jostled around and being de-mic'd until she was finally back across the studio with Charlie. He was subdued as they left the building, steering her across to a quiet bench in the shade of a willow tree on the embankment.

"I just hope that going public will be enough to stop him," she said.

"And what if it isn't?"

She sighed. "Then I'll have no choice but to involve the police. I messaged Nish this morning to fill him in on everything, asked him to make sure Liv sticks to her social media ban for the next few days. He said she's the new queen of Zen, which I can hardly imagine, but thank God right now."

"You know it's going to go nuclear online," he said.

She pulled her mobile from her bag and turned it back on. It had been switched off in the studio and now burst into noisy life.

"Can I suggest something radical?" Charlie said. "A self-imposed social media ban might not be such a bad idea for you either, even if it's just for the rest of today."

She looked at her mobile, the furious torrent of alerts and messages stacking up, missed calls from journalists, and she closed her eyes, exhausted by the whole thing.

"If it wasn't for my family, I'd chuck it in the river," she said, and in that moment she meant it. So much of her life had been taken over by Kate Darrowby's social media.

Charlie reached across and flicked it on to silent. "Better?"

She nodded, dropping her mobile in the bottom of her bag as if it was burning her fingers. If Liv could do it, maybe she could too; a day-detox at least. She'd done just about as much as she could manage for today.

"Stay in the hotel again tonight," he said.

Kate had expected this. It had been Charlie's idea for her to stay at the hotel last night. He'd made the reservation and billed Francisco & Fox; Kate had almost insisted on paying for herself and then didn't, because there was a certain justice to Fiona footing the bill.

"We've been over this," she said. Last night had been necessary to ensure she didn't miss her TV slot, but it was time for her to go home.

"Are you going to open the shop this afternoon?"

"Just for a couple of hours," she said. "I feel bad closing all day—you never know when someone's going to need an emergency Spider-Man mask."

"Or you could just take the rest of the day off," he said. "Get some rest?"

"I'm fine, really," she said. "It'll help take my mind off everything if I'm busy."

"I could take the train back with you, keep you company?"

"He's not going to come in the middle of the afternoon, Charlie, I'm not in danger. In fact, I doubt I'll ever see him again now I've outed him on national TV."

He didn't look convinced.

"It's important to me to do this on my own," she said, more softly. "Going in there today, doing that . . . it felt good, like reclaiming my old self. I'm not scared. I'm not running away. It was my way of sticking my fingers up at the camera and telling him to piss off, and it feels amazing. If I avoid going home now, or let you escort me and keep guard, then it unpicks all of that hard work. I'm going to go home and open the shop, and then tonight when I go to bed I won't lie there worrying about the morning. Bring it on."

49

IT WAS EARLY AFTERNOON BY THE TIME KATE REACHED THE SHOP. SHE WAS surprised to find the door clean, a yellow Post-it note stuck to the glass.

Saw you on TV, wow, so amazing! Hope this morning was the last we see of him. Yushu x

He'd been again, then. She wasn't shocked. Tomorrow would be the acid test. Letting herself into the shop, she threw her bag behind the counter and headed into the kitchenette to put the kettle on. She'd been true to her word so far and not checked social media. Part of her wanted to, but a bigger part of her feared her appearance on TV might have had the opposite effect and escalated the situation. Was she being mocked all over the internet? Was the consensus that she deserved everything she got? The doom-laden thoughts were enough to make avoiding social media altogether the preferable option. It wasn't going anywhere. It would still be there tomorrow, and the next day, and the day after that.

LATER THAT EVENING, SHE SAT alone in her flat, the TV on low, a glass of wine in her hand. Her eyes settled on the shelf she'd put

up with her own hands, a place to display a copy of the book surrounded by Liv's twelve-piece crocheted mouse orchestra. Reaching for her phone, she forced herself to avoid social media and
just check if she'd heard from Liv. There was a photo, Liv with a
cushion up her T-shirt pulling a what-have-I-done face. Kate
touched the screen, wishing she could teleport and be with her
sister.

> I've just remembered we have
> twins in the family

she sent, with a pair of laughing faces.
    Liv appeared online.

>> Piss off. Am eating a massive
>> burger on the beach, so I win.

> I'll let you have that seeing as you're
> all sun-kissed and preggers. Have a
> cocktail on me. Oh, that's right, you can't

Kate sent back with more laughing faces.

>> Ha bloody ha, I'd kill for a glass
>> of wine. Is the shop okay?

Kate felt reassured from Liv's question that she was sticking
faithfully to her social media ban, because after her TV appearance that morning there was bound to be an avalanche of trifle-
gate chatter online.

> Everything's fine! Go have fun xx

Liv sent back a kiss emoji and disappeared offline, and Kate sat pensive on the sofa, tempted to break her own mini social media ban. Then she looked at the twelve small mice again, and because she wanted to linger in the glow of Liv's lighthearted mood, she turned her phone off and threw it back in her bag. Tomorrow would be soon enough.

50

CHARLIE TILTED THE DRIVER'S SEAT AS FAR BACK AS IT WOULD GO, EVERY bit as uncomfortable as you'd imagine a six-foot-two man might be if he was spending the night cramped in a small old sports car. He offered up silent thanks to his father for being of the car rug generation, glad to have something for warmth at least. Not that it was cold, but the suggestion of comfort was welcome all the same. He wasn't sure if he'd imagined the lingering trace of Jojo's scent as he'd pulled it over himself, and he'd closed his eyes and allowed the rug and the car to feel like his father's arms around him. What he wouldn't give. To the rest of the world Jojo Francisco had been a firecracker of a man, raconteur and fierce competitor, but to Charlie he'd been father, best friend, and protector-in-chief. Charlie hoped that if he could see his son right now, he'd approve of the decisions he'd made of late.

He'd parked the car far enough away from the fancy-dress shop for Kate not to spot him, but still close enough to keep watch for anyone suspicious in a balaclava. She'd told him she wanted to handle things her way and he absolutely respected that, and there was every chance she'd already done enough to put a stop to things. But he wasn't prepared to gamble where Kate was concerned. Setting the alarm on his mobile for five A.M., he closed his eyes and tried to find a position where the gearstick wasn't jabbing his knees.

KATE SLEPT BADLY AND WOKE well before her five A.M. alarm, too full of nervous energy to lie in bed and let her mind race down dark avenues. She'd usually pick up her phone and doomscroll in these situations, but she held steady to the pact she'd made with herself the day before. She was going to wait until after she'd opened up the shop at nine o'clock, then make coffee and dive into her phone. By that time she'd know for sure if her TV appearance had worked. If balaclava man turned up again today, she'd made the decision to say enough is enough and involve the police. A hopeful part of her wanted to feel she'd seen him off herself, although even that scenario had its downside. She'd always wonder who he was, what had driven him to such lengths.

She couldn't face food, and coffee tasted like ash in her mouth. She showered and clock-watched, putting the radio on for company as she pulled her hair back in a low bun and dressed in jeans and a T-shirt. Looking in the mirror, she added a slick of mascara and gloss, armor because she was done cowering. She was ready to sit outside, and if balaclava man dared to come again this morning, she was going to film him and file a police report.

51

HEADING DOWNSTAIRS JUST BEFORE SIX, SHE HELD HER BREATH AS SHE checked the door in case he'd been by. Nothing. She hadn't really expected there to be. If he came it was usually half past six; probably en route to whatever it was he did with himself afterward. What did people who committed random acts of petty violence do with their days? It was hard to imagine him carrying on to his office job, washing any traces of cream from his hands before sitting at his desk and cracking a joke with a colleague. The thought of him shoving his balaclava in his pocket and going about his day infuriated her enough to propel her outside to wait.

THE STREET WAS QUIET, PALE morning sun casting the other side of the road in shadow. She'd grabbed her sunglasses from behind the counter, and she hid behind them now as she scanned left and right, on high alert. It was a typical wide suburban road scattered with a mix of shops and residential flats, chosen years ago by Liv for its footfall and passing trade. Not that you'd know it at that hour of the morning. It was usually deserted, but this morning Kate could see a gaggle of people in the distance. She squinted hard behind her dark glasses, trying to make the figures out. It looked for all the world like an eccentric hen party, but they'd have to be pretty hard-core hens to still be on it at six A.M., especially on a weekday. They were making their way along her side of the road. She checked the time again. Six-fifteen. Maybe he wouldn't come. Or maybe he would and get derailed by the hen party, so she'd have to stand outside and wait again tomorrow. *God, please cross the road, girls,* she thought, *I can't stay in this state for another twenty-four hours.*

The crowd drew nearer and, sadly, they didn't cross over. Kate was torn between watching them approach and scanning the street, but they were close enough now for her to spot something that made her heart start to thud. Six instantly recognizable *Bridgerton*-inspired dresses, Liv's beautiful handiwork on full display. Her mind couldn't put the pieces together. The *Bridgerton* wedding had been last weekend, she was sure of it, and the dresses weren't due back in the shop for a couple of weeks at least. But there was no doubt in her head, those bridesmaids were right now marauding their way up the road toward her, along with a gang of other women too, most of them dressed in more usual clothes for a Thursday morning. Except weren't those a couple of the 1930s glam *Peaky Blinders* outfits she'd leased out a few days ago? What the hell was happening here?

She checked the time on her mobile again, thoroughly confused. Six-twenty A.M. One of the crowd spotted her outside the shop and called her name, and they all picked up their pace to a trot, louder now as they approached.

"Morning, Kate," someone said. One of the bridesmaids.

"We've come to help," another said as they clustered outside the fancy-dress shop. There were at least twenty of them, maybe closer to twenty-five. Kate slid her sunglasses into her hair and pressed her hand to her throat, overwhelmed.

"What . . . ? I mean, how . . . ?"

"We saw you on TV," someone said, threading through to the

front of the crowd. "No way we're letting some guy harass you like that."

Kate looked at the women grouped around her, dumbfounded. And then she spotted a face she recognized: Claire, the supermarket assistant whom Liv had thrown the trifle at in the first place.

"We're all book people, and we get it now, you're one of us," Claire said, a tremor in her voice. "I hate how this trifle thing has gotten out of hand, it was all something and nothing and should have stayed that way. I'm really sorry, I wish I'd never posted it."

"We saw people talking in our online book club about gathering here to help you today," one of the bridesmaids said. "Liv has been so great to us, we wanted to show our appreciation."

"Same," one of the Peaky Blinders said, her feathered headband quivering as she nodded her head.

"*The Power of Love* is the best book I've read this year," someone said.

Everyone started to speak over one another about the book, and Kate took a moment to pull herself together as a car drew up.

"Is he one of this lot?" Claire jumped to attention as a bunch of guys tumbled out of the doors.

Kate sucked in a sharp breath; she recognized those soccer shirts.

"Did someone order security?" One of them laughed, rubbing his hands together as if he'd come for a rumble. Kate remembered him as the guy who'd first offered her a beer on the train.

"What are you all doing here?" she said, her hand on his arm.

He shrugged. "We know a thing or two about being judged a certain way," he said.

"Thought you might fancy a beer," his mate said, pulling a can out of his pocket which he'd obviously had there for comedic effect.

Kate started to laugh, slightly hysterical as the gold soccer shirts threaded among the *Bridgerton* dresses and the *Peaky Blinders* girls.

Six twenty-four A.M. "Okay, form a line in front of the shop," someone called, and everyone shuffled haphazardly into a rowdy barricade.

"He might not even come," Kate said, still wrapping her head around the idea of these strangers all wading in to defend her and Liv. She stood near to the door, flanked on each side by *Bridgerton* bridesmaids.

"The absolute nerve of him," someone whispered, and they all turned their heads in unison to see a bike approaching from the far end of the street.

"Quiet, everyone," Claire whispered, like the floor manager on a costume drama. They were scattered in a line, a statue-still bracelet of color and drama.

An expectant hush fell over them, like guests waiting for the lights to flick on at a surprise party. There was no exact plan as balaclava man drew closer, one hand jauntily on his handlebars, the other reaching inside his jacket for his ammunition. It was as if he hadn't spotted the difference that morning, distracted maybe, by his task. He was too close, slowing to a stop almost, by the time the crowd erupted, lunging toward him with a battle cry that filled the air with expletives and heaving bridesmaid cleavage. To give the guy his credit, his reflexes were sharp, throwing trifle down the front of his jacket as he whipped his bike around and pedaled hell for leather in the opposite direction. He'd probably have made his escape too, if it wasn't for someone else coming toward him down the middle of the road.

"Charlie," Kate breathed.

The rider tried to swerve but Charlie was faster, blocking his path, sending the bike in one direction and the rider sliding on his backside in the other. The crowd swept forward like a wave, encircling him to block all possible escape routes.

Kate stepped up and pulled the balaclava off his head, staring at last at the person who'd been making her life a misery. Messy blond hair, defiant gray eyes, a twenty-something nobody of note, not recognizable to her at all.

"Oh, for fuck's sake," someone hissed behind her, loud and disgusted. Claire moved forward to stand beside Kate, staring at him in disdain. "Ciaran?"

The guy on the road wiped his hands down his legs, smearing trifle and grit on his jeans.

"I was only doing it for you," he said, scowling at Claire. "You're so obsessed with your blog and your bloody love stories. This book, that book, every fucking other book."

The crowd gawped. If the *Bridgerton* girls had had their fans, they'd have flapped them furiously.

"Don't even, Ciaran," Claire said, hands on her hips. "Of all the people, my own sodding fiancé . . ." She raised her eyes to the skies. "I can't believe this is happening. I want the ground to literally open and swallow me up."

"Swallow *him* up more like," someone said. "Dissing love stories."

"How are normal men ever supposed to compete with twatty book heroes?" Ciaran moaned, wiping trifle through his hair.

"By not throwing pudding at us, for starters," an older woman in a straw hat shouted from the back.

"Or terrorizing us every day," Kate said.

"Maybe you should read some of those love stories instead of insulting them, you might actually learn something," Claire said.

"You could start with Kate's book," one of the *Peaky* girls said, taking an elegant drag from her elongated cigarette holder, even though there was no cigarette in the end of it.

"It's not mine anymore," Kate said, not prepared to go down that particular road again.

"Oh, trust me, everyone gets that after yesterday, but it kind of *is* still yours too," Claire said. "You were really heartfelt on TV. I felt like such a cow. I think most booklovers would have done the exact same thing if they'd been in your position. I know I would."

A ripple of agreement went round the crowd, and out of the corner of her eye Kate saw Ciaran try to get to his feet and sidle away. Charlie was behind him, a heavy hand on his shoulder to hold him down.

"Not until they say so, pal." He looked at Kate to give her the choice, and the crowd fell quiet, many of them enthralled by Charlie's cool presence. They had no idea who he was or where he'd come from, but they were totally here for whatever it was zinging between him and Kate.

Kate stared at the trifle-splattered man spread-eagled on the road. He was no further threat to Liv. She turned to Claire.

"It's your call," she shrugged.

Claire stared at her fiancé, the look of a truly disappointed woman. "Just go to work," she sighed.

Ciaran clambered up, a sticky, undignified mess, and when he opened his mouth to plead his case, Claire held her hand up, not ready to listen. The crowd parted for him to leave, their arms folded, their faces all set in the same "don't mess with the book community" expression.

He scuttled away and picked his bike up, giving it a shake before pedaling off, not daring to glance back.

"There's not enough flowers in the world to make up for this one," someone shouted after him.

"Or diamonds, or chocolate," one of the bridesmaids chipped in.

Kate cupped her hands around her mouth and yelled, "Or books," and the women erupted into noisy whistles and applause.

52

KATE HAD NEVER SEEN THE SHOP SO FULL, AND SNAPPED A QUICK PHOTO for Liv to get a kick out of at some point. The soccer fans had crammed themselves back into the car and driven away blaring the horn, and then everyone else had crowded inside the fancy-dress shop. Kate stood on Liv's alterations stool so she could see them all.

"I wish I had some champagne to pop," she said. "Because that was bloody amazing! I can't believe you all came down here, you've blown my mind." She made hand explosions in the air around her head and laughed, giddy. "I haven't even dared go online since yesterday, I didn't know if I'd said enough, or too much and made it even worse, but that . . . this . . . the way you all came marching up the street out there . . . it was like a scene from a film I'd pay good money to see."

"Readers united," the woman in the straw hat said. "We should start an online group with the soccer guys, one of them was right up my street."

"Did he happen to have husky-blue eyes?"

Kate turned to the Peaky Blinder giving her the speculative side-eye and shook her head. "If he did, it was a coincidence.

That whole first-love-on-the-train story was a throwaway line that got wildly out of hand."

One of the *Bridgerton* girls standing near to Charlie over by the door turned and studied his face briefly. "Brown," she stated, earning an under-the-breath laugh from most of the room.

Claire held both hands up. "Can I please apologize again for my dick of a fiancé? I could have literally died when I realized it was him."

"In his defense—not that he's entitled to any—he was right about one thing. Fictional men are the best," one of the *Peaky* girls shrugged, knotting her long string of pearls.

"Probably because it's usually women who write them," someone said, raising a laugh.

Kate caught Charlie's eye at the back of the shop. She had no idea how he'd even come to be out there this morning, but in the moment, it had seemed to make total sense.

"Maybe he thought he was making a grand gesture?" someone suggested.

"I'd have preferred a bookstore gift card," Claire said, making everyone laugh.

"Well, I'm just glad to know who it was and why," Kate said. "And you know what the worst thing is? I bloody love trifle, but I'll never be able to face it again after this."

THE GATHERING THINNED QUICKLY, THE morning pull of jobs or family claiming everyone now the day was firing up.

"And then there were two," Charlie said, closing the door.

Kate pressed her hands against her cheeks, incredulous. "Wasn't that *wild*? I half wish Liv had been here because she'd have loved it, although for Ciaran's sake, it's probably better that she's in a different country." She shook her head. "I can't get over it, all those people."

He nodded, then checked the time. "I hate to say this, but there's somewhere else I need to be."

"Oh." Disappointment crashed through her. The morning had been such a roller coaster, so many unexpected turns and euphoria-inducing moments. This was the first time she'd been able to catch her breath and there was so much she wanted to say, to ask.

"I'll call you later," he said, aviators on.

She didn't try to waylay him, because she could see his mind was already somewhere else.

FOR A DAY THAT HAD started with such momentum, the morning soon settled down to a steady ebb and flow of customers. Her phone notifications were off the scale, and every time she checked social media she found it ablaze with that morning's events. As with everything, someone unconnected had caught the scenes outside the fancy-dress shop on their phone camera and shared it with the rest of the world, and the story had been added to and embroidered as it spread across reader groups and book blogs like wildfire. It was obvious from the comments that some of the people who'd actually been there that morning had tried to add proper context, but the angle of the phone footage didn't quite catch Ciaran's face and no one had exposed his identity. Kate found herself relieved; having been at the center of a social media scandal herself, she didn't wish it on anyone else, even if he kind of deserved it.

Her mobile buzzed, a message from Charlie, a pin dropped on a location map at a hotel bar she knew of but had never been to.

Meet me at seven?

She studied his words, looking for clues that weren't there. She tried out several long-winded replies and deleted them all, and in the end she sent back just one word.

Yes

53

CHARLIE TAPPED FIONA'S OPEN DOOR AND, OUT OF POLITENESS, WAITED to be invited in. The atmosphere between them had been decidedly frosty since their showdown about the proposed American tour, and she hadn't yet said a word about Kate's impromptu appearance on the sofa with Niall and Ruby.

"Come," she barked. "And close the door."

He took a seat opposite her. She let out a long, exaggerated sigh and lowered her glasses to stare at him.

"Charles," she said, with the smallest shake of her head.

No one else had ever called him Charles, not even his father.

"We need to talk," he said.

"Evidently so," she said.

She wasn't someone who fidgeted with the end of a pen or bit her lip. She laced her fingers on the desk, diamonds flashing, a power move she'd perfected over the years.

"I release you," she said.

He stared, thrown off his stride. He'd come to talk to her about his place at the agency. It was so like her to pre-empt and control the direction of the conversation.

"You *release* me?"

"You're a good man, Charlie, and you've got the makings of

a decent agent, but you simply don't want this the way your father did. You don't have his fire. You need to want it with every fiber of your being to be the best in this business."

She was right, of course.

"The other day," he said, "when you said I'd become too personally involved with Kate to have sound judgment—it's true."

She rolled her eyes. "Business and pleasure don't mix. You have to choose one or the other." She paused. "Choose wisely, Charlie."

He glanced at Fiona's tell-tale blue-and-orange-marbled pen tray, and then at a framed photograph on the windowsill. To the casual eye it was just a natural shot of his father laughing at someone off camera, Fiona presumably, but the now-familiar riverside setting behind him told a much more personal story.

"I went to the Henley apartment," he said, watching her eyes, seeing nostalgia soften her resolve as she glanced at Jojo's photo too. The prolonged silence sat between them like a third person in the room, someone in a wrinkled linen blazer with a decidedly loud bow tie.

"He and I were too alike," she said eventually. "Too driven by our reputations, too aware of what other people would think." She stopped, choosing her words carefully. "We'd been business partners and friends for a very long time. He was a tower of strength for me when Bob died."

Charlie could remember Fiona being around when his mother died too, her no-nonsense presence holding his father together. He'd never picked up on any sense of romance between them, but then he'd spent little time around them in their later years, too busy living his own life in the United States. He realized now that they'd become more to each other in the years after Bob died, that somewhere along the line their friendship had deepened into love. The Henley apartment made perfect sense—

a place out of time, somewhere only they knew, impersonal by design, personal to them.

"I remember Kate," Fiona said, jumping around the time-line. "She was a loose cannon even back then, too much hair and a laugh that rattled the office windows. All that vulnerability and strength came over clearly onscreen, she was a director's dream." She shook her head, still looking at Jojo's photo. "Your father adored her, said she reminded him of Jane Fonda in *Barefoot in the Park*."

Charlie swallowed the sudden lump in his throat, moved to know his father had held Kate in such affection. "Thank you for telling me," he said.

"He was crushed when she left. I feared history might repeat itself when she blew back in, another Francisco heart to break." Fiona sighed and looked back at Charlie. "Hugh's book is selling because he speaks with such tender truth about grief. He used the manuscript almost as a portal, somewhere to release the enormity of his emotions. Readers can relate, because sooner or later we all lose someone we love."

She was talking about the book, but also, he realized, about Jojo. Fiona's personal connection to the story had always been the driving force behind getting it published, and perhaps also the reason she'd begrudgingly accepted Kate's involvement too; in her own inimitable way, the whole thing had been about honoring the memory of the man she loved.

"What will you do if I leave?" Charlie said, because however serious she was about releasing him, he couldn't imagine her running the agency alone.

She shrugged. "I've been considering winding things down since he died."

An unsettling thought crossed Charlie's mind. "You didn't keep things going because of me, did you?"

Her eyes flickered to the photo of his father, then back to him. "Oh, don't give yourself so much credit, Charles. I think I'll try a longer cruise. Eat shrimp. Read some books."

Charlie looked away, choked up. Fiona had been in his life forever, and in his parents' absence, she'd been watching over him without him realizing it.

"I release you, Fi," he said. He wasn't certain, but he thought he saw tears gather in her eyes. "Can I hug you?"

"You most certainly cannot," she said, sliding her glasses back up her nose. "Ask Felicity to bring me some coffee on your way out."

He nodded, getting up to leave.

"Oh, and Charlie?"

He turned back in the doorway.

"Kate might want to watch the *Good Morning Show*"—she looked at her watch—"in about five minutes' time."

54

KATE FLIPPED THE OPEN SIGN OVER TO CLOSED AND DASHED UPSTAIRS TO turn the TV on. Charlie's text had been short and sweet, passing on Fiona's message, leaving her with an ominous sense of anticipation in her gut. The show had been on for a while and she was beginning to worry she might have missed whatever it was she was supposed to catch, when the camera panned to Ruby and Niall on the sofa.

"And now for our special guest, international bestselling crime author Hugh Hudson," Ruby said, as the shot widened to include a distinguished guy sitting on the sofa opposite. Kate leaned in, remembering how it felt to be under that exact spotlight.

"Welcome, Hugh," Niall said, a hardback sample of Hugh's upcoming novel in his hands. "I have to confess to being a major DI Rivers fan—this copy might just be finding its way home with me."

"It's been a long time coming," Hugh said, and Kate slid forward in her chair, her eyes glued to the screen. She'd know that voice anywhere. Hugh Hudson. *H.* So it hadn't been a random letter after all. Her mind went back to Charlie's advice when she was choosing a pseudonym—stick to something that still feels like you. Hugh would have known that perfectly well, of course.

She drank in the details of his face, slotting him in to her memory as the man in the T-Rex costume, the guy she'd been swapping emails with all of these months. She listened as he answered a few perfunctory questions about his latest book.

"I'm afraid this won't be in the bookstores for a little while yet," he said, prying the hardback from a disappointed Niall's hands. "And they say you should never judge a book by its cover." Hugh's rich Welsh baritone was music to Kate's ears. "Which happens to be especially true in this case."

He peeled the DI Rivers dust cover from the book and revealed a second cover hidden underneath: *The Power of Love* by Kate Darrowby. It was clear from their slack jaws that neither Ruby nor Niall had seen it coming, and Hugh took advantage of the lull to control the interview.

"I'm the mystery author who wrote this book," he said, swallowing. "It's about my beautiful wife, Eleanor, an attempt to navigate my way through my grief. It was a meditation and a relief, of sorts—balm for my soul, if you will. I didn't intend it for publication, that all came afterward, and I certainly didn't intend for anyone else to get dragged into the whole circus it's turned into."

Ruby had recovered herself enough to take the reins. "Wow, Hugh, that's a real bolt out of the blue! Of all the names in the frame, I don't think I've ever heard mention of yours."

"A grisly old crime writer doesn't fit the bill, eh? Especially a male one?"

He was doing himself a great disservice there, but neither of them corrected him because he was right about one thing—everyone had assumed it was a woman.

"I'd like to publicly apologize to every author whose name has been dragged into this, I owe you all a drink or ten. But most of all I'd like to say thank you to Kate Elliot, the woman who's

taken so much heat about this, it's a wonder she hasn't spontane-
ously combusted."

"We had her here on the show just a few days ago," Niall said.

"I know you did," Hugh said. "I watched it. And I hope she's
watching this now, and that everyone will listen when I say that
without her this book would never have seen the light of day. It's
been agony watching her name dragged through the mud, she's
an absolute diamond."

"What's made you decide to come forward now, Hugh?"
Niall said.

Hugh rubbed his hand across his eyes and sighed. "I'm a
crime writer, Niall, I don't like loose ends. I thought in the beginning that this book was too different for my readers to stomach,
and if I'm honest, part of me didn't want to be labeled a romance
writer."

"And now?" Ruby said.

Hugh shrugged. "Now I know I was being a prize fool," he
said. "Losing Eleanor ripped my heart out. I'll never get over it,
and nor do I want to. But I wrote this book for her, and it did her
the greatest injustice for people not to know that our love story
inspired this one. She'd have wanted the world to know, and so
do I."

Ruby looked misty-eyed. "I love that, so romantic," she said.

Niall nodded. "But just to be clear, you *are* still releasing the
next DI Rivers soon, aren't you?"

"Of course." Hugh looked at the book in his hands. "But
right now I'm proud of *this* book, and I'm proud to call myself a
romance writer."

Ruby and Niall wrapped the interview up, and Kate sagged
against her chair, tear-stained and overwhelmed with affection for
Hugh Hudson: the man, the T-Rex, the romance writer.

Dear Hugh,

Thank you, you didn't need to do that, but I'm so grateful that you did, and that you're proud to claim the book as yours. Your love story deserves it.

Yours,

Kate x

Dear Kate,

It seems to me that you've experienced everything about being an author except for actually writing a book, which is a shame.

I've something to run by you. The publishing team are desperate for more where *The Power of Love* came from, and the way I see it, it came from you and me.

I happen to know a thing or two about writing novels, and nothing at all about writing love stories, other than my own. Would you consider riding the author horse again, only this time in the saddle rather than underneath the hooves? Working with you has been the unexpected joy I have found in all of this and I'd selfishly love to continue our partnership.

Yours,

Hugh x

55

KATE ARRIVED A LITTLE EARLY AT CHARLIE'S SUGGESTED MEETING POINT, so she took a moment for herself on an empty bench in the square to people-watch. A jogger in 1970s-style piped terry shorts and huge headphones weaving around an older couple, grandparents perhaps, pushing the kind of vintage pram you might see in royal baby photographs. A woman in corporate dress and trainers, her thumbs flying over her mobile screen as she strode along the path without glancing up. A guy snoozing on the grass with his hat over his face and an open book flat on his chest. Kate absorbed the random snapshot of life, letting the relaxed mood settle her nerves. The vague scent of restaurant food being prepared for evening dinner dates, the distant, ever-present rumble of London traffic. A slow burn sense of anticipation.

Her eyes moved to the hotel entrance, the low-key elegance of the stone facade, navy canopies above the windows and timeless brass revolving doors. It was an if-you-know-you-know kind of place, loyal customers who only told a handful of people about it for fear of it becoming well known. Very Charlie, in other words, she thought, composing a text to Liv in her head.

A small dog veered close by on an extendable lead, and its owners took the hint and clustered around the other end of the bench, a young family with ice-cream-faced kids, a stroller, and the dog.

"Sorry," the mum laughed as her toddler clambered up in the middle and almost upended himself onto Kate.

Kate smiled, reminded of Alice at that age, looking forward to experiencing the baby days again secondhand with Liv.

"It's fine," she said, taking it as her nudge to get going. "I was just leaving, you guys can spread out."

She wandered toward the hotel, enjoying the flick of her skirt around her calves. She'd known straightaway what she was going to wear tonight, a midnight silk Max Mara–inspired halter-neck Liv had made for her a few years ago. It was a confidence-booster dress, cut to skim and flatter, backless with a thigh-grazing split on one side revealing enough skin to feel daring. It felt appropriate: she'd dared to do difficult things over the last few days—baring her soul on the *Good Morning Show,* stepping outside to confront balaclava man alone, or so she thought, this morning. And now she was here, tonight. Meeting Charlie in her favorite dress. She'd made several weighty decisions over the last few weeks, and she knew he'd been wrestling with some hefty ones of his own too.

Twenty years previously, she'd walked into Jojo Francisco's office for a life-changing conversation. It didn't escape her notice that she was here again now, walking into a conversation with a different Francisco, knowing that, one way or the other, it would change her life again.

Placing her hand on the brass door bar, she lifted her chin and stepped inside.

56

IT WAS INSTANTLY COOLER IN THE QUIETLY LUXURIOUS HOTEL LOBBY, scented with the heady old-school opulence of fresh flowers and decades of expensively perfumed clientele. Kate glanced around and spotted a sign for the Library Bar, her stomach vaulting as she took the winding steps up through a stone arch, following the sound of live piano music. Books lined the walls, and a few scattered customers sat in deeply upholstered leather chairs clustered around polished wooden tables. A focal-point bar formed the centerpiece of the room, intricate stained-glass panels backlit to create a soft, inviting ambience, a wall of spirits, mirrored shelves containing endless different liqueurs and cocktail ingredients. It reminded Kate of a grand old cruise liner, the kind of place you might take a seat at and order a glass of champagne. She couldn't see Charlie at first glance, so she perched straight-backed on one of the tall barstools, shaking her head when the uniformed barman glanced across.

"I'm waiting for someone," she said. She wasn't concerned Charlie wouldn't show, and it wasn't many minutes until someone took the seat next to hers.

"Can I buy you a drink?" Smoky words, fingertips skimmed lightly down her exposed spine.

She turned to look at him, two strangers in a bar.

"Champagne would be lovely."

The barman popped a bottle and poured them both a tall, chilled glass, leaving the rest in an ice bucket for them to help themselves.

"You look incredible."

She sipped her champagne. Everything about tonight felt different, as if the world had tilted a degree or two on its axis, an invisible glitter of possibility in the air.

"How was your day?" she said, angling her body toward him, her knees grazing his. Every move felt choreographed, slow-burn sexy, a promise waiting to be fulfilled.

"It started out pretty wild," he said. "After that it got a bit"—he wavered his palm flat in the air—"rocky. But this part"—he gestured between them—"this part is my favorite bit."

"Funny thing," she said. "My day started out pretty wild too."

He sipped his drink. "Is that so?"

She toyed with the stem of her glass, thinking back over the craziness of the day. "All kinds of hell broke loose for a while, like a scene from a movie, and then this guy appeared out of nowhere to help me. He's done it enough times now for it to feel like a habit, as if he has some kind of magic knack for knowing when I need him."

"Like Superman?" he said. "I don't think he'd look good in tights."

"More *Top Gun*," she said, touching the aviators he'd put down on the bar.

"Only taller," he said.

"He looks at me sometimes with his beautiful whiskey-cola eyes," she said, holding his gaze over the rim of her glass. "And I want to ask him what's really going on behind them, but I don't."

She wasn't certain if she'd moved forward or he had, but her knees were inside his now, his hand on her leg.

"Why not?"

She sighed, bit her lip. "Because we met under really bizarre circumstances which didn't allow space for us to have feelings for each other."

He nodded and looked down into his glass. "And now?"

She lifted one shoulder. "I know what I want, but I don't know how he feels."

He swallowed. "He's probably working out how to tell you he's realized the best way to honor his father's memory is to follow his gut rather than walk in his footsteps."

She nodded slowly. "And where is his gut leading him?"

"Here. To tell you he's decided being a talent agent isn't what he wants to do with his life."

He splayed his hand on the side of her leg, his thumb a slow, warm stroke over her kneecap that became all she could focus on.

"He'd also tell you he signed over all rights to the film script in L.A., because he doesn't belong there anymore. He can write new scripts anywhere."

Kate watched his eyes, the fullness of his mouth, the movement of his throat as he swallowed. He was standing now, closer again than he'd been before.

"Where does he belong?" she said as he took her glass from her fingers and placed it on the bar beside his own. She slid to her feet too, their bodies pressed together from shoulder to hip.

"Wherever you are," he breathed, his palm hot against the small of her back.

She laid her hand along his jaw. "So you're not my agent anymore?"

He shook his head. "We're just Kate and Charlie."

"Two people in a bar," she said.

"You're so damn beautiful." His eyes adored her, a look that told her everything she needed to know.

"I love you," she said. "With every single beat of my fragile, messy heart."

"I've loved you since the first day you walked into my office," he said.

"Smelling of baby sick," she said.

"Your hair fastened back with Hugh's tie."

She paused, remembering that morning, the guy leaving Francisco & Fox just as she arrived. She couldn't believe she hadn't made the connection herself. "Oh my God, you're right, it was Hugh."

"He'd just been in and had a shouting match with Fiona because he wasn't prepared to go through with it, then he ran into you downstairs and called up to say he'd changed his mind. Seems you had quite an effect on him too that day."

"So many random things have happened," she said. "We could so easily not have been here."

"I don't think they're random," he said, sliding his hand down her arm. "It's all about you. Your bravery in sending the letter, your kindness in holding that baby, your strength in protecting the people around you when things fell apart. You make things happen, Kate, you're a beautiful, chaotic magnet holding everything together."

"I don't feel very together most days," she said.

"You were luminous this morning," he said. "People turned up because they wanted to be part of your story." He brushed the back of his fingers along her jaw. "I want to be part of your story."

"You're my whole book, Charlie."

He lowered his head and kissed her, slow and searching.

"You're sure about L.A.?" she said.

"I knew even as I boarded the flight," he said. "All I could think about was coming home to you." His fingers stroked her spine, his other hand in her hair. "I tortured myself with thoughts of you and some husky-eyed guy."

"I'm so sorry about him," she laughed softly. "I prefer whiskey cola anyway."

He kissed her full of champagne-tomorrow promises, and she kissed him back with you-make-me-actually-shiver wonder.

"You're killing me in this dress," he murmured, making her laugh and melt against him, because the freedom to finally say the things they wanted to was headier than the champagne in their glasses.

She closed her eyes and rested her head against his shoulder, feeling as if, for the first time in forever, she was exactly where she should be.

"Let's get out of here," he said, quiet against her ear.

"Where will we go?" she said, not wanting to move out of his arms.

"Wherever life takes us."

"Can it be Cornwall?"

"It's a long way to go for dinner."

He reached into his jacket pocket and handed her a flat, gift-wrapped package. "I got you something."

She pulled the string and opened the paper, revealing a leather-bound notebook. Opening the cover, she fanned the blank pages.

"For our deleted scenes," he said, sweeping her hair over one shoulder, his fingertips lingering on her collarbone.

She pressed it against her heart. "We might need more pages."

"I'll buy more books," he said.

Epilogue

THE RELEASE OF A NEW HUGH HUDSON NOVEL ALWAYS CREATED A frenzy of excitement among his loyal army of thriller fans, never more so than for his long-anticipated first book after the loss of his beloved wife, Eleanor. They'd been impatiently patient, turning out in their pre-Christmas droves to welcome him back at book signings up and down the country.

Kate had been queuing for over an hour by the time she neared the front, a hardback under her arm. She'd stuck a cap on and pulled her hair back, not that people tended to recognize her these days. Things had gotten a little wild in the weeks following the whole Kate Darrowby thing, so she'd erred on the side of caution to make sure no one saw her as anything but an avid Hugh Hudson fan, which, to be fair, she absolutely was.

She watched as he chatted easily to the couple in front of her, signing four or five books for them at the same time. The signing table had been placed just far enough away from the queue to allow fans to have him to themselves for a couple of minutes, and a Christmas tree set up to pose beside for a photo with the man himself.

Kate took her cap off as she approached his table. "I didn't recognize you out of your T-Rex costume," she said, handing him the hardback book.

"Kate Darrowby, as I live and breathe," he laughed quietly, his rich, Welsh baritone instantly recognizable. His eyes lingered on the book title, different to all of the thrillers he'd signed that day.

"It's good to see you," he said. "How's life in Cornwall?"

Kate couldn't keep the smile from her face. "It's bliss. Charlie worried it might feel isolated, but people visit all the time, Alice especially. You should come and see us in the spring."

Hugh and Kate had been working together over the last year on the next Kate Darrowby book, exchanging chapters instead of emails these days. It was a work in progress, one they both found profoundly satisfying.

"Thank you, Hugh, for everything."

She knew from Charlie that it was Hugh who'd arranged Pink Cottage for her rather than the publishing team. He'd also insisted she receive a full half of the royalties from *The Power of Love*, which given its bestseller status around the globe, had turned out to be a not-inconsiderable sum.

His pen hovered over the page for a few long seconds before he wrote anything, because his usual stock greeting wasn't going to cut it for this one.

Kate swallowed down the ache of emotion in her windpipe as the queue manager approached to move things along, oblivious to the momentous meeting happening in front of her eyes. She nodded, moving to pose for a photograph together beside the Christmas tree.

"Just one second," Hugh said, as she handed her phone to the assistant in charge of taking photos. "Come here, Diz."

A massive Irish wolfhound climbed out of a basket beside

Hugh's signing table and ambled over to pose between them, clearly used to being called for photo duty. She was a very Hugh kind of dog: grizzly exterior, gentle on the inside. Her presence at the signing didn't come as a surprise to Kate. Dizzy had been the star of Hugh's social media pages ever since he'd adopted her from a rescue center the previous winter. She was as much in demand at his social events as he was.

"I tried calling her Dismal but it didn't suit her," Hugh said quietly. "She's just too damn sweet."

Kate laughed, her hand resting on the dog's huge head, Hugh's arm around her shoulders as they looked down the lens and smiled for the camera.

"Give Charlie my best," he said.

She nodded. "Happy Christmas, Hugh," she said.

"You too." He hugged her quickly and pressed a kiss against her cheek. "Now get out of here before these avid detective fans put two and two together and mob you," he said, handing her the book back.

She smiled and pulled her cap down low, leaving the shop with the book pressed tightly against her chest.

For Kate,

The best guardian angel this book, author, or T-Rex could ask for.

With our eternal thanks and admiration,

Hugh, Eleanor & Dizzy x

ACTUAL DELETED SCENE . . .

Prologue

"I KNOW YOU'RE IN THERE, HUGH, SO DO US BOTH A FAVOR AND OPEN THE bloody door, would you? The motorway was hellish and I'm a woman of a certain age in need of the bathroom and a G&T, heavy on the G, four ice cubes, and a good squeeze of lime. Don't even think about bullshitting me with lemon, I'm not in the mood."

Low evening sunlight glinted off the eye-watering antique diamond on Fiona Fox's hand as she drummed her fingernails against the sun-bleached doorframe of the impressive Cotswolds pile, secure in the knowledge that Hugh Hudson would eventually do as she'd demanded. More than twenty years spent as both his literary agent and his friend told her that he was in need of intervention, hence the reason for turning up unannounced on a Friday evening with her weekend case and iron-will determination.

She lowered her huge sunglasses on their golden chain and reached for the handle of her suitcase as she heard movement in the hallway.

"Well, you look rough," she said, when he finally opened the door.

"I wasn't expecting visitors," he said.

"Ever again?" she said, eyeing the dark shadows beneath Hugh's eyes and the stubble that was more of an unkempt beard.

"Hello to you too, Fi," he sighed. "Is there any point in me saying this isn't a good time?"

"I mean, you can try," she said, pushing her case at him. "Take that, will you?"

"I'm going away." He glanced at his wrist where his watch used to be. "Tonight, actually. In about half an hour."

Fiona completely ignored him, her heels clicking on the terracotta tiles as she headed through the house toward the kitchen.

"Is Dilly away?" Her nose twitched as she took in the mess of used glasses and empty bottles, the unwiped surfaces, the piles of clutter.

Hugh pushed a hand through his hair, irritated. "I let her go."

"You let the one person standing between you and dysentery go?" Fi said. "When?"

He shrugged. "I don't know. A month? Three months? Who are you, my mother?"

"If I *was* your mother I'd move in, so you better be glad I'm not," she said.

"My mother doesn't give a damn as long as I keep paying the rent on her condo. She certainly doesn't come round here being unnecessarily pissy over a few dirty glasses."

Fiona pinched the bridge of her nose. "Let me help you."

"I don't need anything."

She looked at him, really looked at him, and she didn't say how exhausted he looked, or how truly broken her heart was for him that Eleanor died, or how she was painfully aware that eighteen months is both a long time and a blink of an eye to get over losing the love of your life. His disordered home was a reflection of what was going on behind his eyes, of his solitary descent into quiet chaos. She resisted the urge to load the dishwasher or empty the overflowing bins and reached instead for two highball glasses, placing them down beside an age-shrunken lime from the fruit bowl on the windowsill.

"Mix the drinks while I go upstairs and unpack. And roll that lime a few times before you cut it, or it'll be drier than a camel's hump."

SEVERAL HOURS AND A HASTILY cobbled-together carbonara later, Fi sat in the armchair cradling a mug of black coffee, thinking. Hugh had passed out on the sofa, having whiskey-bared his soul and the fact that he'd not written a single word of the chronically overdue manuscript she'd come to talk to him about. Didn't even have a vague outline. His publisher had been understanding, of course—Hugh Hudson's smash-hit DI Rivers series had more than earned him their loyalty and patience—but everything has a limit and the public was baying for the eighth book in the series. As was his editor.

She looked at him, his scowl finally smoothed away by sleep, and wished she could wipe the last eighteen months from his memory and see him smile again. He'd always been a self-assured sort of person; readers loved his easygoing style at public events, Eleanor always by his side adding star power. They'd been the gilded couple, the handsome writer and the luminous theater actress. And then she was gone, wiped off the earth by an abrupt and tragic riding accident, and it was as if someone had turned Hugh's sun off.

Fi rose to settle a blanket over him and was about to turn in herself when an email alert illuminated the screen of the computer on his desk in the bay window. Instinctively, she wandered across to dim it so it didn't disturb Hugh. Not that it was likely to—he was sleeping the sleep of the dead, one arm flung above his head, the other trailing toward the oak floorboards. She'd taken his half-empty glass from his hand awhile back, remembering how much Eleanor had prized the huge Turkish rug beneath the coffee table.

Clicking a random key on Hugh's keyboard, Fi squinted at the suddenly glaring brightness, raising her glasses with a quiet jangle of chain. She wasn't planning to look, especially, or to not look, especially, but she couldn't hold back her agent instinct when she noticed the flashing cursor on an open manuscript.

"What have you been writing, Hugh?" she whispered, leaning closer to the screen. Within a couple of minutes she'd abandoned her plan to allow her client his privacy and settled down in his leather desk chair, unable to tear her eyes away from the screen.

"MORNING," HUGH SAID, BLEARY-EYED AND sheepish. "Did I pass out?"

Fi handed him a coffee, careful not to pounce too soon.

"Mexican eggs," she said, laying him a place at the table she'd scrubbed.

"You really didn't need to cook for me," he said, scraping his chair back on the flagstones. "But thank you anyway, smells good."

In the same way a mother might roast a chicken for incoming teenagers on a particularly cold Sunday, Fiona Fox had mastered a small but reliable menu of dishes for occasions exactly such as this, comfort food designed to engender trust and lower raised guards.

She sipped her coffee and sat opposite him as he ate, safe in the knowledge that the food was restaurant standard.

"I read your manuscript," she said.

His body stilled, then he lowered his cutlery and raised his gaze.

"I haven't written one."

She looked at him over the rim of her coffee cup. "Yes, you have."

"You had no right."

"It was just there, Hugh, and I'm your agent."

"It's not for sale."

She nodded, knowing everything has its price.

"Your publisher has been incredibly fair with you," she said, pitching her voice low and neutral. "They haven't applied pressure, but we all know you need to deliver a book, and believe me when I say I get it, Hugh, your mind isn't in the right place to write another DI Rivers yet."

"Bear with me, that's all I'm asking," he said. "A couple more months."

"You know that's not realistic," she said.

He banged his cutlery down with a clatter. "I can't, Fi. Don't ask me to share that manuscript, because I just cannot."

She held his gaze steadily across the table, warming up. She was Fiona Fox, and she never failed at the negotiation table, whether in a London boardroom or a Cotswolds kitchen. "It's easily the most beautiful love story I've ever read, and you know how many have crossed my desk over the years. Or maybe you don't. Think of a big number and times it by fifty."

"I don't write love stories."

"And yet you have."

Hugh looked away and shook his head, exasperated. "But I don't want to. There won't be any more where that came from— Christ, I don't even know where it came from. I just . . . I felt this *thing* stuck inside me, this physical block. This fucking deadweight,

Fi. It eased things to get some of it out onto paper. I could breathe around it, at least."

"Grief, Hugh," Fiona said. "It's called grief."

"Yeah, well it's my grief, and it's private. You're asking me to share Eleanor with the world, and I won't do it."

Fi chose her line of attack in accordance with his. "She dances across those pages like Ginger Rogers, Hugh. I felt her twirl and breathless spin around every word you've written, heard her laughter slide between the fragile lines, saw the blur of her tears through my own. It's jubilant and magical and it's tragic on the spin of a dime, because that's what she was, wasn't she? You've somehow captured her essence in a way that only a man in love could, distilled her into words in a way only *you* possibly could, because by God did that woman adore you."

"And now you want me to share that intimate part of me, of us, with every Tom, Dick, and Harry on their sun loungers around the pool at some godforsaken two-star hotel in Spain? Have her hang around next to disgraced politicians' autobiographies on the reduced stand in the bookstore? Can't you see how impossible that would be, how utterly fucking disrespectful to her memory?"

"I see the exact opposite," Fi reasoned. "Eleanor lived for the performance, for the audience, for the spotlight. What more magnificent thing could you do for her now than let her take center stage one last, unexpected time? You've immortalized her with your words, given her a new role to play, first-night glory every time someone opens the book."

Hugh eyeballed his agent across the table, and she stared right back, knowing her words had landed on a tender, exposed place.

"But all the questions, Fi. The bandwagon, the interviews, the publicity." He shrank into himself like a kicked dog. "I can't face it."

Hugh didn't know it, but Fiona had spent a sleepless night working out counterpoints for all of his potential arguments. She wanted that knockout manuscript almost more than she wanted Hugh Hudson as her client.

"A sweetener like this could buy you another six months. Nine even, to write the next DI Rivers. Space to think, get away maybe."

"Except there'd be no space, would there, with edits and publicity. You can't fool me with empty promises, I'm too long in the tooth for that."

She steepled her fingers over her coffee cup, blood-red fingernails resting against one another. "Unless it's put out under a different author's name."

He blinked, uncomprehending. "A pseudonym?"

She clicked her tongue, as if making up the meticulously thought-out plan on the hoof. "Not exactly. If it does well, which it will, a pseudonym without a face could easily track back to you, given how adored Eleanor was. Is."

He sat back in his chair, scowling. "Then what are you suggesting?"

She paused, just long enough to be convincing. "We splash a completely unconnected author's name across the cover. A woman, even. I could find an unknown actor to act as the public face, someone to deal with any publicity. Eleanor would have rather enjoyed that, don't you think? Reaching a hand back to help the next girl up the ladder?"

Hugh dropped his gaze to his coffee cup and Fiona waited, never one to overplay her hand. She knew she had him when he sighed, bone deep and weary.

"A year, Fi. Twelve clear months to write the next DI Rivers book without any pressure, and your cast-iron guarantee that my name will never be publicly linked to this manuscript."

"Have I ever let you down?"

Hugh Hudson had spent the last twenty years honing his craft, and it had all come together in this once-in-a-lifetime manuscript poured straight from his tender, lovesick heart onto the page. It had made the hairs on the back of her neck stand up.

She'd have bought him two years if he'd asked for it, because that unicorn manuscript had bestseller written all over it.

Acknowledgments

Thank you to my agent, Nelle Andrew, for being all-encompassingly fabulous, I love being one of your authors! Wider thanks to everyone on the team at RML, I feel in very safe hands.

Many thanks to my UK editor, Harriet Bourton, and the lovely team at Viking, I hugely appreciate everything you do for me. Thank you also to the amazing rights team at Penguin for spreading the *Slow Burn* love overseas.

Extra thanks to my copyeditor, Karen Whitlock, for your help, good humor, and kindness; you really went the extra mile on this one and it's so appreciated!

Buckets of endless gratitude to my U.S. editor, Hilary Teeman, and all of the legends on team Dell—your support, wise editorial advice, and cheerleading has really kept me going. I am a lucky lass to have worked with you guys for so many years.

Much gratitude to all of my overseas publishers. I am always thankful for the opportunity to work with you and the thrill of seeing foreign editions never gets old.

Sally and Rose—you're the best! Thank you for the many years of friendship, and especially for the initial spark for *Slow Burn Summer.* You ladies are my writing rocks.

Kim and Emma—totally love you ladies and our writing breakfasts!

Last and never least, thank you to my beloved folks—my husband, James; and my boys, Ed and Ali; my mom and dad; my sister, Jackie; and my brother, Andy. You're all my shining stars.

Slow Burn Summer

JOSIE SILVER

Random
House
Book Club

Because
Stories Are
Better Shared ™

A Book Club Guide

Questions for Discussion

1. How did you perceive Kate's evolution throughout the story? What were some pivotal moments for her character?

2. Discuss Charlie's journey from being Jojo's son to finding his own path. How did his relationship with Kate influence this transition?

3. The book explores themes of grief and love. How do the characters navigate their grief, and what role does love play in their healing process?

4. The concept of a "guardian angel" is mentioned several times. How does Kate embody this role for the book and for Hugh?

5. How did you feel about the use of the "deleted scene" concept in the narrative? Did it add depth to the story for you?

6. Discuss the dynamics between Kate and Liv. How does their sisterly bond influence the decisions they make?

7. How did you perceive the relationship between Kate and Charlie? What were the key moments that defined their connection?

8. What were the main conflicts in the story, and how were they resolved? Were you satisfied with the resolutions?

9. Do you agree with Kate's decision to play the role of author? If you learned the author of a famous book was actually an actor hired to play the part, how would you feel? Would it change your opinion of the book itself?

10. Have you ever faced a situation where you felt misunderstood or misrepresented? How did you handle it, and how does it compare to Kate's experience?

Playlist

"Slipping Through My Fingers"—ABBA

"When We Were Young"—Adele

"I Was Here"—Lady A

"When Someone Stops Loving You"—Little Big Town

"Goodbye"—Mimi Webb

"The Power of Love"—Frankie Goes to Hollywood

"With You"—Caissie Levy, *Ghost: The Musical*

"A Safe Place to Land"—Sara Bareilles feat. John Legend

"Rescue"—Lauren Daigle

"Compass"—Rascal Flatts

"The Reason"—Hoobastank

"Knots"—Anna Nalick

"Come Away with Me"—Norah Jones

"Until I Found You"—Stephen Sanchez

"Somewhere Only We Know"—Keane

JOSIE SILVER is a writer of love stories. She is the #1 *New York Times* bestselling author of *One Day in December*, which has been published in more than twenty-five languages, *The Two Lives of Lydia Bird*, *One Night on the Island*, and *A Winter in New York*. She lives in the UK with her husband, their sons, and an ever-changing cast of animals.

About the Type

This book was set in Baskerville, a typeface designed by John Baskerville (1706–75), an amateur printer and typefounder, and cut for him by John Handy in 1750. The type became popular again when the Lanston Monotype Corporation of London revived the classic roman face in 1923. The Mergenthaler Linotype Company in England and the United States cut a version of Baskerville in 1931, making it one of the most widely used typefaces today.

RANDOM HOUSE BOOK CLUB

Because Stories Are Better Shared

Discover

Exciting new books that spark conversation every week.

Connect

With authors on tour—or in your living room. (Request an Author Chat for your book club!)

Discuss

Stories that move you with fellow book lovers on Facebook, on Goodreads, or at in-person meet-ups.

Enhance

Your reading experience with discussion prompts, digital book club kits, and more, available on our website.

Join our online book club community!

f **g** randomhousebookclub.com

RANDOM HOUSE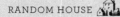